Set in the attractive and mundane, seaside-town of Southport, HER FATHER is a contemporary and emotional psychological thriller about a troubled teenager: Mara Aneka Bones.

HER FATHER is the second novel in this electrifying trilogy, HIS MOTHER being the first and SISTERS being the last in the series.

***

It is on the evening of Valentine's Day that Inspector Folkard's short break away is interrupted by an urgent call. The bodies of two teenagers, both male, have been discovered at a local park: one is in a critical condition the other one is dead. With a possible double murder on their hands, Detectives Inspector Hermione Folkard and Sergeant Catherine Shakespeare struggle to find any concrete witnesses willing to come forward; it also proves difficult to wade through the many versions of what exactly was going on in Botanic Park that evening.

Mara is fourteen and a lonely recluse. Her mother died during childbirth, or so her father says. The closer the detectives get to their killer, the more the reader learns about Mara and her father. Inspector Folkard must tread judiciously – she could after all, have a teenage, serial killer on her hands.

To Lesley and Adrid: Don't have nightmares!
Sally-Anne
xxx

HER FATHER

SALLY-ANNE TAPIA-BOWES

For my brothers Ramón Felipe (Philip) and John-Thomas (JT)

my 'iron-willed brothers', whom I love dearly.

Copyright © 2019 Sally-Anne Tapia-Bowes

purplepenguinpublishing.com

FIRST PUBLISHED 2016

ISBN-13: 978-0993191954

Cambria font used with permission from Microsoft

***

With thanks to the many friends and writers who have both supported and inspired me on my journey.

In particular, a big thank you to Bob Stone and Stephen Beattie for their advice and support.

My love for books was probably ignited by my parents. They always read – every day.

Reading has been my saviour on many an occasion. Writing exorcises, cleanses and heals. It is a courtship between the heart and soul – a dance worth dancing…

'All fathers are invisible in daytime: daytime is ruled by mothers,

and fathers come out at night.

Darkness brings home fathers, with their real, unspeakable power.

There is more to fathers than meets the eye.'

Margaret Atwood

1

ALTHOUGH IT IS already quite dark, the striking full moon generously basks her brightness from far overhead. At this time of night, it is usual to hear the voices of teenagers who are lurking in the shadows, all of them gathering for different purposes in the nearby local park. It is cold tonight, bitterly cold.

Mara rubs her gloved hands together; she is walking through the popular park alone. She passes a sign, KEEP DOGS ON LEAD. Although she feels excited, she is also quite afraid - there are times when even her own shadow startles her.

Although Mara has never been in Botanic Park at this time of night, she is still fairly familiar with its general outline. By the look on her pallid, thin face and wide-open eyes, she is possibly lost or looking for someone she knows.

In order to tidy her hair, Mara spits into her hands before she simultaneously smooths downwards, with both palms, her unruly shoulder-length dark mane that is parted in the middle; she then nervously pushes back the waif-like strands that refuse to conform behind her ears. Mara looks back once more over her left shoulder. In the near distance, the sound of two or maybe three supermarket trolleys can be heard crashing about; in the far distance, an ambulance wails – the blue lights permeating through the smudge-like foliage.

For a few moments, Mara considers how everything looks around her; it is so different in the nightime. She looks at her watch before squinting, nearly seven. Directly, an unexpected flutter ripples below her ribcage. It is similar to the ones she has been experiencing all day, except this one was much stronger. For a moment, Mara thinks she needs the toilet but she does not want to be late. Joseph said he'd meet her by the swings at seven.

Suddenly, unsure which way to go, Mara remembers what Joseph had told her earlier that day, on the playground. He had repeated it twice to her, '... as you enter the park by the front gate, there is a path that goes right. Stay on that path. Keep going until you reach the swings. I'll meet you there.' When Mara looked at him suspiciously, he smiled before adding, 'I'll be there. I'll be waiting for you.'

For as long as Mara can remember, boys have never been interested in her – they have rarely spoken to her unless instructed to do so. In school, Mara is often the butt of some joke or another. But Joseph, Joseph Rawcliffe is different; he is thoughtful and kind. He rarely joins in with the others; he's even on occasion asked after her following yet another unnecessary affray with someone or another along the corridor. The popular girls usually giggle when he walks past.

In the last week, Joseph has spoken to Mara twice – the dreamy smile always follows. It is difficult to concentrate when he is about. Joseph is handsome; he has a tanned complexion with dark features to match. His large, sincere eyes ooze trustworthiness.

Joseph attends the same 10:30 Sunday service at *St Patrick's Catholic Parish*, on Marshide Road. He always sits on the same bench each week - fourth from the front, on the left hand side of the church, as if facing the altar. Joseph sits the closest to Mara, although Mara sits on the right hand side of the church, on the sixth bench. Mara's father sits to her right. Joseph's mother always sits between him and his older sister Niamh. On occasion, he has looked over his right shoulder towards her; he does so in order to roll his eyes upwards to make her laugh. Mara's father never notices. He rarely notices anything.

***

A sudden scream in the distance is quickly followed by uncontrollable laughter. Mara responds quickly by looking left. Mara is worried she is going to be late; she is now walking a little faster. She does not want to trip, nor spoil her clothes. Directly ahead, she is sure she can hear whispering, as well as some faint laughter. Mara shivers; although she is wearing a thick coat and gloves, the freezing cold fastens itself crisp onto her cheeks and forehead.

Ahead there seems to be a familiar tunnel. For a few moments Mara hesitates; it's mouth is pitch-black like a wolf's throat. Mara takes a deep breath. She knows this tunnel; it is not very long. Mara knows that as soon as she enters it, it will snake a little to the left before she will have sight of the outside of it. Mara thinks of Joseph and heads for the passageway.

'Happy Valentine's!'

Laughter. Raucous laughter. Perfidious.

A freezing, dense liquid is upon Mara; she stops dead in her tracks. Some of the freezing fluid trickles through her hair, along her neck and into her dark-green duffle coat; the cold pierces her all over - a knife jabbing incessantly. As she looks up, she hears the familiar laughter of at least two people overhead. Their hilarity is deafening - overpowering.

Mara is now screaming. She instinctively runs through the tunnel only to find in the bright glow of a nearby council lamp that she is covered in blood. For a moment she looks at her hands. Mara is unaware that she has wet herself. She turns around. She is terrified, unsure of what she should do next. When Mara looks up again, to where the laughter is coming from, she is astounded.

Unbelievably, and above the tunnel, stands Joseph - her Joseph. He is accompanied by his friend Jacob

Lamb, the wolf in sheep's clothing. Jacob is holding what seems to be a bucket in his right hand. He is still laughing; his body is slightly bent forward, like he is in pain, like he has a stitch. His left hand is resting on the upper half of his leg. He keeps flicking back his blonde quiff, each time he laughs, each time he draws breath. Mara's eyes move across from Jacob to Joseph. Joseph is laughing less now – he has noticed that Mara is crying.

A furious rage that has always existed somewhere deep inside suddenly takes over. Gone are the stomach spasms and the butterflies, gone is the fear of the dark. Mara marches in the direction of the right hand side of the tunnel, up the side of the bridge-like structure, stepping forward on a variety of unseen pastel-shaded croci, carelessly breaking the backs of numerous snowflake plants, instinctively stepping over two bulging tree roots – thick like a fat woman's legs. Mara is heading straight for the culprits.

As soon as Mara arrives to her final destination, she makes immediate contact with Jacob – off he disappears from the edge of the tunnel. Immediately after, Joseph follows.

For several moments later, Mara looks at them both in disbelief; they lie uncomfortably flat on their backs on the black tarmac below. Cheap mascara has now blackened her eyes and cheeks. Although she didn't watch what happened to Jacob at the time, she heard the crack of his head slamming onto a rock or stone, most likely on one of the many boulders fixed decoratively along the ascent to the other side of the tunnel.

Jacob's attempt to hold onto Joseph resulted in him falling backwards too. At the time, Mara looked down upon Joseph as he fell quickly away from her – his arms outstretched – his eyes wide-open – a look of horror upon his face as he sunk into the darkness below. Subsequently, Mara descends the side of the tunnel. Both boys are still lying on their backs - neither of them moving. There is already a dark pool of blood leaking sideways from underneath Jacob's head.

Feeling even colder now, Mara shivers uncontrollably. Her eyes are full of tears again; she is now aware that she has wet herself – the smell of urine is potent. The sound of a car alarm, probably in the distant car park, startles her. Suddenly enlightened by the reality of it all, Mara steps backwards. Mara can hear voices nearby; she can hear laughter as well. In that moment, it was as though time itself had frozen rigid. Right now, the park is alive once more, a dog barks repeatedly in the remote distance – the trees make a strange rustling sound as the wind picks up, whipping the nearby branches into a frenzy.

Mara tries to think; she knows that if she continues to follow the path, it will take her past the swings and out through the back gates onto Balmoral Lane and straight home. Mara looks down at her gloved hands. Inside the sticky liquid has gathered itself in every tip. Sickened by the feeling of it, she removes her gloves and places them into her coat pocket. Mara's shoes are wet on the inside too. She removes her thick coat, turns it inside out and pulls it over her head. From here it is a twenty minute walk home. Her father won't be home until after nine.

Darkness envelops Mara like a long lost friend. She is shaking violently now; tears well up once more in her eyes. It does not matter that she cannot see her way ahead clearly – she has found her way home in the dark many times before.

2

ONCE AGAIN, The wide open gates belonging to Comlongon Castle welcomed the Folkard clan back like a long lost friend.

Darcy and Zita emerged instinctively from the gap that existed between the two front seats. All four waited with baited breath as Walter's ageing red convertible trundled along the straightish wide path, the crowded foliage above them obscuring what they knew to be right ahead of them.

And there she was. There she stood – proud like an Inuksuk stone guiding them home - elegant, waiting for them. The squarish, pink-dressed sandstone structure, with its rubble insert, said to be four metres thick, had a portcullis-like metal grid, hung guillotine fashion above the arched front entrance. The castle was even more impressive at this time of day.

Like a spotlight on any given set, the glaring winter sun did its best to present the venerable edifice in all of its glory. The lookout tower was visible in the near distance. Even now, the girls were yet to learn of the apparent ghost of Lady Marion Carruthers who had supposedly leapt to her death from the very top in order to avoid marriage to a man she did not love. For sure, Zita, who was all grown up now she was eight, would have refused to accompany them had she known of such a legend. Although Darcy was now fourteen, she too was still susceptible to any suchlike tale; most likely she would have talked herself into having heard this or that when left alone.

On one of the longest of corridors, on the fourth floor, a few years back, she stood considering the impressive stone-carved corbels on the ceiling when suddenly she realised she had been unintentionally left behind. When her father found her, she was looking backwards over her left shoulder, as if something had alarmed her – although everyone laughed later, she made sure she was never left behind again, not at any given point.

The desire to run about the place was too much for the youngest. As soon as the car ground to a halt, she exited, raced from the gravelled car park along the left hand side of the castle before disappearing. Habitually, they followed - their first destination, to soak up the impressive grounds and walk along the paved path that ran along the middle of it all. There, at some point, they would pause on their ceremonial flagstone and look down affectionately upon it. Although they had done it many times before, both parents would habitually read their names and date of marriage out loud, as if checking something that had since been forgotten. Like picking at a scab, Walter had a habit of cleaning it. It irritated him that it was always seemed soiled; had he foreseen this at the time, he would have insisted on the flagstone being placed away from the left edge of the path adjacent to the grass.

A little further down the path, they paused again; there they stood, hand in hand, looking far out. Panoramically, everything from left to right was a decorative landscape that had been sculptured with the precision only an artist could muster. An ever present mixture of emerald, mulberry and mottled-green shades - picturesque for as far as the eye – adorned the spectacle before them. In the near distance ahead, a familiar sound, Walter's favourite, a hardy herd of Highland cows. The long-horned beasts majestically meandered about purposefully, their rusting wavy overcoats warming the rich landscape. Everything was as it should be, for this was Scotland, their favourite place on earth.

Laughter and a mixture of frolicsome screams were now coming from close behind them. They mechanically turned and smiled at the girls. How different the stronghold looked from the bottommost part belonging to the grounds, the width of it, almost one-hundred feet, its entirety a postcard. All of the largest windows could be seen from here; without a doubt, the stone mullion frames with their carried leaded windows complimented the imposing vertical structure.

Hermione Folkard wandered off to the left towards the circular bench that surrounded an established wych elm. From there she watched Walter routinely photograph this and that, a large red admiral hovering about his left shoulder. The girls continued to shriek between laughs. From a round bridge-like structure, surrounded by a large and deep circular pond, the fat koi carp that rose like seals, amused them greatly. Their great triangular heads protruded out from beneath the icy water, thick grey whiskers like cats.

For Hermione Folkard, the sound of no traffic, no wailing emergency services, no shouting, was bliss. Instead, the flurry of alternating bird noise was pleasurable to hear, to say the least. Their intermittent high-pitched variations, according to their size, type and distance, was both reassuring and relaxing, like a breath of fresh crisp air to the lungs.

There were four grand floors to the residential part of the castle – yet only fifteen rooms in total. In contrast, the non-residential quarter was used mostly for conducting the ceremony of marriage; this quarter was tucked at the back of it all. There, little had altered since the fourteen hundreds. It was on the first floor, below the many full-sized flags, and in front of the burning fireplace, the width of a small house, that the Folkards had married, almost a quarter of a century ago. On the outside, the narrow vertical slits from which the castle's defenders launched their arrows many moons ago, appeared almost randomly.

Bags unloaded and now indoors, the familiar and courteous-as-always staff welcomed the family back. There had been an addition – a new member. An overfriendly and adorable Jack Russell, by the name of Ernest, leapt forward - literally into the arms of Zita. The frisky terrier with its patchy coarse overcoat energetically moved around the youngest – his almond-shaped eyes alert and intelligent.

It was impossible to pass this and that without noticing and remembering. Hermione Folkard pointed to the right towards some large wooden double doors, not long after they had entered via the tall and slim turret-like entrance.

'We had our reception in there.'

Dutifully, and having heard this account many times before, Darcy and Zita had looked right before quickly disappearing left towards the reception area.

Three impressive, large knights awaited them by the foot of the large and wide staircase. They stood to attention in their tailor-made, full-plate metal armour; each must have weighed individually about fifty pounds. They all exhibited some proof of having been worn on some battlefield or another. For a moment, Hermione Folkard pictured herself walking down the extensive stairs on her wedding day, her right arm tucked into her father's.

'Hello you two. Aren't you the lucky ones accompanying your parents on a Valentine's weekend?'

The receptionist, who had undoubtedly returned from a recent holiday from somewhere quite hot, smiled kindly; she did so despite the girls refusal to reply. They simply half-smiled before shyly taking a small step back.

'Wouldn't be the same without them.'

The girls automatically looked up before inching a tad closer to their father. Hermione Folkard nodded in approvement. Yes, this was a place for all of them to visit as a unit, a place to return to time and time again, a place where once their dearest and nearest had gathered in celebration – sadly some of them were with them no longer. For many, returning to a favoured place could permanently alter special memories. For the Folkards, any return had only served to enhance the latter. Comlongon Castle remained much the same, unspoilt, precious, magical.

There was a uniformity on the corridor and landings belonging to the four floors. The tasteful emerald-green, belonging to the upper half above the dado rail on the walls, complimenting the decadent crimson-red below it. Everywhere else, from floor to ceiling, was a dark polished wood, oak-linenfold panelled walls, made up like parchment sheets - the consistent plush crimson carpet marrying the decor. Yet, that was where the uniformity ended. Once indoors, each suite was unique, as was the accompanying bathroom – in itself, a large room of its own. In addition, an impressive array of weighty furniture featured in all the necessary places; one could have easily remained indoors, cosiness oozing from every quarter.

***

That evening, once the girls were finally fast asleep, Hermione Folkard nestled half-a-slumber in Walter's right arm, whilst they watched from their bed a rerun of a well-known Columbo episode. It was one of Hermione Folkard's favourite – the one where he sympathises with the killer because her son-in-law drove her daughter to suicide; for a moment, it looked as if he was going to let her off.

Walter and Hermione lay like spoons in a drawer, contentedly surveying the detective's tactful arrest from their curtained Jacobean four-poster bed - that was, until Hermione Folkard's work mobile rang. Although Walter's arm did not move, his almost inaudible sigh said it all.

The familiar voice of Catherine Shakespeare, sounding worse for wear herself, resonated in her right ear.

'Hermione,' she began, 'the bodies of two white males, schoolkids, have been found in Churchtown's botanical park. One of the boys, identified as Jacob Lamb, is dead – a nasty head injury, looks like he's suffered a significant fall.'

Sergeant Shakespeare paused momentarily.

'The other, Joseph Rawcliffe, appears to have suffered a similar but less aggressive injury to the head – he's is in intensive care, in a coma, at Southport's General Hospital. They're talking about moving him to Walton's Neurological Unit – critical condition – may not make it. Superintendent Reid is on site now. I arrived about half-an-hour ago. George Davies is on his way.'

After a short pause she added, 'Happy Valentine's'.

3

THE HALF-GLAZED, HALF-PANELLED off-white front door closes noisily behind Mara's father; he is heading off to work. Today is Saturday; like Fridays, he will not finish work at the Italian restaurant on Lord Street until nine. When Mara's father arrives home, he will have already eaten but, as customary, he will expect some soup and a meat sandwich, not long after he enters the front door, not long before nine-thirty.

Mara's father will not make much conversation; he will have his fill, down a large glass of whisky, take a walk down the garden path to check on his shed full of birds, lock everything up and head for bed.

Sitting upright now on her single bed and staring blankly ahead towards her bedroom door, Mara feels relieved that her father did not look in on her. If he had seen her duffle coat, gloves and shoes, still wet, drying out on the radiator, he would have gone mad. Mara's father rarely enters her bedroom. Most of their conversations, if there are any, are one sided; they talk mostly on Sundays – her father's day off. When they talk, they talk mostly about the birds.

Mara looks about her cheerless room – it has never been painted, not since they moved in. The terraced house is situated in one of two cul-de-sacs belonging to the area of Crossens. They moved here nearly eleven years ago. Her rectangular bedroom is at the front of the house; the two square windows let in very little light. Mara's desk is in front of one of these – in front of the left window, adjacent to her bed; an almost unoccupied dressing table is below the other. There is an eyeliner and a mascara tube in a green glass tumbler, the colour of grass; to the right of it, a worn-out wooden paddle brush – matted dark-brown hair trapped at the root of each needle, bobbled fur gripping each bristle tightly at the root.

The walls are a pale apricot, faded, especially around the windows. The outdated Aztec patterned curtains and quilt-cover match them perfectly. Nothing else in the room matches really – feeble pine-like furniture rests on a common dark-brown carpet with inconspicuous tram lines running along it, the rough texture similar to the black outdoor mat afore the front door.

The room's misery is cheered by Mara's collection of aesthetic literary posters. The school librarian, Mrs Cassidy, has been passing the odd poster or two to Mara since she asked for one in Year Seven - one with *The Diary of Anne Frank* on it. Next to it, to its right, is a poster with a picture of a book turned into a film called *The Boy in The Striped Pyjamas*. In the background of this picture is a tall wire fence.

At either side of the fence sit two boys facing one another; they are about the same age but look quite different. One boy has got no hair. Despite that, they seem to like one another – they are smiling. Both of these posters are above her white, tessellated, metallic headboard.

***

Mrs Cassidy is an *Alice in Wonderland* fan. Her longish, black hair is always crimped like potato chips were in the eighties. It suits her. Mara has tried a few times to copy this style by plaiting her hair at night but has never managed to get it to look quite right. Sally Conway laughed at her in Year Seven and said she looked like she'd had an electric shock after sticking her finger in a socket. Mara hasn't plaited her hair since.

Going in the library is like falling down the rabbit hole. Mara could lose herself in there for hours. She has often left this wondrous wonderland late, late. Mrs Cassidy knows when to not ask questions; she reads Mara's eyes like a priest waiting for a confession. Once she touched Mara on the back of her right hand. It felt strange. It was then Mara truly wished she had a mother.

Mara can't remember much about their last home, although she knows somebody once pushed her to and fro, from behind, whilst she was on a swing in the back garden. Later, that someone had picked her up when she fell forward and cried. Mara is sure the person was a lady because of the voice inside her head. The voice that sang a lullaby to her is always a woman's voice – she is sure of that. Mara is also sure the voice sang the song after she fell from the swing.

Hush little baby don't say a word,

Mama's gonna buy you a mockingbird,

and if that mockingbird don't sing,

Mama's gonna buy you a diamond ring.

Mara can't remember much after that; she knows there's a bit that says something about a looking glass getting broken but that's about it. Mara decides that at some point when she's in the library again, she's going to look the lullaby up, there's something haunting about it – maybe the words will help her remember the face of the lady that pushed her on the swing – if there was a lady.

A sudden spasm in her stomach, not one of excitement, but one of sheer anxiousness, accompanies a recollection of the events from the night before. Mara tries not to think on it but Joseph's face haunts her still; even with her eyes closed she keeps having flashbacks. His sweet dark eyes look up at her as he falls backwards. There is confusion in his face. He is frightened too.

Unsure if either of them are even alive, Mara half-convinces herself to wait until school tomorrow – she is sure to find out how they both are on the grapevine. An uncomfortable feeling in the pit of her stomach makes her wince – fear building up inside her once more – a small fly lying in wait for the spider to advance. Mara is now sobbing; she has gone back to bed. She lies curled up like a quaver underneath the covers for another forty minutes before she finally rises in order to begin her Saturday ritual.

***

Mara has been crushing and grinding glass downstairs on the kitchen table for almost an hour now. It is important to persevere until the right powdery consistency is reached - it regularly needs checking. Like the tiniest grain of sand hidden in a busy sandwich, any trace can easily be detected by most palates, and more importantly, go undigested. In front of her is a large recycled paint tin containing bird seed. Mara taps the dark-green granite pestle lightly on the side of the small and matching mortar bowl, before she continues reducing the content into a fine, white powder once more.

It was in primary school when Mara learned that these tools were once invaluable to any pharmacist, essential in the preparation for prescriptions. The better the reduction, the better the medicine could be absorbed, ingested or even inhaled. Some ingredients need pounding for a very long time, for example, for the purpose of insufflation.

Mara was shocked when her father gave her the pestle and mortar for her tenth birthday-come-tenth-Christmas present. She opened and closed her mouth like a fish. He has never since asked what she would like for her birthday. Looking back, it was obvious really; they had had numerous visits from social services that year.

Mara's father has been doing this for as far as she can remember. Her birthday is on the second of December; her father gives her one present for both her birthday and Christmas, at some point between the two dates. Mara has never received a present on Christmas Day. Her father says they are not religious people. Mara would like to believe in something – Mara would like to believe in someone.

To date, the pestle and mortar is the nicest thing he has ever bought her. Dating back, even before Roman times, in fact, even mentioned in the Old Testament, these ancient pounding tools are now deemed to be some of the oldest examples of medical equipment, the apothecary's symbol.

Mara has always liked reading. To Mara, books are her only escape from life – they brainwash her momentarily into places she wishes she could be – transport her into worlds that exist in paintings – that exist in the illustrations of various artists – a birch wood, an Italian garden, an orchard of pears.

The first book she ever borrowed was from the library at her primary school; it was a bulky medical dictionary. On every page there were pictures and symbols. Mara had not realised until then, that books that apparently told no story, books that were not fictional, did in fact, and quite often share many stories too – shorter ones usually, lots of shorter ones – lots of facts.

For example, under the subheading *Pestle and Mortars*, there is a reference to a Slavic tale, a tale about a woman called Baba Yaga who mothered her folk but was feared because she had a bony leg; she travelled through the air in her mortar, with her pestle in hand. She lived in a chicken-boned hut, dressed in firebird feathers – her long white hair wildly surrounding her.

Books are truly splendid, like the paperback she is reading now. It is a book about a boy with a dog who is not a lawyer but seems to know almost everything about the law; he is helping several people with their problems. The boy is a bit younger than her, but he is confident and very clever, so confident. Mara loves dogs. Theodore's dog is truly awesome, clever too. His dog is called Judge. Theodore has two very busy but very loving parents. Mara wishes she had just one.

In contrast, birds are truly stupid – why people choose to keep them as pets, when they do not want to be petted, is anybody's guess. They're dirty too. They take everything from people like her father and give nothing in return. Like the popular girls in Year Ten, they attract others because of their colourful plumage. Her father would rather spend time with his canaries than anyone else in the world, even her.

Mara has always wanted a puppy of her own, to raise, to love. When she was a child, and for as far back as she can remember, Mara used to help her father with his business, a family business he used to call it. Her father used to breed Dalmatians. They had a female dog called Lara – she eventually died whilst giving birth to her sixth litter, when Mara was ten. The third pup was so big, it got stuck. Her father, for fear of having to return the deposits that had secured each customer a pup, took Lara to the emergency vet, but Lara was almost dead by the time they got there. The vet reported her father for animal cruelty - overbreeding – wasn't resting her in between litters.

Mara loved Lara. Mara shudders uncomfortably at the thought of her father kicking Lara every time she chewed anything up at home. She was too young then to walk her, to help her get away. When the RSPCA turned up to take away the two puppies, it was a relief - for this time would have been the one and only occasion when Mara would not have been made to drown off the last third of the litter. Her father had heard Dalmatian runts were often blue-eyed and deaf – he didn't want to take any risks.

Mara looks across the table and out into the bleak and rectangularish garden. The orange bucket is still there by the side of the shed, adjacent to the bird house, at the bottom of the garden. It is now used to clean his bird house out. Mara tries not to recall the painful images. In them she is crying whilst holding the puppy below the water; it eventually stiffens – its lungs full of water – its mouth open – tiny bubbles frothing the water's edge - its eyes still closed from birth – closed forever. Dead. Brown bread.

Once her father had drank so much whisky that he missed two puppies being born. He'd returned to the living room to watch television and had fallen asleep; he lay sprawled on the settee like gossip under the bedcovers. The pups drowned there and then in their own sacs. Lara was too tired to break the sacs open and consume the afterbirth. When her father woke, he couldn't exactly kick Lara, so he chased after Mara and beat her instead. The puppies where white like new pages in a book - fat rats. Unlike Mara's bruises, the dark spots appeared days later.

Sometimes Mara can see the anger in her father's eyes, the frustration building up inside him. This especially happens when he has been drinking. Now Mara is older, taller, a little stronger and colder, he is conscious of something that did not exist before. He is conscious of her ability to judge him. It's in her eyes. The ability to judge. Her father may have never taught her much. But she knows the difference between what is right and what is wrong.

Regardless, Mara truly does not understand him. When Social Services became involved, when she was still in primary school, when the first bruises appeared, he could have got rid of her, burden someone else with her. Mara heard them ask about foster care. Each time he said no. Mara is grateful he liked her enough to keep her.

There are other girls in her class that do not see their fathers, girls like Sally Conway. Sally Conway used to tell everyone in Year Six that her father was a loser – that she was better off without him. The Friday before Father's Day last year, in Year Nine, Sally Conway slapped Spudhead Ted across his face for saying her father looked like Norris Cole in Coronation Street. She was seen later that afternoon by Summer Sinclair crying in the toilet. Sally Conway is the cock-of-the-back-of-the-Crown – she's earned the name through fighting other girls, outside school, in the carpark at the back of the Crown pub.

As well, Mara has no idea why he goes to church every Sunday. For as far as she can remember, they have always gone to church – even at midnight on Christmas Eve. Mara's father never prays, not even in church. He sits throughout the entire service, never kneels, never stands. When others line up for communion, he stays put like a stiff rock. Mara always goes to communion regardless; Mara hopes it might make her a better person.

***

Now the dark-green pestle and mortar has been carefully washed, Mara opens two tins of tomato and lentil soup, ready for later, for when her father comes home. There is no point making the sandwiches this early; her father likes them freshly prepared.

Mara replaces the lid back on the red tin before she puts the bird food away, back under the kitchen sink. Mara washes her hands. For a girl of fourteen, her hands are incredibly rough, the skin around the tips of her fingers hardened and wrinkled like she's been in the bath for hours.

It is almost eleven now. Mara prepares some porridge before taking it in with her into the white and textured anaglypta-papered living room, there she will watch television for most of the day. As she turns on the small screen, the local news channel is reporting a local story that is about to end.

A young female news reporter, wearing a smart black dress with a white scarf about her neckline, is standing outside the ornate, metallic main gates belonging to their local park. Mara just about catches the last two sentences. '...dead teenager whilst the other is believed to be in a critical state. It is believed that later this afternoon, he will be transferred to the Walton Neurological Centre in Fazakerley, Liverpool.'

4

IT WAS TEN O'CLOCK in the evening when Hermione Folkard finally arrived home following a long day at work - the solitary household almost in near darkness. How friendless everywhere seemed – as friendless and as clinical as a hospital ward. Without her brood, her house just wasn't a home. Silence had taken over what once was a canvas to the senses; it now filled every room, reached deep and occupied even the smallest of corners. Ordinarily, any silence at all was golden; today, it was stony, unwelcome, a lonesome graveyard.

Hermione Folkard inclined towards the kitchen counter and turned the radio on; the soothing melody should have helped.

Well it's not far down to paradise,

at least it's not for me

And if the wind is right you can sail away

and find tranquility…

A visible note, lemon paper, rested effortlessly against the letterbox-red toaster. It was from their neighbour's eldest son; he had slept over during her short absence and attended to the dogs. One of them had been sick that morning. Still, the note went unread until the following day.

Hermione Folkard looked towards the back door; the relentless scratching at its lower half, was beginning to irritate her. She quickly made herself a mug of coffee before she surrendered and let the two Labradors in. 'Come on girls, that's it, come on.'

Slipper's chocolate-brown body trundled forward, needy as always, restless. Her tired and ageing body said she needed more exercise; her attention-seeking eyes pleaded for more food. Similar in colour, yet thinner and a tad taller, the younger of the two, Socks, followed. She didn't really care for the food, right then, at that point in time, she was too pleased to see a familiar face back home. From the look of them both right then and there, one would have dialled immediately for the RSPCA, their eyes oozing neglect – a psychological protest for anyone interested, anyone willing to hold eye contact.

***

Almost twenty-four hours earlier, Friday evening, she had been happily settled at Comlongon in bonnie-wee Scotland. Her brief romantic break was then followed by a monotonous three hour drive south and an even lonelier drive back home to Southport, their much-loved seaside resort. It took twenty minutes before the heated seats managed to fight off the intense cold that had somehow breached the vehicle like a thief in the night.

Inspector Folkard arrived at the crime scene not long after Chief Superintendent Reid had left – small blessing she supposed. Unsurprisingly, Sergeant Shakespeare was still there. Inspector Folkard headed for the familiar unmarked vehicle and rapped gently on a window belonging to the driver's side. It didn't take long for Sergeant Shakespeare to awaken. Her tiredness was obvious – she was clearly relieved that her colleague was finally there.

'Thought you'd never get here!'

Relief etched across her face, Sergeant Shakespeare exited the police vehicle. She ran both palms back over her dark wispy hair, checking her short ponytail was still intact. She quickly altered the odd pin here and there before she pulled a thick, woollen navy hat over her head. Even in the obscure light, her pallid skin seemed almost transparent, the streetlight glare failing to warm her appearance in any way.

Overalls on and latex gloves affixed, the two detectives headed together for the park gates. Beyond there, about four hundred metres ahead, the crime scene - the tunnel.

'Any sign of which entrance to the park the boys used?'

Inspector Folkard rubbed her hands together, it was freezing cold. The sky was cloudless, a merciless wind blowing.

'Most likely, the back of the park – evidence of spillage from a bucket we think – its contents - must have carried the bucket from one of their homes to here.'

'Where do the lads live?'

'Jacob Lamb, the deceased, resided at 200 Preston Road, a few minutes in a car – fifteen walking. He's at the Hospital Mortuary. The other, Joseph Rawcliffe, not far from the park either, top of Balmoral Lane itself, number 4, five minutes walk.'

'Bucket?'

Sergeant Shakespeare pointed ahead.

'At the crime scene. Empty. From the little left behind, it looks like it had been filled with some sort of liquid - sticky stuff. Red liquid, I think. Possibly fake blood - seems too sticky for food colouring, although it could have been mixed with water.'

From the sub-zero temperature, it was hard to believe next month would mark the beginning of spring. Mind, it was nearly three in the morning. It was almost impossible to prevent the cold taking hold of them – it fastened its grip-like-vice and refused to let go. How Sergeant Shakespeare had managed to wait for her, even inside the car, in such unforgiving conditions and for so long, was anyone's guess.

'SOCO still here?'

'Yep. Up ahead.'

'Which one?'

'George Davies. Doesn't look too happy.'

'We'll miss him when he's gone though. Great dry sense of humour. Heard he's retiring – end of Easter, I think.'

Together they quickened their pace. There was little to be seen anywhere. Black contours belonging to the various vegetation, some with branches that threatened to take hold as they passed, merged into the background like grotesque statuettes. Bulky, bulbous-shaped bushes, like giant candyfloss clouds, closely surrounded them. There were no lampposts or ground lights of any sort once inside the park; right now, their only illumination came from above. The obliging moon, her grey spotlight glowing like a gigantic firefly, had now temporarily become their only overhead torchlight.

The path they followed was at intervals a little brightened by a crass ginger glow coming from the occasional street lamp outside the park. How quiet it was now – like walking through a churchyard – peaceful and yet eerie.

Within a few minutes they arrived – the tunnel ahead of them, about twenty metres long, snaking to the left – the top of it three metres from the ground, all greyish mottled stone, with large boulders up the left side of it. No bodies though – just the usual demarcations ahead.

'Morning George. So what have you got for us.' A short man raised himself slightly. His wavy grey hair, was now tied tightly back in a ponytail. His hatchet face rendered him ageless; he could have been in his early forties, he could have been in his late fifties. When he looked up, only the lower half of his face was truly visible. Although his mouth opened, his lips remained fixed, like he had lost all ability to smile – taut.

'Retiring this summer. Can't wait. Can't wait to spend every night, on every weekend, without being disturbed. Seems like the entire Merseyside Police waits for me to go to bed before they pick up the phone and call me in.'

'What happened to Easter? Or shouldn't I ask?' uttered Inspector Folkard tactfully.

Davies shook his head before he finally smiled wryly. He paused momentarily before he spoke again. 'No can do. Only daughter's wedding, wedding number two – the last one cost an arm and a leg too!'

For a moment nobody spoke. 'The deceased was identified by a group of three kids,' began Davies. 'PC Clark has the witness statements and a bus pass, found in his coat pocket.' He pointed to a space where Jacob Lamb had originally been found. 'Sustained a head trauma, consistent with having fallen directly onto two of these boulders, almost certainly these two - here and here.'

With some kind of a writing implement in his left hand and a torch in his right, he pointed to a moss covered boulder the size of a medium cardboard box. 'The obvious of course - skin and hair here – on this one too – but no blood – no blood until he hit the ground. Nasty fall. Died almost immediately.'

'How do we know he didn't just fall?' interrupted Inspector Folkard.

'The footprints at the top of the tunnel. Both boys were facing away from where they fell – soil indicates they moved backwards – besides, there are no abrasions to the forward-facing part to their bodies – their faces clean too. If they didn't fall backwards – they were most likely pushed. That's of course where you come in.' For a moment he paused, as if expecting another question. Inspector Folkard rubbed her gloved hands together before securing her invisible collar tighter about her neck.

'How many involved George?'

'Not sure at the moment – that's the problem with parks - visitors, lots of them – dogs too.'

'Come on George. At a guess, how many do you think were involved?' George Davies stood up. He signalled for them to follow. With his torch he illuminated a recently formed man-made footpath consistent with persons walking up the side of the tunnel. The lilac crocuses looked translucent under his direct torchlight – the snowdrops a ghostly white.

'Recently, and at a guess, one. Maybe two. See here, the flowers that are snapped, broken – they're fresh – latex-sap still oozing.'

Davies paused momentarily before he advanced to the top of the tunnel. Now the light from his torchlight was thrown towards the soil that had been dragged backwards from the edge.

'When the body was discovered by a group of kids, others came – can't guarantee it but there weren't many at the top of the tunnel.'

All three advanced. Inspector Folkard crouched.

'There is a set of clear shoeprints up the side, still moist – smallish feet though – about a size six. Could be male or female. Most likely male. The two victims were of medium build, approximately one-hundred and seventy-three centimetres tall, weighing about sixty-five kilos each.'

'So not an adult then?'

Sergeant Shakespeare was rubbing her gloved hands too. She looked like she was trying to start a campfire with a couple of dry spindly sticks.

'Could be any age – maybe even another teenager. These footprints contain the most moisture – size six again. There's a strong smell of urine where the footprints are – someone wet themselves – none to gather though.'

'Maybe the killer,' spoke Sergeant Shakespeare, 'the person that was pranked? Clear shoeprints. Bit like Cinderella – find the slipper, secure the killer.'

Davies began to descend the tunnel via the other side. The others followed.

'I've taken samples of the soil.'

'And the bucket? A prank would fit?'

'Not for me to say.'

'Thanks George. Anything else?'

'I'll know more after the post-mortem. I'll be in touch tomorrow once I know more. May have the toxicology report then too. I took the first victim's temperature when I arrived. Had only been dead about an hour.'

'What about the other lad? Joseph Rawcliffe? How did he fall?'

'Much the same. But fell clean onto the tarmac. Nasty fall too. Lucky to survive. The injury to his head was less aggressive – as you know, he's in a coma. The super reckons he'll be moved to Walton's Neurological Unit in the morning – critical - fingers crossed he pulls through. Would save you a lot of trouble.'

'If we're lucky,' began Sergeant Shakespeare, 'he'll be able to tell us who did what – that's if he's not sustained any cerebral damage. His parents are with him now. McKenna went down to interview them.'

'Thanks George.'

Inspector Folkard knew how cruel boys could be. There was a time in school when she herself had been subjected to a school prank. When urine ran down the back of her legs after she had used the toilet with the cling-filmed ceramic, she was the laughing stock of Year Nine. Her form tutor, Mr Witcherley, refused to send her home. He walked away when she began to cry. It wasn't funny then – it still wasn't funny now.

'Might as well pack up now. Potential evidence has been contaminated – too many kids passing through – difficult to know what's what – footwear marks everywhere.'

With that Davies started to pack his samples away. It was time to head back to the office - time to set up a board in the incident room – almost everyone else could go home. Hermione Folkard considered returning home. There seemed little point; there was plenty of work to be done, statements to collect - a statement for the media to prepare. Already a local reporter had published online, a photograph of the scene outside the local park – the recognisable blue and white banners strewn across the entrance – the Chief Superintendent not looking best pleased.

Several hours later, Inspector Folkard witnessed from her office desk the dawning of a new day. Having acquired no sleep at all, she listened to the ticking of the conventional black and white analogue clock, whilst compiling a list that would be delegated to the investigating officers later that morning. Only then would she return home for a few hours sleep.

Walter was still on her mind. Hermione Folkard had looked up at the mechanical clock – it appeared to be ticking louder than usual. It was still far too early to call. She pictured him asleep, alone in the four-poster bed. She sighed before she frowned.

Dutifully, Walter had walked her to the car before she had set off back home; understandably, the rest of the family had opted to stay put. Who could blame them? It was late. The rooms had been paid for. Besides, Hermione Folkard would be knee-deep investigating for God-knows-how-long. They were better off there, enjoying what was left of the weekend – enjoying what Scotland had on offer.

Hermione Folkard stood up and looked beyond the almost empty car park. For a moment she scowled. Had she imagined it? Did Walter really peck her dutifully on the cheek? She was sure he had kissed her like one who submissively bids an acquaintance goodbye. She also thought she had caught him smiling, robot-like fashion, in the rear view mirror and then before she had another chance to wave once more, he was gone, gone far too quick, gone back indoors.

***

Finishing her coffee first, Hermione Folkard turned the radio off before dimming the kitchen lights. As she was about to ascend the stairs, alone, she affectionately touched an updated portrait of her family. Unusually, she had worn her hair down on this occasion; her grandson Mark was in her arms, his small right hand in hers. The girls were at one side, Harry on the other. Walter stood behind her, smiling. For a moment she studied his smile. Hermione Folkard's smile reappeared reassured. The youngest, Zita, was scowling at their grandson – she didn't much like sharing her mother.

5

IT IS ALMOST nine-thirty in the evening when Mara's father enters the front door. Mara is in the kitchen stirring the tomato soup with an old wooden spoon that has an unusually long handle. The spoon is older than Mara will ever know; it used to belong to her mother. Mara's mother used it religiously every year to make marmalade - in a large copper pan with cast-iron handles. By the time her father has removed his coat and entered the kitchen, the soup is poured; a plate of three ham sandwiches awaits him.

Mara sits opposite her father. She tries not to sip her soup too loudly. She is about to begin eating her sandwich when her father suddenly speaks.

'A lad's been killed in the park. Have you heard? A lad in your school.'

Mara is taken aback; her father is usually silent for a considerable while, once he arrives home. She is about to speak when he continues, his mouth half full.

'Two lads attacked. One dead, his best friend left for dead, the radio said. Passed the park on the way home, police everywhere – all sealed off. They'll have trouble keeping the kids out of the park tonight. Like to see them try!'

Understandably, Mara struggles to join in in the one-sided conversation. Her face has reddened like a robin's redbreast but her father does not notice.

Mara's father finishes his first sandwich before he continues.

'Have you seen the news? Goes to your school. They said *Stanley Secondary* - I'm sure they said *Stanley Secondary*. Did you know them?'

Mara's father stops eating, he is waiting for an answer.

'I only caught the last part of a news story,' states Mara, 'I thought I recognised the park?'

Mara's father stares at her for a few moments. He stares at her as if in disbelief – his mouth has stopped moving - the contents visible. He shakes his head from side to side before he begins eating his other sandwiches, quicker this time, like he is in a rush or angry. Mara's plate is empty now. She wasn't hungry in the first place.

Mara's father looks to the back door; she knows he is thinking about his birds. Like a cantankerous customer interacting with a well-trained waiter, he signals with his right hand for her to come forward and collect his bowl and plate. There's something about the way he signals with his right hand that has always annoyed her. His fingers are always positioned sideways, like a four-fingered Kit-Kat, whilst his thumb points upwards. When he signals to her, he sort of waves his hand by making small circular movements that resemble a non-committal regal wave. He waves them towards himself when she is beckoned, usually to collect something, and the opposite way when she is to retrieve, like a dutiful servant.

Regardless, Mara is deferential; she is at the sink when he exits the kitchen through the back door, the birds now solely on his mind. In his right hand he is holding a tumbler half-filled with whisky; under his left arm he holds the red tin with the bird food.

Grateful that her father did not draw her into his one-sided conversation, Mara remembers the words on one of Mrs Cassidy's large posters behind her main desk in the library. The words belong to a Greek playwright called Euripides: *Question Everything – Learn Something – Answer Nothing.* It's the last bit Mara's thinking about. From now on, she must avoid answering questions – avoid becoming drawn into any conversation about Jacob or Joseph, especially at school. In reality, few people ever talk to Mara. The *Answer Nothing* bit should be straight forward.

The kitchen sink is both adjacent to and below the only kitchen window, to the left of the back door. Only ten minutes have passed when Mara's father returns with the tin of bird food in his left arm in a headlock. Instinctively, Mara moves quickly aside, to the left, so that he is able to replace the container back under the kitchen sink, his large hands almost cupping the entire tin. Not long after, the television is switched on in the living-room; the sound of the television is heightened before he calls out to her.

'Mara, Mara. Come on Mara. Come through and see!'

It is difficult for Mara to know how she should react. She is thinking about looking surprised when she suddenly feels nauseous. Her father is standing in the position often adopted by football fans at the match; he is pointing at the television. A reporter is speaking outside Southport General Hospital, outside the A & E Department.

'Joseph Rawcliffe,' her father shouts, even though she is standing only five feet away, 'that's him, Joseph Rawcliffe. Do you know him Mara?'

'I don't know him very well. I've seen him around.'

Mara wonders whether to point out to him that Joseph, his sister Niamh and his mother, sit nearby to them every Sunday service, when he starts to point to the television screen once more.

'Jacob Lamb. Do you know him? His best friend. Dead.'

For a few moments Mara's father grows silent, then he looks at Mara. He fails to notice she has gone deathly white.

Mara is aware that he is awaiting a response, but getting the words out proves difficult. She shares two lessons with both boys, Maths and History. Her thoughts are jumbled – she is like a visiting tourist – the native language uncommunicable.

'No. I didn't really know him. Just seen him hanging around Joseph after school. They walk home together.'

A look of disappointment quickly develops on her father's face, before he sits back down. For a short moment, he gazes at Mara before quickly looking away – back to the television – back to the news report. Mara's stomach is hurting once more; the abdominal pain is getting worse. On top of everything else, her mind is a whirlpool. She leaves the living room and heads for the kitchen.

The pots and pan are dried and back in their cupboard before she has time to figure out what must have happened. Reality dawns. Mara shivers. She killed Jacob. He died from the fall. He died because she pushed him. Joseph is not dead, though from the brief report on television, it seems he is in danger of dying too. Although Jacob caused Joseph's fall, Mara knows, that in reality, it is all her fault.

'The one that is still alive,' Mara's father shouts from the living room, 'they've moved him to Walton Neuro Hospital – you know the place where they fix your head if you've banged it, like Steven up the road, after he came of his bike.'

Mara re-enters the living room, a wet and threadbare yellow tea-towel in her hand. Mara looks to the photographs that are now exhibited on the screen – passport-like photographs of Joseph and Jacob, side by side, laughing. For a moment, Mara looks at Jacob's photograph on the left of the screen; he looks so different – he has a kind looking face, gentle eyes. Her eyes move right, from Jacob to Joseph. Joseph looks much the same as before, handsome, caring, confident. Mara's eyes fill quickly with tears. For a brief moment, she considers talking to her father. She is about to say something when he speaks first.

'Go make a brew for us Mara. Run me a bath too.'

6

SEVEN-THIRTY AM. Hermione Folkard fastened her navy raincoat over her newly-acquired Harris-Tweed suit. Her thinning dark eyebrows needed plucking, especially towards the bends that headed slightly downwards. It had taken seconds to quickly pencil them in – like a magic wand, instinct guiding her right hand and making up for her diminishing eyesight.

Hermione Folkard tied her hair back into a neat ponytail. Her roots no longer needed doing; in the near past, it had always been a priority; for as long as she could remember, she kept putting it off. Now, she had returned to her natural dark-brown colour, she no longer needed to concentrate on what she viewed as vanity. Something rebellious, something deep within her, liked to avoid the demands set about by women, for women and essentially for the approval of men. As a tomboy, and for most of her childhood, Hermione Folkard had never gone in for the pristine look; she neither had the patience nor the time needed for what seemed to be an excessive triviality.

Thick eyeliner to the top eyelids belonging to her greenish-brown eyes and some tinted Vaseline to her cheekbones and lips, had been her make-up routine for as long as she could remember. On the occasional night out, she would still wear a brownish lipstick. Brownish with a red tint to it. It warmed her ageing skin, reminded her she still had something about her. Darcy had bought it for her last Mother's Day; she wasn't sure – it seemed too bright, her lips fuller. When she wore it on an evening out, she learned Walter liked it – it suited her he said.

The two Labradors accompanied her faithfully to the back door before they were expelled into the back garden; Slipper looked back dejectedly whilst Socks headed forward, straight for the bucket of water. Hermione Folkard hoped her brood would be home before her. Walter would give both dogs a good walk. At times like these, no-one really knew at what hour she would return home. Now the girls were getting older, they complained less; their default position set to Walter – he was the one that could be counted upon – and by everyone. When was the last time she checked he wasn't feeling taken for granted?

Upon closing the black metallic gate, she looked back at what seemed to be an idyllic life, her family caged in domesticity, secured from the outside world, it was a world that had at times frightened her horribly, especially since becoming a mother.

Time seemed to be passing by so very quickly. Like the silence she had experienced only the night before, it was unwelcome and friendless – the children were growing-up too fast. Hermione Folkard sensed something deep within her, something that she recognised immediately – had recognised it on a few occasions before today. It gripped her insides from somewhere deep within, warning her: she looked about for red admirals but there were none to be seen. A familiar sound announcing the arrival of a text from Walter grounded her; *Missed you, love you. Hope all is going well. Don't forget to eat xxx.*

7

THE STOMACH CRAMPS are so painful that Mara is unable to get up this Sunday morning. Her father bursts into her bedroom just as she rises and moves towards the edge of her single bed. He is about to say something, when he suddenly stops.

For a moment, Mara's father looks confused, even uncomfortable. His eyes glance quickly from her bedsheets to the window. For a moment, Mara thinks he is about to pass some comment possibly about his birds. It is raining heavily outside. Mara's father turns around and walks out of her bedroom; he does so in a much quieter way than when he entered - he even closes the door behind him, slowly.

Mara moves backwards in order to settle back into her warm bed. She is about to curl up, the pain is now almost unbearable, when she unexpectedly notices a dark patch of what seems to be blood, about half-way down the bedsheet. Mara panics. It is the colour of dried red roses.

For what seems to be quite a long while. Mara wonders if the stain has really been there since Friday evening – she hadn't noticed it before. Maybe she had not washed it from her back properly, it had after all seeped right down her neck.

Another sharp cramp and the reality of it all begins to dawn on Mara. Mara has heard other girls talking about their periods. Some girls started talking about them in Year Eight, most girls talked about them in Year Nine. When she first heard of it, in a PSHE lesson, she could not believe it, nor really understand it.

Mara is grateful to the internet for many things. At home she has no computer. She is the only teenager she knows, that does not possess a computer; she is the only teenager she knows that does not possess a mobile phone. It is fortunate that her father arrives home not long after half-past five, from Monday to Thursday. This enables her to remain behind after school, in the library with Mrs Cassidy, in order to complete her homework. Literally every homework now in Year Ten necessitates a computer but her father doesn't want to know.

In addition, Mara receives no pocket-money. Her bus pass and school dinners are provided for by the State, benefits she rarely benefits from. At school, she pays for everything with her fingerprint – either of her two second fingers from the thumb in work. Until it was put in place in Year Eight, bullies like Sally Conway used to take her dinner-money on a regular basis.

Mara knows there is always paracetamol in the cupboard, her father often wakes up with a headache. She does not have any money to buy *the stuff*, whatever it is, whatever it is that is needed to line her underwear, towels maybe? Mara thinks about the adverts on television; she can picture a glass tube filled with blue liquid being poured onto a pad of some sort – that is all, she must pay more attention from now on.

The last few years, her father has given her an envelope with a twenty pound note for her Birthday-come-Christmas-gift. Last year, Mara bought herself some mascara, a new paddle brush and some gloves; the rest she spent on sweets – liquorice allsorts. Mara likes the black and white ones best. They're minty; their firm cube-shaped stacks remind her of a zebra crossing. This year she planned on getting her ears pierced. She has since began stealing this and that to get by. It will be harder to steal a pack of towels – Mara will need to speak to her father.

***

Later that evening, Mara enters the living room still in her dressing gown. Her father is watching the news again. Mara abruptly places her right arm on the back of a wide chair, the second arm follows – her head lowers – she is feeling dizzy. Her father notices her pallid complexion. For a few moments it appears as though he is about to speak, but he does not. When Mara asks for some money, he does not wait for any explanation; he goes into his trouser pocket and passes her a ten-pound note.

'Thanks dad'.

For a moment they both look at each other – the word *dad* sounded strange to them both, almost unnatural.

By nine, Mara is feeling better. She has just finished reading her latest paperback novel, borrowed from the school library. Mara smiles – it was a great book. Theodore has saved the day – overcome so much, despite the odds. For a thirteen-year-old, he is remarkably brave; there is no doubt he is destined to achieve his dream of becoming a great trial lawyer.

Mara thinks about what she'd like to be when she is older. She looks in the mirror; her transparent, pale skin is a perfect advertisement for soap, although it unfortunately draws even more attention to the shadows below her dark and large luminous eyes.

'Nothing,' she whispers quietly. 'Nothing at all.'

Moments later Mara picks up the much-loved novel. She pauses over it momentarily, before putting it away in the green plastic carrier that is also her school bag, Mara reads a line from the front cover *The Perfect Murder. Theo won't stop until justice is served.*

Not long before bed, Mara is having a cheerless, bubble-free bath when she hears her father swearing loudly. Her father is not speaking to anyone in particular. He is not a great communicator.

'Another God damn one of my canaries is dead. Some bleeding little bastard's been at it again. Bloodied up as well. I'm going to have to isolate some of the males until I find out which little shit is doing the fighting.'

For a few moments Mara's father goes silent before he comes up the stairs.

'Another bloody dead bird Mara!' he directs as he passes the bathroom door on the left.

Mara lowers her shoulders once more below the comforting hot water. She holds her head just below the water – her hair swirling in slow motion like smoke. Despite the grim and challenging weekend, she decides she can afford herself a smile.

8

BY TEN AM. the incident board was taking shape. Photographs of the two victims, taken at the crime scene, had been affixed to the centre; a structured mind map assembled from each point of information, in black, what they knew to be true - in red, what they still needed to know or verify – alternative viewpoints too.

A close-up shot of the deceased, Jacob Lamb, was to the centre-left of the board – Joseph Rawcliffe was to the right. Above them was a blank space but larger – the size of two photographs, a grave for the guilty party to lie in. The edge of it had been drawn in thick black marker – three red question marks to the middle. This indicated the possibility of more than one suspect.

Inspector Folkard knew only too well that the longer the space remained blank, the more unlikely it would be that the killer would be caught. Once any suspect was identified, TIE would follow. Inspector Folkard hoped to begin the trace – interview – eliminate dialogues, that all too often proved a waste of time, as soon as possible. Regardless, they were essential to any investigation; on average, one in ten interviews revealed something that could support their enquiry in some way, identifying that singular source, according to Chief Superintendent Reid, cost too much of the tax-payers money and dented their depleting budget. Their suspect or suspects, could not only be charged with murder but with manslaughter too. There was no time to waste.

'Any change in Joseph Rawcliffe's condition?'

Inspector Folkard looked up from the preliminary post-mortem report she then held in her hands. PC Clark, having only entered the room, hot drink in hand, responded casually.

'Nope. Sorry. Still critical. Just came off the phone.'

'Do me a favour Juliet. Get down to the Neuro ward and speak to the team caring for him. Speak to the parents too. Try and find out, as sensitively as you can if he is likely to pull through.'

PC Clark's face looked downwards towards her mug of coffee.

'Sure. Ok if I finish this first?'

Sergeant Shakespeare looked in the direction of Inspector Folkard.

'Jacob's post-mortem report?'

Still encased in her swivel chair; she used her two legs, staccato fashion, in order to move in jerk-like phases towards Inspector Folkard. Although a little pallid still, she was looking much better.

'Yes. What we expected really, more of what we already knew – severe head trauma, back injury consistent with the fall, punctured right lung - a fracture to the right shoulder that had gone unnoticed at the time. We'll know more when George calls us in for the full post-mortem.'

'Estimated time of death?'

Sergeant Shakespeare leaned over.

'According to this, the estimated time of death has been recorded as anytime between six and eight in the evening. The boys were discovered just after eight. The discovery helped. George's initial examination, using his thermometer, wasn't as reliable as he would have liked it to be - the weather too cold.'

'Fits in with both parents' accounts – Jacob called for Joseph before they went out – between five-thirty and six that night.'

'More interesting is the lab report, ' began Inspector Folkard, 'there were traces of human urine in the soil taken from the side of the tunnel – possibly the same urine found in a dried up, frozen patch on the concrete where the liquid patch was found.'

Sergeant Shakespeare shook her head.

'That could mean anything. Unfortunately, traces of urine is most probably found almost anywhere in a park.'

'I know. Unfortunately contaminated – but, what if,' continued Inspector Folkard, 'our killer, who was the victim of a prank of some sort, passed through the tunnel, was drowned in fake blood before he or she went on to wet themselves in response.'

Sergeant Shakespeare stood up before picking up a red marker, adding the words *Victim of a Valentine Prank*, followed by a question mark to the incident board.

Inspector Folkard unfolded her right leg from her left before speaking once more.

'Lab report also states that the trace of liquid frozen on the ground contained chemicals used in theatrical or stage blood, bought most likely from a local dress-hire shop. Although fake blood washes off with soap and water – it can stain clothes. We need to bear that in mind when any clothing, belonging to any suspect, is sent to the lab.'

'Shall I see if any local dress-hire shops can confirm any of these details?'

PC McKenna, as always, was on hand to assist. He liked to be kept busy – liked to be useful. His lanky frame contrasted greatly against Juliet's. Luke McKenna was always trying to put weight on; Juliet was always on a diet. Together, and both in their late thirties, they had worked alongside each other for the past four years – two peas in a pod.

'Yes, thank you Luke. Myself and Sergeant Shakespeare will revisit the site again, now it's daylight. We will meet up again shortly after lunch; I'm hoping George will fit us in later this afternoon. Sergeant Boardley, PC Cunliffe – how are you getting on with the statements? Other than the two lads that found our victims, do you have a list from the TIE interviews?'

A tall Scandinavian-looking female in her late twenties, wearing round spectacles and an extremely lengthy pigtail looked down at a neat pile of collated paper, her left hand resting upon it. As she spoke she rested three of her fingers, from her right hand, on the side of the frame belonging to her spectacles. At times, usually when pausing, she would take her fingers away, only to replace them again as she began to talk once more. Although her spectacles never moved much, she seemed to be pushing them back further up her slim nose each time she spoke.

'These are pretty much straight forward,' she began, 'they're consistent in their stories and tell us nothing that we didn't know.'

'However, this lot,' began Sergeant Boardley placing her right hand on a scattered pile of statements strewn fan-like fashion, 'this lot,' she repeated shaking her head from side to side, 'have several inconsistencies – the perils of listening to teenagers who are either deliberately being difficult or were too drunk or stoned to remember. Many are certainly hiding something, most likely in case their parents discover what they were really up to! '

Sergeant Shakespeare was about to say something when Sergeant Boardley spoke suddenly again.

'There are even two statements taken by two unhappy and anxious couples, interviewed in the car park at the time, doing God-knows-what, all of them married but none to each other. In reality, I'm dealing with a bucketful of liars!'

Sergeant Boardley continued to shake her head from side to side, her immaculate bob moving rhythmically in accompaniment.

There were at least ten years between the two officers organising the witness statements. Despite this, they too had found much common ground since they had begun working together last year. They both operated in a highly organised fashion. Inspector Folkard knew she could count on both of them to neither misplace any paperwork nor to slack on any duty given. They both admired and respected each other's qualities. Together, small miracles could be counted upon – at times like climbing up a hill yet coming down a mountain.

'So nothing concrete for us to go on.'

'Not a sausage.' Came Sergeant Boardley's exasperated reply.

'Not a sausage.' added PC Cunliffe.

'And CCTV in the area?'

'Omar is onto it.'

'Good.'

At that point, Inspector Folkard received a text.

'George will see us at Southport's mortuary for the post-mortem as soon as we're ready.'

Sergeant Shakespeare nodded. Despite the clear screen – she disliked intensely watching George working his magic. In contrast, Inspector Folkard found it fascinating – at times she had been known to leave the room and join George for a closer look.

***

The drive to Botanic Park was pleasant enough under the circumstances. Even though the cold was unforgiving, sunshine bathed their faces. Hermione Folkard tilted her head back and for a few moments closed her eyes.

'I remember my brother Philip saying something about keeping your face to the sun and never seeing a shadow – I never really understood that. Haven't heard from him in a while. I'll call him this weekend.'

'Walter and the kids home later?'

'Yes.' For a moment it seemed as if Inspector Folkard had nothing more to say. 'Walter wasn't best pleased though, when I received the call – ruined our

Valentine weekend away. We were so looking forward to the break as well.'

'Wendy wasn't best pleased either. Nearly ruined ours too.'

For a moment, Catherine Shakespeare seemed to smile absentmindedly. Hermione Folkard noticed something different about her. Even her driving resembled a Sunday outing.

'Well! What's the mystery? Or shouldn't I ask?'

A few moments passed before she replied. 'Wendy asked me to marry her.' After a pause, she added, 'and of course, I said yes!'

Hermione Folkard was almost speechless. Despite their close friendship, she found herself feeling a little sad, surprised even. Why she felt like this, she was not sure? They had been friends a long time – it was as if the younger sister she had never had was leaving home, leaving and never coming back.

Catherine Shakespeare afforded herself yet another smile before Hermione Folkard finally spoke.

'Congratulations. The girls will be elated, everyone will. I'm really happy for you both. Wow. Any idea when?'

'Yes,' came the prompt reply. 'Summer. This summer. August.'

'Well, we'd best get cracking this case. Last time, it took us eight months before we wrapped it all up. We've got six until then. Fingers crossed.'

Hermione Folkard smiled. News of Wendy and Catherine's wedding had brought some much needed cheer to her day.

'It's not as if we have a serial killer on our hands this time. No obvious evidence of premeditation. Shouldn't be long before we learn who did what. Kids tell on each other all the time - always have - always will.'

Hermione Folkard began to laugh.

'You're probably right of course. Let's hope you haven't spoken too soon Catherine Shakespeare.'

Moments later she added, 'I myself am determined, this time, to get away with Walter, undisturbed. I may even post a notice in the form of a public appeal in *The Southport Visitor*, asking the residents of our quaint seaside town to behave themselves for the duration of my break for the sake of my marriage!'

The two women exited the car still laughing as they gathered their possessions and headed for the park. How naturally a physical detachment grew between them as soon as they were within the company of anyone else – their formality re-established, their professionalism unquestionable - a sturdy ship on murky waters, both sails juxtaposed, complimenting one another, heading in the same direction.

In daylight, the botanical park didn't seem much different, although the scene of the crime seemed to appear sooner than they had anticipated – the visible blue and white tape safe-guarding and securing the area was still there – a tent now erected before the tunnel.

Together, they studied the scene, played out the possible scenario. A yellow indicator had been placed where the liquid appeared to have fallen onto the ground. Several others appeared at intervals, mostly by partial or full footprints. Inspector Folkard found herself feeling some empathy for the one who may have urinated with fright on the spot – more likely to have been a girl.

Carefully, they ascended the side of the tunnel. They witnessed once more the carnage enacted upon the spring bouquets of crocus; even the odd snowdrop had fallen victim under some weight or another. From above, the height that seemed insignificant from below, took them by surprise.

'It's quite a drop isn't it?'

'Indeed it is,' remarked Inspector Folkard, 'quite a drop.'

The dried up blood, directly below was barely visible from above. The markers allowed them both to see things from the right perspective.

'Plain as the nose on your face,' stated Sergeant Shakespeare.

'A teenage boy is less likely to urinate on the spot like that. Remember what George said about the possible footprint: Size 6? I think we could possibly be dealing with a female, likely a teenager.'

Sergeant Shakespeare looked back over the scene before she replied.

'But the crime? I suppose a girl could push two strapping lads like them if she caught them unaware.'

'Well,' replied Inspector Folkard, 'by the speed she may have ascended the side of the tunnel, I think there is every chance she caught them unaware – was angry - although it seems less likely she managed to push both of them off at once.'

'Why a teenager? It could have been a woman – even an elderly woman. Equally anyone, more likely a boy could have been the one to urinate, maybe even from above the tunnel.'

'The width of the patch suggests the person did not move as they urinated – stood right here.' Inspector Folkard continued to look around her. 'And, if they left one of their homes with the bucket – there's premeditation to consider. Did they plan to soak any passer-by or someone in particular?'

Forty minutes later and their work was all but done. There were so many ifs and buts – nothing concrete. The interviews at the school in question needed to be conducted methodically – most likely, if it were another teenager, they would have attended the same school as them both; *Stanley Secondary*. Also likely, the boys would have boasted to others about their prank beforehand, maybe to some of the other boys that they hung around with.

***

George Davies, in his white scrub suit, gown and shoe covers, removed his plastic face shield before smiling candidly. There was no doubt now that he was in his element - the glass screen separating the audience from the action. The young unclothed corpse of Jacob Lamb lay on a metal slab ahead of him, a familiar range of equipment and tools arranged on a working table to his left by the head of the bed. Some of the tools had already been bloodied – a post-mortem for murder usually taking an entire day.

Jacob's head was being held in Davies' gloved hands. For a moment, it reminded Inspector Folkard of a scene from her favourite musical *Sweeney Todd*. Sergeant Shakespeare remained quite still whilst Inspector Folkard leaned eagerly forward. The microphone was already switched on.

'Good afternoon ladies. Well, let's get on with it, shall we?'

Inspector Folkard smiled warmly back whilst Sergeant Shakespeare only managed a polite grimace. Looking back, even the very first time she witnessed a post-mortem, it didn't put her off – she'd even questioned if she'd chosen the right profession. The most difficult, about eight years back, was a procedure involving a child – at the time she had only just returned from maternity leave. Catherine Shakespeare left after a few minutes, crying. It was dreadful. But necessary. Without the evidence – the perpetrator would have never been caught.

'I've already carried out most procedures as you can see. The subject Jacob Lamb was fourteen years old at the time of death, estimated between six and eight pm He has no distinguishing features to his body – no piercings, visible scars or tattoos. His muscle tone is average. He received several blows to the cranium, resulting in severe head trauma. His back and spinal injuries are also consistent with the type of fall, and in accordance to the crime-scene report.'

Davies moved round to the corpses right side, this time facing the officers direct.

'He suffered a punctured right lung which caused some minor internal bleeding. The fracture to the right shoulder is consistent again with the type of fall.'

Davies had now picked up a steel bowl from a working table behind him; he waved it before them before it hovered above the victim's chest – a Y shaped incision on it.

'From the few contents in his stomach, he had a ham and cheese sandwich for lunch - chicken and fries for dinner. The extent of the digestion tallies with the estimated time of death.'

Davies returned to his original position hovering above the teenager's head. Sergeant Shakespeare took a step back as Davies insouciantly began to peel back the flesh from the head using a small, hand-held electric saw.

In a nutshell, George Davies was especially gifted at separating the skull ahead of examining the brain. It didn't take long for him to remove it in one piece; he had now reached a point in his career when he could carry out this procedure in his sleep. Here, he was an artist in his own right – his mastery unquestionable.

'The occipital bone is cut first.'

Davies picked up a small flat tool before he began to saw at either side of the skull, back and forth like a tree-logger, keeping the same straight line. A tool, a little like a screw driver, now aided Davies to lever the skull underneath. He picked up the saw once more; seconds later and the whole of the skull had been removed in one piece. Davies afforded himself a half-smile, as did Inspector Folkard. In contrast, Sergeant Shakespeare unintentionally placed her right hand across her mouth, as if holding back a muffled scream.

Davies' stage was set – the audience in his theatre in complete suspense. He teased the brain outwards and upwards with the tips of his fingers by rocking it from left to right – left to right – a little gentle tug. Moments later and he tenderly held the victim's brain like a new born baby – the organ pale, meninges giving it a glossy appearance. It was like a scene from a horror movie for Sergeant Shakespeare who looked like she was about to faint.

For a few moments Davies examined the victim's brain before speaking once more.

'Straight-forward. Some parts of the skull have naturally broken upon impact. As you can see here and here, pieces of bone have dug into the brain and torn a fair amount of delicate brain tissue. Most likely, had the victim survived, he would have sustained some significant brain damage.'

'Thank you George. So the official cause of death?'

'Neurogenic shock caused by severe blows to the head and vertebral column.'

Sergeant Shakespeare breathed a sigh of emancipation. The time to go had finally arrived. She was about to speak when Davies spoke again.

'The usual damage – a presence of blood, not unusual for such head-trauma – the swelling underneath has since reduced. There are no shallow lacerations of the pontomedullary junction with stretching to the mid-brain. In short – the head injury caused a quick death for our young man in question - always a bonus - to communicate to his parents that he did not suffer – very sad though - so young, his life no longer ahead of him.'

***

Once back at the station, Sergeant Shakespeare shared her news with the investigating team that had quickly surrounded them. Juliet and Luke both embraced Catherine whilst Charlotte and Barbara smiled warmly from where they sat. As news spread so did the congratulatory exchanges. How times had changed, thought Inspector Folkard, even in the last few years, about time too.

Brew over, PC Clark began by reporting on Joseph Rawcliffe's condition. 'I managed to speak to the attending surgeon. In the last hour, not long after I had arrived, the surgeon had removed a part of the skull away from the brain to relieve pressure. The fall had caused a lot of swelling and an unreasonable amount of excess fluid had built up around the skull – needed lifting. Joseph should be more comfortable now, but still, he is in a coma; he is in a critical state. A team of surgeons are to meet later this afternoon to discuss brain activity – check for grey matter.'

Sergeant Shakespeare's smile had disappeared instantaneously. There was only so much talk about the cranium and what lurked beneath that she could withstand in one day.

'Grey matter?' Inspector Folkard returned with interest.

'Grey matter. Grey is not good – when parts of the brain die or are dying, they turn grey.'

'Thank you Juliet – good work. Did you manage to speak to the parents?'

'Both parents were at his bedside. They could not recollect anything else that would be of any help to the investigation. They looked worn out. I didn't want to push them further. I did though manage to get some interesting information from Mrs Lamb. She had no idea of any possible Valentine prank planned by either boy but when I asked them both if they owned an orange bucket, she seemed a little defensive. She eventually blurted out that both boys had been watching the latest version of the film *Carrie* last Saturday evening, on the 8th. '

'Carrie?'

Inspector Folkard looked incredulously at the younger generation in the room – their faces both perplexed and curious.

'Really? A famous American horror film – 80's? – Stephen King? I think there's been a remake since.'

From the blank faces about the room she knew it was up to her to share further.

'A prank is played on a shy and unpopular teenage girl – bullied of course. She is humiliated by her classmates at the senior prom when a bucket of pig's blood is tipped onto her as she stands on the stage. Horrible really.'

'Sounds awful!'

'Must get a copy – sounds gruesome.'

For a moment everyone stared at PC McKenna before he spoke once more. Juliet's face was a picture. It was as if she'd seen her colleague in an altogether new light.

'Good news from me anyhow,'

'First and only fancy dress shop I entered in the vicinity of Crossens - CCTV as well – confirmed that Jacob Lamb entered the shop alone at 15:48 precisely; he purchased a large bottle of fake blood, paid £6.99 cash, left twenty-two minutes later after pretty much trying one mask on after another.'

'Great work both of you. Thank you for coming in and working all weekend. All coming together nicely. The full post-mortem report has been e-mailed to us already. Copy to be printed and distributed in the next hour by PC Stanfield. No surprises - straightforward.'

PC Stanfield, who had sat quietly listening on a desk by the incident board, raised his left arm before interjecting.

'Nothing from CCTV in the area. Very little of it – mostly in Churchtown village – none of it seeming important. There was CCTV around the park's entrance but none around the back. Neither Jacob nor Joseph appear on any footage, so by means of elimination, we can assume the boys entered the park from the back entrance, from Balmoral Lane.

Unfortunately, the CCTV outside the park's own café wasn't working. It is also possible that the lads, as well as the suspect, and many others could have both entered and exited the park by simply hopping the wall's perimeter.'

'A nightmare, thank you Omar – what about a possible suspect?'

Omar's striking face looked taut with frustration. The lines on his bronzed forehead gathered about the centre of his forehead.

'We have been able to eliminate some teenagers that left before six in the evening but I am struggling to identify many of them in that two-hour window, too many are wearing hoodies – lots on bikes too. Too many groups - like herds camouflaged by the dark.'

'Does anyone leave looking upset in any way? In a hurry. Alone?'

'I'll have to get back to you again on that one. It's taking quite a while. Lucy is on it right now; she's trawling through footage in the AV room. She is following a few possible leads taken from a number of freeze frames. We'll let you know as soon as we have anything. Sorry, that's all we've got so far.'

Inspector Folkard stood up and pointed to the photograph of *Stanley Secondary* on the Incident Board.

'Tomorrow, a team of our officers will be stationed at *Stanley Secondary* following a brief assembly. We want students to be able to come to us if they want to – we need to encourage it. The suspect will most likely be someone they know. Somebody must know whom they'd planned to prank, maybe even whom they had possibly arranged to meet.'

Inspector Folkard looked to the incident board before she spoke again.

'We need to interview all school friends, including all students the two boys share lessons with. We also need to make a note of all students wearing size six footwear. Find out the names of any students who are considered to be at risk – recluses – our everyday Carries. Interview them – interview them all, in all years.

Sergeant Shakespeare, please contact the headteacher to make the necessary arrangements. For those who are not familiar with *Stanley Secondary*, it is on Marshide Road, directly opposite the house that once belonged to Mr Rimmer.'

PC Cunliffe looked towards Sergeant Boardley. She had joined the team not long after but knew little about the case.

'The teacher from *St Williams* – serial killer – multiple personality disorder. Had at least five bodies buried beneath his granny house at the bottom of the garden. They found the last victim just in time. Believe it or not, she's now working herself, as an English teacher, in *St Williams* of all places.'

9

MARA'S FATHER IS in a foul mood on this drab Monday morning. Approximately fifteen minutes before he leaves for work, each day, he takes a walk down the path, into the back garden. and heads to his beloved bird shed. There, he will check that the canaries have enough food and water.

Almost always, as he heads down the path, he whistles to them – emulates them – communicates with them. The pitch he projects varies according to the pitch of the birds themselves – quite wonderful to witness. It is alien to Mara, at times like these, how affectionate her father can be.

When Mara hears the back kitchen door slam noisily behind him, as he heads off down the path, she rises quickly and slips into his cornflower-blue painted bedroom, adjacent to hers, with windows that overlook the wide, back garden. Carefully, Mara positions herself behind the furthest of the two windows, bending down in order to spy on her father. From here, from this diagonal viewpoint, she can observe him and the shed, undetected.

Mara's father is already at the bird shed door, whistling most likely, taking out the key to the outbuilding from his right trouser pocket. He opens the door and quickly closes it behind him.

Mara begins to count, 'one, two, three, four, five, six, seven, eight, nine, ten, eleven, twelve, thirteen, fourteen, fifteen, sixteen, seventeen, eighteen, nineteen, twenty, twenty-one, twenty-two, twenty-three, twenty-four, twenty-five, twenty-six.' The bird-shed door swings wide open.

From the pace of Mara's father's footsteps, even from the stride of them, Mara knows instinctively he has found at least one more dead bird. Mara smiles triumphantly. In his hands he is cradling something – he looks down at it, at least twice, his face the very picture of wretchedness. For a moment she wonders if he ever held her like that, when she was a baby, but the fleeting thought disappears from her mind like a shadow thrown by a passing cloud. She exits his rectangular cheerless bedroom just as the kitchen door closes noisily behind him.

Ten minutes later, Mara's father leaves for work. From her first window, the one furthest from her bed and closest to her bedroom door, she can see his ageing grey estate parked on the drive. Although she cannot see his face from this angle, Mara can see his large hands gripping tightly the steering wheel. Inside the car, he places some post on the passenger's seat;

Her Father

Mara's father always takes the post to work – it never really returns back home.

It is eight o'clock now. Mara's father reverses carelessly out of their drive. He swishes it around one of the gate posts before heading straight out of the cul-de-sac like a bat swooping out from a cave. Mara breathes a sigh of relief – it is a sigh that is as long as the drive itself, longer even.

Mara has fifteen minutes to herself before she heads off. It has been a long time since her father has offered to drop her off at school; saving her the bus ride before the short walk alone, would be nice. If she had a mobile, she could pretend she is busy on her phone as she walks friendless on a daily basis but Mara has no mobile. Instead, Mara is used to walking with her head in the clouds – the books that Mrs Cassidy suggests for her to read help tremendously.

For a moment her stomach crunches – Jacob and Joseph, Joseph and Jacob – everyone will have something to say today, but fortunately not to her.

Mara heads downstairs for a drink of water – a headache is looming. She taps the left breast of her blazer; she has plenty of Paracetamol in the inside pocket. Mara picks up some soiled underwear to wash it in the sink.

Sun-streaks slicing through the gaps in between a tall and established mother-in-law cactus, cast dagger-like shapes along the back of her shoulder-length hair as she descends the first four steps before turning right for another three; the carpet along the stairs is awash with sun beams. They meander across her black school shoes as she heads towards the downstairs entrance hall. As she moves ahead towards the kitchen, rays ascend her black and white uniform, caressing her forehead as she moves, highlighting the top of her head where her untidy parting ends.

'Good morning,' she says out loud, her golden coarse hands held ahead of herself as if waiting to catch a ball. For a few moments, she looks at the shimmering light held in them – for a few moments, she is truly contented.

Moreover, the warm winter sun glows generously through the square windows belonging to the upper-half of the wooden front door. It warms the kitchen lino ahead. Mara closes her eyes before she deliberately jumps from the carpet into the blob of sun on the lino. It's a pool in a holiday resort, far, far away. Mara opens her eyes and smiles.

She moves ahead into the kitchen, her bloodied underwear crumpled up in her right pocket. She walks straight ahead to the sink below the kitchen window. Water pours from the tap like molten lava; it gradually heats up to the desired temperature. The sun is yet to arrive in the back garden; the back of the kitchen is mostly dark, dark and grey, like an old movie.

As Mara bends down to open the cupboard below the sink, in order to retrieve the soap powder box, she notices from the corner of her right eye some newspaper on the kitchen table by the back wall. As she turns, a sight to behold awaits her; not one dead bird but six!

Leaving her underwear in the sink to soak in some powder, Mara heads over to the table. Her father will bury them later – he always does this when they die – takes his time burying them, so that the next door's ginger cat won't dig them back up and play with them - he has a nasty habit of pulling the wings off.

For a few moments, Mara stands stroking the smallest of the six canaries. They are all lined up like chicken drumsticks – yellow and already a little stiff. Her middle finger rests on a feathery breast, as if searching for a heartbeat. She strokes its head downwards for several moments – the feathers white underneath. Mara's throat tightens; they didn't stand a chance.

It only takes twenty minutes for Mara to get to school - a small ten minute walk, left out of the cul-de-sac then along North Lane before she reaches Preston Road. The double-decker bus will then take her to the end of the picturesque and leafy wide road, into the centre of Churchtown, before it turns right onto Marshide Road. At the bottom of Marshide Road, not long before the marshes themselves, to the left, is *Stanley Secondary*.

Opposite is a beautiful bungalow – its mustard overture is pleasing to the eye. It has three ponds in it but no fish. Mara has always wanted to cross the road to look into the garden; there is something unique about it, magical even.

Next door to the bungalow's left, lives Sally Conway's father. He can often be seen sitting in the front-room bay window with Sally's grandmother also sitting at the table, opposite him, as if they are playing cards. Sally has bright-red hair like her mother, her dad has hardly any hair, like his mother. Mara has overheard Sally speaking of him twice at least. She hasn't seen him for years. From the tone of her voice she sounds very angry. Maybe that is why she bullies anyone she takes a disliking too. One of those people is Mara.

In Year Seven, within a fortnight of starting school, Sally Conway and Amanda Wells demanded half her dinner-money. When Mara hesitated, Sally pinched her hard on her arm. Mara didn't mean to yelp so loud – the few close by, walked away. The pain brought tears to Mara's eyes. Her father ignored the bruising. At first, Mara made sure he noticed, then she got the message – he wasn't interested.

Pinching Mara and other select students hard is something Sally and her ever changing roulette of bullies like doing on a regular basis. Since Year Ten began, the bullying has lessened – boys are their main priority now – God help them thinks Mara.

The bus chugs along steadily. It is noisier than usual today, packed with the same bunch of kids making the same exaggerated boasts that inform others of their incredible and unlikely weekend. Nearby, at least three separate small groupings are talking about the death of Jacob – and to her surprise the death of Joseph, that is, before a tall girl with long curly hair and false eyelashes corrects them, stating he is still alive but on a life support machine but still, at death's door from what she's heard.

'Tammy and Danny were in the park too. As soon as they saw the coppers they ran and got off home.'

The tall girl jerks backwards one step as the bus stops suddenly.

'If Tammy's mum knew she was in the park with Danny, she would have killed her. There'd have been three corpses for the coppers to find!'

Laughter. Wild teenage laughter.

A pretty blonde girl with skin like milk begins to speak.

'I couldn't believe it when I heard. I can't get my head around it; can't believe we'll never see Jacob again. I know he can be a div' but he's funny, he's...'

'Was funny,' interrupted the tall girl. For a few seconds they grew silent.

Mara looks away from the group that is now talking about some new talent show on television. She looks out of the dirty bus window. The windows are cloudy; yellow graffiti informs everyone who looks through it that *Cameron is a WANKER.*

They are about to reach their final destination. The bus passes their school before it arrives to their stop. The school always greets them from its side, the front entrance, right to the building, faces a large field. The car park is before the school; it casts a sideways shadow across neighbouring homes.

The unexpected sight of two police vehicles, in the school car park, sends a sudden flutter of alarm that etches itself internally across her stomach like lightning. It grows and fades at intervals like the beating of a heart. Mara wonders if they have come for her. It takes a while for Mara to regain composure; of course they have not come for her. If they knew what she had done, they would have come for her, to her home, sometime over the weekend. They are here to fish, sling their hook – they have no idea she is involved – why should they?

Mara is walking down a brightly decorated Art display corridor; she is on her way to her form room. Mara often arrives first. There she can take out her latest book and read – reading might calm her nerves. As she is about to reach for the handle of the door, the familiar nasal-like voice of Sally Conway reaches her like a witch's finger from behind.

'Hey! Marrowbone! We've all got to go to the assembly hall this morning.'

'Thanks.'

Mara is surprised by Sally's short outburst. Sally and her gang are like frenzied hyenas. It is strange how tragedy evokes so much excitement; in books the characters almost always cry – or at least show some sympathy.

But as Mara walks on ahead, she can hear titters coming from Sally and her crew. Although she cannot make out what they have said, she can guess - marrowbone no-frills, bought in the no-frills aisle, probably born in the no-frills aisle too, sure dresses from the no-frills clothing range. There are many different variations to the no-frills chant; the girls tend to reuse the ones that make the majority cackle.

Five minutes later and Mara is sitting at the rear of the assembly hall, about five rows from the back, just in front of the Year Elevens and about twenty rows behind the Year Sevens, eights, nines and most of the tens. As she enters the hall, she does not see the others standing on the stage. She only notices the stranger with dark hair like herself; she is standing like an unknown soldier, at the back of the hall, observing everyone as they enter. She even occasionally appears to be checking out their footwear.

At no point does this woman smile at anyone, just looks on. Her formality and aloofness sets her aside from everyone else – a police officer of some sort or an OFSTED inspector perhaps. There is no visible ID or badge of any sort. Mara thinks for a few moments that she would like to grow up and be like her, together, collected and seeming in control. Her hair is neatly tied back, a little eyeliner to the eyelids, simple, smart. When Mara gets home, she might try such a hairstyle – she has enough change to buy a hair bobble.

Mara is about to follow the single file of Year Tens into a row of chairs when the woman at the back of the hall looks her way. She looked at Kevin, then Fortune, then across to herself. Mara is sure she is looking at her longer than the others. Mara unintentionally stares back; she inadvertently smiles before putting her head down.

The assembly has finished now. Mara has avoided turning around. Mara has listened abstractedly; she has not been able to stop thinking about the female officer with the neatly tied dark ponytail. She is sure that if she turns around, she will discover that she is looking directly her way.

The children have been informed by the headteacher, Mrs Hart, following a prayer for Joseph and his family which followed one for Jacob and his family, that the police are in school to make some enquiries as well as to invite anyone who may know anything regarding the unfortunate incident, 'however trivial it may seem'.

Mara will, of course, not be visiting anyone in the room set aside for helping the officers in school today.

It is good that she is not in either of the boys' form classes, although she is in the same class as both boys for Maths and History. The police will probably interview everyone in their form. Some of the girls in Year Ten, from the row in front, are crying now. Mara stands. Her row is being directed out of the assembly hall, single file. Mara glances quickly in the direction of where the female officer stands at the back of the hall but she is no longer there.

10

STANLEY SECONDARY WAS a cheerless and unwelcoming building from the outside. It's overall concrete-grey structure now emerged into clear view. Ill-fitting amongst the leafy dwellings along Marshide Road, it stood three storeys high on its side; from overhead, an aerial view of a parenthesis-like-structure – encased within, several rectangular-shaped mobile huts.

Despite the investigating team's early arrival, there were still several stragglers hanging about the presentable high-school's double entrance, the glossy dark-grey doors rejecting any attempt to enter the building before the allocated time.

A thin boy, with hair that stood on end like an exclamation mark, rubbed his white hands fiercely together – all nails bitten; at intervals he would stop and hold them as if in prayer, blowing into the gap between them for warmth. Soon he was met by the arrival of another similar looking student, this time a girl. Coatless, they smiled awkwardly at one another. Before long they were circling the entire site as they talked – kindred spirits of some sort – the morning sun barely heating their thin faces as they turned left around yet another fruitless corner.

By eight, a team of four officers had stationed themselves in an oblong conference room, a salmon wallpaper with a lined pattern that rose upwards and sideways and spread across the walls like varicose veins. As they entered, a large horseshoe, made up of light-grey desks with chairs, awaited them. A functional whiteboard on the back wall had been partially cleaned; on it, the names of the attending officers in the room. In each corner, a two metre high, glossy cheese-plant cheering the otherwise clinical environment. With the exception of noticeboards and shelves, there were no pictures of any kind to be appreciated – a truly sterile environment.

The team set about placing a singular wooden chair opposite each interviewing officer, comfortable bloodshot-red seats. A gathering of small bottles of water, pens, tissue boxes and interview forms still needed sharing between the four desks.

The headteacher's administrator, a short and thin lady with very short white hair, possibly in her fifties, entered the meeting room pushing a trolley with tea and coffee flasks, an orange tin of assorted biscuits on the shelf below. She looked about bewildered, her grief apparent. The general mood in the school was a mixture of both solemnity and excitement. It was obvious on the faces of too many students that the news had spread like wildfire – some looked genuinely upset, others indifferent - too many seemed animated by the whole experience.

'Awful, all this. Absolutely awful.'

She shook her head before looking at PC McKenna.

'I've worked here for over thirty-years. I've never known anything like this to happen. I'm lost for words.'

PC McKenna smiled before she introduced herself, 'Dora. Dora Daniels.'

Immediately, they began the type of conversation that only occurs under such morose circumstances; this was filled with the type of soothing platitudes that are often present when someone is willing to listen. PC McKenna appeared to listen intently; his head nodded at the right points, his hands held together behind his back.

Mrs Daniels had just began to blow her nose when Inspector Folkard entered with the establishment's headteacher. A tall and slim female, possibly in her late thirties, dressed in an all navy suit that complimented her fair skin-tone, looked towards Mrs Daniels with slight irritation.

'Help yourself to tea and coffee. About five minutes before the assembly bell, Dora will bring you over. I'm sorry, I'll have to go now. I have two school governors waiting for me in my office.'

Inspector Folkard watched Mrs Hart leave before the white painted door closed firmly behind her. Her thin long hair had hung neatly at either side of her face, in tubular curls. For someone so young, and in her position of responsibility, she seemed ordered and unwavering, despite the circumstances – skills attributed to any decent sea captain used to steering the mammoth ship through choppy and unchartered waters. Yet, despite her composed appearance, her deep and large blue eyes bore the lines of someone ten years her senior. Inspector Folkard had admired her long, lanky fingers - piano fingers, her grandmother would have called them.

PC Clark held the door open as Dora Daniels was about to leave. She was about to close it, when she spotted Sergeant Shakespeare and Sergeant Boardley approaching.

'Great, you're all here. Stick to the agreed line of questioning. One more thing, ask them for their shoe size. If they're not sure or look like they are about to lie, offer to look at their shoe for them. Keep a list of all students with size six feet, girls in particular.'

***

From the back of the assembly hall, Inspector Folkard watched the students file in year by year. How solemn they looked; she was sure that, under normal circumstances, they would have been far chattier upon entry. At the sight of strangers, some of them laughed nervously. Many of the students did not really notice her at the back of the hall, their attention caught up with the visitors at the front.

From the back, most students looked the same. Few stood out and if they did, they did so for the wrong reasons – trainers instead of shoes, no tie, bronzer about the girls' shirt collars. One of the few students to catch her eye was a girl with shoulder length dark hair, skin as pale as milk. Her gaze, although momentary, was somewhat entrancing. She looked at her just a little longer than most, maybe because although she was surrounded by other students like her, she seemed totally alone. The others had looked away in order to talk to someone, do something. She with the dark hair and penetrating eyes smiled ever so briefly before looking away – a smile like a row of pearls. Like many of the girls, her feet looked about the right size.

Sergeant Shakespeare, now standing at the front, ahead of the school stage and behind a glass lectern, introduced the team of officers available to any students willing to share any information, however trivial.

'Let us decide what is trivial and what is not. Not only ourselves, but the families of Jacob and Joseph, would like to thank you, in advance, for your cooperation.'

The students sat very quietly; only occasionally did one turn to another to pass comment. There was nothing like a suspicious death to captivate an audience at this impressionable age. At intervals, some students began to cry – their collective grief obvious - the room holding them close together. Mrs Hart then spoke briefly before delivering a prayer, a prayer for Joseph and Jacob and their families and friends.

It was evident from a few blank faces in the room, mostly from the younger ones, that news of the incident had not reached them yet – they sat dumbfounded like sculptured stone statues. Two of those included the shy and thin wavering couple who had met so very early on that very morning. They looked at each other bemused, before they looked around them – aware now of the misery invading the room.

Along the sides of the hall, teachers stood like bewildered soldiers, the second nearest to the stage kept lifting her right hand upwards and wiping her eyes. She wore an all-black outfit, fit for a funeral. This contrasted with her nail colour, a deep red, the colour of altar wine.

By the time the assembly was over, Inspector Folkard had moved from the back of the hall, up the right-hand side. The room was momentarily silent, as if everyone was waiting for someone else to speak. A few seconds passed and everyone was talking again. Their chatter was inaudible, like bees buzzing. Rows of children were dismissed year by year, file by file.

They headed right and out of the hall, many, if not all, looking up at the stage at some point.

Inspector Folkard observed the older girls from the side of the hall; her own daughter was now in Year Ten. All heads facing away from her, it was difficult now to see the young girl she had detected upon her entry to the hall. Moments later and she had located her. Whilst many chatted, looked towards the lectern or filed out looking towards the exit, the dark-haired individual looked towards the back of the hall, towards the very spot where she had stood earlier. The students directly behind her prevented Inspector Folkard from checking out her footwear. She was only about 163cm in height – about the same height as Darcy.

11

MARA ARRIVES HOME after a good day. There have been no more inquisitive visitors to the school, although everyone is still talking about Joseph and Jacob – Jacob and Joseph. It is impossible to know what the truth really is – some say Joseph has since died in the night – others say he is knocking on death's door. No-one seems to really know anything.

When Mara first heard that Joseph had died *in the middle of the night*, she felt sick. She was in registration looking out of a window, the angry sun brightening the noisy classroom. She was looking at the horizon, the stretch of it, wondering whether the word *period* was related to a *period in time*. Just how long was this period in time going to last?

At first she didn't hear what Ged had said. What exact time constituted *the middle of the night*? When others joined in the conversation, it became apparent that Joseph had most definitely died, in the middle of the night. How did they know? Nobody was really sure. Ged had heard it from another group of kids on the bus. Mr Quinn eventually managed to quieten the ring-leaders but the gossip had spread like spilled milk – it found almost every groove possible and filled them like tormentors working on their victim's fears.

Towards the end of the day, Mara heard a teacher telling another on the corridor that Joseph had made no progress, was still critical. Sally Conway and her on and off best pal Amanda Wells looked dumbfounded on the bus when tea-leaf Tom said Joseph had woken up in hospital and was eating tea and toast. In reality, the frenzy of gossip and assumption behaved much like the metachronal rhythm of a Mexican wave – it rose then subsided, copied, exaggerated, rested before it was eventually re-born.

Mara approaches the cul-de-sac having not long got off the bus. For a moment, Mara's stomach lurches uncomfortably as she suddenly becomes aware that her father is home. In the near distance, its front end sticking out, she can see a familiar ageing vehicle. Parked on the drive, at almost half-past four, is her father's silver car. Silver is meant to gleam – it is meant to gleam like water pouring from a tap, shine like the knife on the front cover of the book she is now reading - her father's silver car is more like the wrong side of aluminium foil.

When Mara enters the front door, she is cautious to close it quietly behind her. Mara is scared. He must have somehow found out about the birds - her game is up. Her father has worked everything out and has come home to teach her a lesson – give her the hiding of a lifetime. For a moment Mara stands in the pool of sunshine that has been emitted from the front door. She doesn't want to step out. She looks at her feet and listens. Silence. Mara pictures her father sitting at the kitchen table waiting for her, the red bird-seed tin in his hands.

Eventually, Mara enters the kitchen – the house is still silent. Mara wonders if her father is hiding somewhere when she notices the back door is slightly ajar. For a moment, she considers locking the door shut - her father must be in the garden. If she locks him out, it will take a while for him to break the door down. This would give her enough time to run out from the front door – but where would she go?

Mara tip-toes forward; she takes the handle with her left hand before she quickly glances through the gap that is a wide crack, in order to make sure he is really outdoors. Mara sees him straight away; he is on his knees burying the stiff yellow birds in the rhubarb patch, not far from where the path starts by the back door. Mara fingers the key that is already in the keyhole when he calls out.

'Is that you Mara?'

'Yes. It's me.'

Mara has detected an almost friendly tone in his voice. Her father stands up and rubs his trousers down with both his soiled hands – there is a small damp patch to each knee, one is the shape of Canada. Mara's father smiles awkwardly. In return, Mara opens the gap of the door wider. Her hands are still trembling – guilt like a cat scratching on the inside of her stomach.

'Go and put the kettle on. I'll be in in a mo.'

Mara breathes sigh of relief – her father suspects nothing. He must be home early for some other reason – but why? Although today has been less troublesome, Mara is still feeling nauseous from time to time. Mara decides that after putting on the kettle, she will take a bath. She fills the kettle up fully in order to make herself a hot water bottle. Her father suddenly enters, just as she was about to fish the rubber bottle out from under the sink.

'Got a phone call today from the police – in work. They got my number from the women in the office at your school. They're going round interviewing kids who knew the two lads – said they'd be round about five. I told them I didn't think you knew them.'

For a few seconds, Mara stares dumbfounded at her father. She is not entirely sure what he has just said. She is sure he said something about the police coming round.

'Did you say the police where coming round? Here?'

Mara's father is using the friendly voice again. It has a tone that sounds careful, concerned even – he used to use this tone when Social Services used to come round, in the early days.

'Yes – to interview you. You must be in a class or two with one of them – or both of them. Said it wouldn't take long. Should be here in the next half-hour.'

For a moment, Mara contemplates running straight out of the front door but instead ascends the stairs like a dejected child that has been sent to bed early, having committed an unspeakable crime. She thinks of the book she is reading now. In it Todd lives in a place called the New World; everyone can hear each other's thoughts – they can even hear what the animals are thinking. Mara thinks it's a small blessing no-one can read hers; sometimes her thoughts bother her, even surprise her.

As she enters her bedroom, she is startled by a poster she had forgotten she had blu-tacked to her bedroom wall only yesterday. It is written by the same author as the book she is reading now. The poster, which takes up most of the space between her two windows, is mostly illustrated in black and white. Mrs Cassidy had flicked the pages of the book before her like a pack of cards – lots of black and white hand-drawn illustrations – many of a gigantic yew tree with a towering mass of branches and leaves in a human shape. Mrs Cassidy then produced a poster for Mara to take home. Mrs Cassidy's smile is never one that shows her teeth – it is one that shows her heart.

Yesterday, when she arrived home, she raced upstairs to her bedroom. After finally locating the blu-tac, up went *A Monster Calls*.

12

'SO NOTHING. Nothing at all was gained from eighty-two interviews – from two entire form classes, pupils studying alongside them, and sixteen close friends of the boys!'

Inspector Folkard stared at the incident board for a short while, her right hand gently restraining the left, the others sitting in silence. Little had changed in the last twenty-four hours. From experience, she knew this time period to be crucial – as time lapsed, the chances of finding the person or persons responsible lessened by the hour.

To this day, an unresolved crime was yet to be accredited to her name - the culprit would surely be found, sooner or later; he, she or they would be exposed and the case closed, although rarely ever forgotten.

Sergeant Boardley had a forlorn expression on her face.

'We still haven't interviewed all of the children, some were off sick and we have seventeen more home visits to make. We have contacted most of them and will begin interviews from four o'clock.'

Inspector Folkard fell silent for a few moments. She looked to the back of the room before she spoke again.

'Can I see the photographs of all those interviewed so far please?'

From somewhere on her orderly desk, PC Cunliffe produced a vanilla-coloured cardboard wallet. She smiled proudly before passing it over.

'Here you go, all in alphabetical order.'

'Are you looking for something in particular?'

Sergeant Shakespeare had recognised some indifference in the tone of Inspector Folkard's voice, an inquisitiveness in her manner. Inspector Folkard had the look of someone with an idea churning about in her head, a blinking thought that refused to disappear. In the past, her colleagues had seen many of these materialise into something beneficial or significant to an investigation.

Inspector Folkard looked through the photographs carefully. When she reached the back of the folder, she searched their faces once again - a look of disappointment then imprinted on her face.

'And the ones still to be interviewed?'

'Here.'

PC Cunliffe produced a similar wallet to the last one, thinner this time.

From the look on Inspector Folkard's face, Sergeant Shakespeare knew something interesting was now on the agenda. How long it would take before she'd share these thoughts, was anyone's guess.

'Sergeant Shakespeare and I will interview the third name on your list: Mara Aneka Bones, 25 North Lane.'

Inspector Folkard's sudden announcement raised immediate curiosity in the room. PC Cunliffe adjusted her spectacles without comment. Sergeant Boardley starting chewing on the end of her pen. PC McKenna and PC Clark looked meaningfully at one another. Only Sergeant Shakespeare followed her colleague back to her office. Behind her, the remaining investigation team had gathered around PC Cunliffe's vanilla folder. They looked upon the school photograph of Mara Aneka Bones with inquisitiveness before returning to their work.

Mara's photograph had clearly been taken when she first started school – she must have been about eleven years old. She had thick dark hair and eyes to match; this complimented her pallid skin. PC Clark skimmed and scanned the other photographs on the page before she spoke.

'Doesn't look too happy. One of the few that's not smiling.'

'Yes. Looks sad – troubled.' Sergeant Boardley added before she looked a little closer still. 'Think I'll check with Social Services – might be some history.'

Sergeant Shakespeare followed her colleague into her office. She stood there silent for a few seconds before speaking. It was intriguing watching her colleague's facial expression at that very moment; she looked like she was recalling an event of some sort, maybe something recent.

'So, what's on your mind?'

'Close the door will you? I'm going to nip home for a couple of hours to see Walter. I'll be back in time for us to interview Mara Bones.' Inspector Folkard was giving nothing away.

'Interesting name Bones?'

Inspector Folkard did not reply. She looked directly through the internal window of her office towards PC Cunliffe's desk – the congregation had now dispersed. Although attending a different school, her own daughter was in Year Ten too; in comparison, Mara had appeared much younger than Darcy, shorter, less sociable, vulnerable. There was something she had recognised in the eyes of Mara before assembly had begun, something she had seen many times before. It wasn't a coldness as such – more of a loneliness. There was something in her smile too – a child's smile – a smile that was never over-friendly, a solemn smile that kept everyone at bay because there was a nervousness to it – a nervousness created by a tension of some sort.

***

It was just after two by the time Hermione Folkard reached home; she was already running late – lunch would be waiting and so would Walter.

'I'm home!' Hermione Folkard had a habit of throwing her voice ahead of her. In return, and almost always, someone would bellow back a response. There was a short pause.

'In here!'

Hermione Folkard quickly checked herself in the mirror – as always, her eyeliner had smudged a little above each eyelid.

'Sorry I'm a bit late. I got here as soon as I could. It's great coming home and finding someone here – someone other than the dogs!'

They both smiled before they laughed – a nervous laugh. At the kitchen table was a sumptuous salad, made up of spinach, roast peppers, tuna, anchovies and olives. The table was set for two, a pale blue glass containing water to the right of each dish – a larger plate with two iced Danish pastries to the centre, her favourite, a small vase with bluebells too – lovely.

Walter was at the kitchen counter, preparing some sort of dressing to accompany their lunch. As he turned, a sincere smile welcomed her – she advanced and they kissed. They didn't kiss any longer than they usually did; it lasted no longer than a peck. But the kiss was different. They looked at each other for a split-second, not a moment longer than it would take a wasp to sting its recipient. Nonetheless, the look said something. At the very last fraction in its time-frame, Walter had looked down at her hands held in his before he looked back up sharing a much-needed reassuring smile.

On her behalf, the look said – *I love you very much. I'm truly sorry that my job comes between us from time to time*. His apologetic eyes said something similar yet something different too. Was it a warning of some sort? Could it have been a complaint even? Maybe it was a protest, one she had not taken seriously, maybe for years – how long had this gone on she was not entirely sure. Maybe Walter was simply saying – *you are taking me for granted*. It needed resolving – Walter mattered too much. He meant everything to her. Her mother had always said that it was the small things that mattered in a relationship. Unresolved they snowballed and grew undetected until suddenly the problem was far too large to handle and sometimes too difficult to resolve.

***

The drive towards Crossens, along the undulating coastal road, was pleasant enough for the two colleagues. The sun was shining brilliantly and the sky was mostly clear. The unblemished leftward view across the water, and along the coastline, settled as far out as Blackpool - the tower and circular rides at the foreground, a familiar postcard to the eye.

Crafty white-breasted and grey-winged seagulls swooned back and forth like the motions of a harpist – their angry squawks menacing, their beady red eyes weighing-up the variety of take-away items held by the most vulnerable.

Close-up their wingspan was at least a metre wide, their beak hell-bent on getting something, discarded or not. Inspector Folkard detested their mobbing behaviour. They seemed able to take off with a relatively short amount of space around them, their legs spread neatly back, like a well-trained dancer, taut, chest proudly protruding.

Ahead, also on the left, the disused salt factory had finally been removed, a fresh-water marsh in its place. Since the Marshide Nature Reserve had been created, about twenty years ago, huge expanses of salt marshes had formed and extended for many a mile; a network of popular footpaths, visible to the eye, had since appeared. The odd canvas-clad enthusiast, bearing bags and binoculars, stood rooted to the spot – emerald iron-men sculptures of the north, but clothed. There they lingered faithfully looking as though they had learned of something undiscovered, most likely invisible to the untrained eye.

The greatest spectacle of all came from the right, just past the only road at the latter end of the coastal road. Diagonally, and for as far as the eye could see, huge flocks of water-birds flashed about in ripples, breaking off at times before coming back together. Inspector Folkard marvelled the speed and agility as they wheeled and swooped across from the right, over the coastal road, to the left. They then made off along the tide line, passing through the resident wildlife before returning once more to resume their dance.

'Nice lunch?' Sergeant Shakespeare interrupted in the knowledge that they were minutes away from their destination. She had noticed her colleague had been quieter than normal, unusually distracted.

'Lovely. Just Walter and I. A lovely lunch.'

'Mara Aneka Bones. When did you meet her? What did she say to you?'

'Nothing. I never met her. I came across her. I saw her in assembly; I saw her and she saw me. She seemed to really see me – and I seemed to really see her. Can't put my finger on it, never can.'

'Well,' began Sergeant Shakespeare, 'Sergeant Boardley eventually got hold of Mara's father. He was at work. Works at the Italian restaurant on Lord Street. No mother. Passed away following childbirth. He has arranged to leave work early – usually gets home about five-thirty. Nothing from Social Services so far.'

'Good. Interesting. Any siblings?'

'No siblings. Just Mara and her father.'

'I've never come across that name before; it's an unusual name. Can't say I've ever met someone with that name.'

The lengthy coastal road came to an abrupt end – they had arrived to the quaint village of Crossens. Third from the busy roundabout, to the right, about half way down, past the historic village church, was North Lane. It began with a series of cul-de-sacs and ended by a disused Mormon Church. Whilst the area was not affluent, it was quaint enough – leafy at intervals, the road wide and generous.

The car slowed down before halting outside the first cul-de-sac on the left. A dark male with black wire-like hair and matching eyebrows was preventing them from entering the orderly horseshoe setting. He stopped half-way across the road and stared cross-eyed at their unmarked vehicle. What seemed to be his support worker, began to speak with the thin child-like male in an attempt to persuade him to finish the crossing. Inspector Folkard smiled patiently before lowering her window. The young man continued to omit sounds that resembled a child imitating the engine of a car. The female support worker smiled back before apologising.

'Not a problem.'

'Pie. Pie,' the young man repeated.

'We're off to get *pie* now aren't we John – off to the bakery for a nice sausage roll,' she explained.

For an instant, he eyed the vehicle suspiciously before he let out a loud hooting-like-screech; he lifted his left hand in robotic, jerk–like stages before he immersed two of his longest fingers in his mouth. For a few moments, he looked directly at Inspector Folkard. Eventually, after a couple of gentle tugs, his thin body staggered across the remaining part of the road. Ahead was a four-by-four garage - he had a bigger vehicle in his sights now. Even seconds later down the road, they could still hear the loud hooting-like-scream from the man who had the innocence of a small child.

An elongated, ageing silver car was parked in the drive belonging to the address: 25 North Lane. The square garden was to the right. There were no gates to the terraced house's drive. A thick green hedge ran at both sides dividing the cottage-like abode from its neighbouring homes. Unkempt and established rose bushes, reaching the height of the downstairs' windows, adorned the only border that ran parallel to the front of the house. Sergeant Shakespeare reversed the car back out. There was nowhere to park.

A white wooden front door, in need of both a wash and a lick of paint, met the arrival of the two female officers. Inspector Folkard looked to the left; the garden was reasonably tidy, although the grass needed cutting. In comparison to the other homes, it seemed the one in most need of some attention. 'Clearly no gardener – mind, he is a widower and in full-time work - a waiter.' At this point in time that was about all they knew, about Mara's father. At this point in time, they knew even less about Mara herself.

A brass knocker was at the top of the door. Sergeant Shakespeare inserted the tips of her two longest fingers before she lifted the triangular knocker and used it three times. Within seconds, the large shadow of a person could be seen moving from the room ahead, into the entrance hallway before unlocking the front door.

Inspector Folkard was looking upwards at the very left window. In the corner, a curtain was being held back – no face could be seen but Inspector Folkard knew she was there – knew she was watching her.

13

FROM HER UPSTAIRS bedroom window, Mara can see two females, in plain clothes, exiting a newish-looking green vehicle. Mara knows they are police officers; it's the way they hold themselves, straight like soldiers, swimming shoulders, pendulum arms. They attempt to casually make their way to the cul-de-sac, but in reality they are walking too fast; there is some purpose in their synchronised stride.

They are about to open the double gate that belongs to the house opposite her own, when one of the officers, the tallest, scans the semi-circular cul-de-sac. Mara recognises her face. She is the woman from the back of the assembly hall. Once at the front door, she looks up and locates her at her bedroom window; despite the distance between them, it is as if a taut gossamer thread exists between them – hanging in the air – connecting them somehow. Mara isn't sure why but she likes her.

Moments later, Mara can hear the voices of the two female police officers, having just entered the house. One of them is speaking.

'Detective Sergeant Shakespeare – Detective Inspector Folkard.'

Mara can hear the voice of her father too – he is being all friendly again; his voice is like freshly-washed cotton hanging on a line. Mara remains on the upstairs landing until her father calls her - he normally yells.

'Mara. Mara come down. The police are here.'

Mara takes a deep breath. Her stomach hurts. It also hurts where her ribs gather in the middle – undulating waves rising and flipping – a sickness inside that refuses to budge. There is no turning back and there is no way out.

Looking often at her shoes, Mara descends the stairs slowly; she looks upwards, as if in prayer, towards the tall and narrow window opposite the second flight of stairs – its church-like glow skirmishes the upper half of the wall – a vanilla haze. For the briefest of moments, Mara looks like one of those sacred paintings where the holy saint kneels as the light of God is cast upon the blessed recipient. Safe in any puddle of light.

As she reaches the bottom of the stairs, Mara crosses the hall and heads straight for the lounge; the door is already open. Her father and the two officers are all smiling when she turns right at the point of entry. In the far right corner, the television is turned off. Her father has put away his bottle of whisky. Outside, behind her, nature's orchestra.

Mara's father told her years ago that most birds sing in the morning, go quiet during the day, before beginning once more in the late afternoon. Mara is grateful for the distraction. She pictures their thin ballerina necks vibrating frantically, their breasts raised. Mara is listening intently as the shortest of the women reintroduces them both once again. For a moment she looks to her father, then she sits down on the chair nearest to the door. The taller one, the one with the dark hair, is smiling now but she hasn't said a word.

The shortest of the two officers, Sergeant Shakespeare, talks for most of the time. The phrase 'general enquiries' helps to somehow settle her. The other one, Inspector Folkard, just watches. Mara avoids her gaze; there is something about her – she could pick her like a lock if she wanted to. On occasion she looks about the room. It occurs to Mara that there are no photographs at all about the house. Her father has never bought the official school photograph.

'Thank you Mara for talking to us today. It's a lovely name – quite unusual.'

'Her mother chose it.'

Mara shoots a glance towards her father; for some strange reason, the unfamiliar revelation means a lot more to her than she could have ever anticipated. Her mother named her. Mara has always hated her name. When she looked it up on a computer in the library, it said that her first name meant 'bitter'. But Aneka, her second name, wasn't so bad. It means 'sweet'. Mara Aneka – bitter sweet. Maybe it is not such a bad name after all.'

'We realise talking about Joseph and Jacob could be distressing for you. If at any point you'd like a break, let us know. We can return on another day.'

Mara's father looks reluctantly about. His eyes are willing her to talk – he doesn't want them in his house any longer than needed.

Mara nods politely. For a while now she has avoided any eye contact with the Inspector. Mara's hands remain clasped together like a clam. Sergeant Shakespeare is talking again. Her voice is formal, like a teacher's but not quite. It is lower, softer, like Mrs Cassidy's voice in the library.

'Mara, how do you know Jacob Lamb and Joseph Rawcliffe?'

Mara pauses for a moment.

'I don't really - they're in two of my classes - History and - Maths – both of them – that's all.'

'Thank you. And have you ever socialised with either of these boys outside class – break or lunch, or even outside school, for instance?'

Mara is shaking her head sideways. Although she is looking intently at Sergeant Shakespeare, she can see Inspector Folkard from the corner of her right eye.

'Are you sure? What about after-school club, homework club, activities, sport, intervention classes?'

'No.'

Sergeant Shakespeare is about to ask another question when Mara speaks once more.

'I only ever go to the library after school. Neither Joseph or Jacob use the library.'

'What are you reading at the moment Mara?'

The unexpected yet authoritative motherly voice of Inspector Folkard surprises them all. Mara looks through the open lounge door and up the stairs. It is as if for a moment she has mentally left the room, exited in order to fetch her novel.

'*The Knife of Never Letting Go* by Patrick Ness'.

'Sounds interesting. Are you sure that you have never seen either of these two boys outside school?'

Mara unintentionally bites the right, lower-half of her lip.

'No. No, I don't know them really – how is Joseph?'

'He is in a critical condition.'

Inspector Folkard's voice is a tad louder now. Mara is unaware that her face is a little pinker, even her chin is pinker – she is perspiring a little. Inspector Folkard is speaking to her father now. They have changed tactics. Sergeant Shakespeare is now talking to Mara. Mara is trying to look at her but listen to both conversations at once.

Her father mutters things like – 'it's always been just us two' – he adds to her question, 'her mother died after Mara was born. When her father added the word 'childbirth', he lowered his voice, she is sure he did. She is also sure that he paused for the tiniest fraction in time before he uttered the word.

Mara is still sitting as Inspector Folkard and her father stand. Sergeant Shakespeare and Mara follow.

'And are you enjoying the book, your Ness book?'

Inspector Folkard is looking straight at her. She is waiting for a reply.

'Sort of. I've only just started it. I've also started reading another book of his.'

'My daughter likes to read. She is about your age. I must recommend it to her. What is the story about?'

'A boy. A boy whose mother is maybe dying of cancer. A tree, the monster, he might help him – he is a yew tree, a healing tree. That is why the book is called *A Monster Calls*.'

'Thank you Mara, thank you.'

Inspector Folkard moves forward in order to shake her father's hand. For a moment he hesitates – he has his left hand on his stomach.

'Sorry,' he begins ', had a virus recently, stomach pains.'

Mara immediately responds when Inspector Folkard catches her unawares by holding her hand out to shake hers. For a second or two, Mara is a tiny bird in the Inspector's warm hand – warm like a mother's breath.

'Good evening to you both.'

'And thank you for your time,' adds Sergeant Shakespeare. Moments later they are gone. For a moment Mara's father stands behind her at the window; they are watching them leave the mouth of the cul-de-sac. Even though Mara is willing the Inspector to, the Inspector does not look back.

14

'YOU'D THINK BY now I'd have some understanding what you're up to. What are you thinking on Hermione?'

A familiar silence had now established itself. Inspector Folkard was most definitely preoccupied with her thoughts. Now sitting in the passenger seat, she gazed curiously through the window – seeing nothing at all; she still held the fingers to her right hand partly closed, in the grip – it helped somehow. Mara's hands had been a little clammy at the time, warm even, but not soft like talc. After a short while Inspector Folkard spoke, quietly at first, then with more certainty.

'It may seem to you that little was achieved from this singular visit. Although I'm not entirely certain, I am sure there is something about Mara - something that we are yet to find out – that will link her to the incident at the park. I'm sure of it.'

Sergeant Shakespeare knew better than to roll her eyes upwards but she did. She continued to drive purposefully but said nothing in response. For years she had learned the routine; she instinctively knew, especially at times like this, that any interruption could prevent what was brewing in her colleague's mind, come to any fruition.

'When we return, I want you to contact the school. Find out who is Mara's best friend, friends even – I suspect there are few. Find out her reading age, her overall progress – get me the last copy of her school report. Find out too if her father attends parents evening.'

Sergeant Shakespeare continued driving ahead. She mentally noted what needed to be done. It was now Cambridge Road all the way, all the way until they reached the station. It was less sunnier now. The large established trees towered vertically on both sides of the wide road. Their limbs gathered high above their torso-like-body – intertwined at the very middle, like old friends embracing. The bluish sky penetrated every pocket – with the movement of the car – an impressionism for sky gazers.

When Inspector Folkard took out her mobile, she looked at it with some concern. Walter had called – Walter rarely rang unless it was an emergency. The girls came to mind immediately. She saw then that she had missed several calls. She went back to the call list and punched the green button, it was ringing. For a while Walter did not answer. Her father came to mind, he'd been ill of late.

'Hello? Who is this please?'

It wasn't Walter who had answered the phone. It was a woman, a woman who seemed of a similar age to herself. She sounded anxious – upset even.'

'Who is this please? With whom am I speaking?'

For a moment Hermione Folkard hesitated; she didn't know why she used her full official title. Speaking in the formal tone of a woman scorned, she requested.

'May I ask who this is?'

There was a shrieking intermittent siren in the background now – a nightmarish sinister sounding wa-wa that grew louder and louder. When the voice spoke again, it was difficult to hear the recipient clearly. The speaker spoke for what seemed to be a long while before the call ended.

Hermione Folkard had not realised they had already arrived back to the station's car park. The sky had grown darker now – a thin veil across the landscape. Her eyes stung – welled. For a moment she was blinded, held her breath in order to combat the instant pain, sickened, drowsy.

15

MARA IS SITTING in the lounge in her light-green cotton pyjamas. Today she has remained at home sick – unwell. Mara never takes a day off school; her father won't let her. This morning Mara knew, following the police visit and her recent ailment, that he'd probably not deny her the day off school.

Her novel is now closed on her lap – her left palm upon it. She puts her right palm onto her tummy, her hand slightly cupped around it. Mara is truly grateful that her first period is almost over. It is hard not knowing what to do - relying on the internet helps. The websites she visited in the first few days advised constantly on the involvement of a parent – a guardian. Mara wishes she had something of the sort, someone to get her through difficult times. Her father relies on his whisky. He has relied on this beverage for as long as she can remember.

The attic.

Mara read a book called *Millions* last year. She cannot remember one of the boys' names but she does remember that even *he* got to see his mother, even though she had already died of cancer, two years earlier. In the book that she's nearly finished reading now, *A Monster Calls*, Conor got to see his mother too, before she died. Everyone seems to get to see their mother, despite tragedy – especially in books.

There are lots of adverts on television about beating cancer these days. Some of them do what her English teacher calls *personification* – what a great thing to use when writing – using a language feature that brings an inanimate object alive. The advert says; 'STAND UP TO CANCER'. For a moment Mara pictures herself standing up to cancer. She pictures herself looking up at the capitalised word floating in the sky like a gigantic cloud – she has her fists raised, poised for a fight, crouched, elbows bent outwards like a proper boxer. The adverts always sound so positive; nothing seems that final anymore – there is always hope – a chance of survival.

Mr Carey, her current English teacher, is a little like Miss Honey in the book *Matilda*. He has warm blue eyes, the shape of almonds; he is always smiling. Mara is not afraid to put her hand up – none of the children are. Even the difficult kids behave in his lesson. Mr Carey has a way of transporting them all to faraway places – his hypnotic voice lulling them across the ocean, miles away. Mr Carey told Mara, at the start of term this January, that she is above target in both of her English grades; he says she is likely to get an A grade in both her Literature and Language GCSE's. Mr Carey says she is gifted – that she will go far.

Once upon a time, Mara thought that she'd like to be a teacher – either a teacher or a librarian – something that involves books. Her father lost his temper last year after she forgot to turn off the bath tap and there was a leak. He said she was a good for nothing. When she was younger, he regularly used to say she was a waste of space; as she has got older, he says this less frequently. Mara knows this is a metaphor; a metaphor that suggests her place in the family home would be better replaced by anything but her.

***

Late morning and Mara has now finished her paperback. The police visit is less on her mind now. Even the image she had of the taller Inspector has faded in her mind – an outline fading on an old photograph. Mara is thinking about the novel again. She is stroking the front cover – the black and white illustrations are so striking, especially the ones of the gigantic elm tree.

It is such a sad story – one of those stories that is hard to forget for days and days. Was it a blessing, as some would say, that Mara never knew her own mother? Can you ever miss what you have never known? Mara would even settle for an elm tree as a friend – a companion – a guardian; she'd be more appreciative than Conor, even if a monster were to call.

The attic.

Mara is now looking across the room towards the window. In Year Two, at St. John's Primary up the road, Mara's teacher, Miss Bushnell, read her a story about a tiger that came to tea; she loved that story. Until last week, nobody interesting had ever called to their front door. The little girl in the book secretly hoped the tiger would return one day, even if it had drank all that there was to drink and ate all that there was to eat. The mother in the story went to the shop to buy special tiger food but the tiger never came back. Mara thinks that deep down she'd like to see *her* Inspector again, but she probably never will.

For a moment Mara's mind begins to wander again – back to school on Monday. Although it feels like a long day at home, by herself, she doesn't really mind. She has ground her glass, washed her bedding, done all of her jobs.

The attic.

Mara thinks about the elm tree again – the healing tree in the book – why couldn't it just cure Conor's mother? It could have but it didn't. So, the moral of the story is to accept what happens to you in life – accept it without much of a fight - accept that change is inevitable – deal with it – accept you have lost someone you love because these things happen in life. Be strong. Deal with it. Put up with it.

Mara shakes her head from side to side; she tucks the wisps of dark loose hair back behind her ears and stands upright. Unexpectedly, her eyes fill quickly with tears – she walks ahead towards the window and attempts to look outdoors, blurred patches everywhere, watercolours that merge across a page. Birds rarely sing in the afternoon. They do not sing now.

Conor has many keepsakes. He has letters and photographs and memories. He even got to spent time with his mother. He had twelve years more than she ever had. In contrast, Mara has absolutely nothing of her mother's, not even a photograph. For a moment she tries to picture her mother – like before, her face is always blank but her hair and eyes are dark like hers. Maybe her mother doesn't even look like her.

Mara turns right, away from the lounge window and heads for the eye-shaped mirror. When she looks into it she sees her father – dark, thick mop of hair; although she is much slighter, her hands are daintier. Mara asked at least a couple of times, many years back really, what her mother looked like…for some reason she cannot remember what her father had said at the time.

The attic.

The attic is smack bang in the middle of the upstairs landing; you have to look up to find it. Mara has never been in the attic. Her father used to often put things up there. He never goes up there anymore. He's never said she can't go up there; something in the back of her mind tells her he does not want her to. She has never looked through his draws – not even to put his washing away. Somehow, an invisible communication, maybe accompanied by regular facial expressions, thrown in with plenty rejection and a little disdain and aloofness, one that has gone on for years, has led her to understand what she can and cannot do.

There is also a large wooden blanket box on the landing; all folded washing lands there, bumpity bump, in separate piles. From there, they go their separate ways, her room, the airing cupboard, her father's room. Mara never really enters her father's room.

The attic.

Mara is upstairs now. She ascended the stairs like a discreet cat – curious; she slinked around the bends, blotches of light on each step like stepping stones to heaven. Mara is looking up now. A panel of wood – light wood – a latch of some sort in the middle, to the edge – no lock – no ladder. Her father will not be back for hours – she has at least four more. Mara looks towards the stairs. Downstairs, in the kitchen, at the back, adjacent to where her father sits, is a pantry. In there is a folding step ladder of some sort that is sure to reach the attic.

Slipperless, Mara descends the stairs quickly. Resolute, she puts the latch down on the front door. She tells herself that she could have done it by accident. The town's local newspaper, *The Southport Visitor* is on the floor. She is about to head over to the kitchen when a photograph of a funeral procession, surrounded by many police officers catches her eye. She picks up the paper, turns it before unfolding and reading the headline: THREE KILLED IN TRAGIC HEAD-ON COLLISION.

Mara is now sitting down on the third step – the skin between her eyebrows has wrinkled into a concerned frown. It is a larger than a postcard, all colour, a church surrounded by darkly dressed mourners; there is a procession of smart elongated funeral cars along the main road. Mara begins to read the first few paragraphs.

THOUSANDS of tributes have been paid to the families of the three members of the public who died tragically following a head-on collision on Tuesday evening. Southport's busy coastal road remains closed.

The service for PC Walter Folkard, a part-time administrator with Merseyside Police, was held at 10am at St. Teresa of Avila's Birkdale Parish.

Whilst the other two victims died instantaneously, PC Folkard was critically injured. He was taken by ambulance to Southport's General Hospital but sadly passed away later that evening.

Deputy Chief Constable Gary Griffin said, 'Walter was an experienced and highly respected member of staff who will be sadly missed by all his colleagues and friends at Merseyside Police. He was a popular man who worked as part of a close knit team – they are especially devastated by his loss.

The loss of this colleague is felt by everyone on the force. Our heartfelt thoughts are with his family right now. We are grateful for the numerous messages of support and condolence that have been received. He leaves behind a wife, Detective Inspector H.A. Folkard from Merseyside CID, three children and a grandchild.'

Mara brushes her palm across the page. In time she finds the familiar face amongst the front line of mourners belonging to *her* Inspector. It is unclear because she looks different – broken; it is a side view too. For a moment she feels anxious; the skin on her bare arms is raised – goose-pimples, she shivers. Inspector Folkard is standing stern like all the others, serious soldiers. To her right stands a younger man – his face is like hers – he is holding the hand of a girl about her own age but with blonde hair. Inspector Folkard is holding the hand of a young child with lots of dark hair; she has a flower in her hand – a red rose.

Mara touches affectionately the face of the young child before looking at all the other faces in turn. Despite their loss, they all appear connected, united in their grief. Mara is sure her father has never held her hand. Something tells her that her own mother once did – but she could not have.

Mara puts the paper down on her lap. She looks at her own hands. She holds them before her as if standing before the priest prior to communion. The powdered glass has made her fingertips rough – she has hands like a witch. She takes her right hand and places it in her left then she squeezes the right hand, lets go – squeezes it a little more – closes her eyes – the left hand is her mother's, the tiny right hand is hers. She lowers her right hand downwards a little down the palm, to make her hand seem smaller. Her mother's hand squeezes her tiny hand lightly. Mara does not move. She does not open her eyes. She sits there for a few moments. The house is still and quiet. Her mother gives tiny squeezes to her hand, reassuring her, loving her.

Eventually, Mara picks up the paper again. Mara looks once again at the photograph of the Folkard family. An overwhelming sadness is quite suddenly replaced by a determination to find out more about her own past – her own mother – what she looked like – more about how she died. She knows nothing about her family. Had her mother been a sister? Who'd been her friends at the time? A vague picture of a make-shift funeral of her own mother was now forming in her own mind. But she wasn't a baby in her picture. She was the little girl holding the red rose in her hand.

Upstairs once more, the attic door is not that difficult to open; the wooden part of it flips down like a waterfall – a gaping dark mouth awaits her. Somewhere in there, Mara knows there is a light to switch on – she is sure that this is the case – mind, the bulb might not work; it's been a long time since she has seen her father up there.

There are not many boxes up in the attic. There are a few bin bags but generally, there is very little up there. Nearest is an elongated cardboard box with the picture of a Christmas tree on it. Her father stopped bringing down the Christmas tree years ago. From the rustle as she passes the bin bag next to it, there is a bag filled with festive decorations too.

Instinctively, Mara delves through the largest cardboard box that stands alone in the furthest corner; it looks timeworn – dented corners – dust – lots of thick dust. Once upon a time, the box had been secured with brown duct tape – sealed with a purpose. Mara places both her coarse hands on the top of it before hesitating. Her father will be angry if he learns she has been rummaging in the attic. It will be difficult to conceal once opened; the tape is unlikely to stick back as it was. Despite a few reservations, Mara begins to pick at the tape with her nails – tiny movements like a guitarist plucking the strings – a melody unfolding.

The box is now open; the tape comes away with ease. It peels back like a banana skin, except it curls a little. For a moment Mara pauses. The delicate, unfamiliar scent of old things - musty even – ignites her curiosity. It invites her to plunge amongst, and to retrieve from within. The contents are dusty too – papers – cards – lots of cards it seems - wrapped packages with colourful ribbon tied all the way round.

Mara takes a thick batch out from the middle; underneath she spies what seems to be a toy giraffe. Mara blows at the front of a large pink card, now held in both her hands; being the largest, it holds many others inside its muzzled mouth. Mara is about to pull back the thick elastic band when it snaps apart with ease – parts of it stick around the card's waistline, like molluscs that colonise decks on wrecks at the bottom of the ocean. Inside, the cards have all yellowed a little, like in movies – some of their curly edges like a Cos lettuce.

On the front of the large pale pink card, at the top right-hand corner, is a large number 1 - silver embossed – slightly raised above the thick card. To the left of the number it says *To Our Daughter on Your First Birthday.* Mara frowns – she is a little confused. These cannot belong to her; after all, her mother died during childbirth.

Mara opens the card that confuses matters further. Her fingers trace what seems to be her mother's words; she does so slowly, like one who is partially sighted, feeling each letter – the dots that don't add up. Mara carefully re-reads the message that means everything: *My little Mara, my precious little miracle, Happy Birthday – Mummy xxx.*

Mara begins to cry.

In contrast, Mara's father has written no message, although he has signed the card just below the word *Mummy.* It says *Dad.* There is no kiss by his almost illegible scrawl. Mara looks at the front of the card – there is a lamb in the picture; it is frolicking and leaping about in a meadow full of blue butterflies and red poppies.

Other cards in the bundle are addressed to her – *To Mara,* they say. Some say, *To Mara Aneka.* Almost all of them are pink in one way or another – pink to make the boys wink. Mara does not know any of these people; she tries hard to remember but she cannot. One of the cards has a date in the right hand corner – Mara checks – yes, it is *her* birthday date, the second of December. These cards really must belong to her. Mara separates her mother's card from the others – she will take this one with her – her mother's DNA surely exists on this card.

Mara begins to lift other paper bundles out from the box. There are similar bundles for the ages of two and three. Mara removes the two cards that are addressed to her from her mother, magical. Despite the excitement, in the pit of her stomach Mara feels something that feels like dread; her stomach tightens anxiously. Had her mother really been alive when she was three. Was her mother actually dead? Maybe her father drove her away – took her away from her, after a fight, kidnapped her. Moments pass and Mara regains some much needed composure. She continues to rummage inside the box.

At the bottom, in the cardboard box is a wooden chest, the size of a large shoe box, it has a keyhole –

gilding to the edges. After a short while, Mara realises it is closed - locked; despite looking everywhere for the key, she has been unsuccessful in finding it. Mara disappears downstairs once more, reappearing in less than five minutes. Mara has a thin, yellow screwdriver and a hammer with her; she is determined to get inside the box.

The box is now on its back – a victim about to be split open, unless it spills the beans beforehand. Having inserted the thin end of the screwdriver into the keyhole, Mara lifts the hammer before dropping it down onto the screwdriver's handle. One gentle swing. One not so gentle. It's open.

The anticipation is half the fun, like now, waiting to lift the lid. Mara is feeling excited; she is like Pandora opening the great big box of the world. There are several folded pieces of paper inside - a few envelopes. But right at the top of the pile, is a singular photograph, a photograph Mara cannot avert her eyes from.

Mara has been looking intently at the snapshot for a few moments now. Her hands are at first shaking and her eyes are filled with tears once more. Then her body takes over. Tremors run through her body like a train track vibrating.

In the photograph, Mara is in the garden. She is sitting in a seat belonging to a small swing. The swing's frame is blue. The seat is red. It is one of those seats for small children that fits the child's lower half like a giant nappy. The child looks about two, maybe three years old – not a baby – her hair is dark and longish. The girl is laughing. The girl has most of her teeth – she is not a baby.

A lady is stood behind the swing; she has a pink patterned scarf about her head, like in the cancer adverts – she is laughing as well. It is impossible to see much of her face, she is looking down towards the child – her arms outstretched, elbows bent outwardly a little - ready to push the swing again.

Mara can't remember much about their last home, although she knew somebody once pushed her to and fro, from behind, whilst she was on a swing – someone who picked her up when she fell forward and cried. Mara remembers falling now. The lady in the picture held her in her arms and sang softly to her.

Hush little baby don't say a word,

Mama's gonna buy you a mockingbird,

and if that mockingbird don't sing,

Mama's gonna buy you a diamond ring.

16

TUESDAY MORNING WAS bin morning. Still in the same blue-checked pyjamas she had worn for days, Walter's pyjamas, Hermione Folkard dragged the heavy purple bin to the front of the house - today was recycling day. She returned to pick up one by one the four separate plastic boxes – some of the tins with paper still on them – some of the milk containers with lids. For years she had moaned to Walter about this – now, reminded of it, she felt bad – did she ever really mind at all? What had all the fuss been really over? How petty she had been.

Hermione Folkard started to cry. She made no noise. The muscles around her hoarse throat knew it – her head knew it. It hurt – it hurt and spread everywhere. Her arms had been heavy for days now, her feet too. Hermione Folkard tried to put down the last green plastic box outside the gate – funny how everything suddenly looks like a small coffin – so many rectangular objects she had never paid attention to - the smell of decay. And death.

She found herself remembering the time when she lost the baby – a long time ago now. For months she kept seeing prams everywhere – everybody had a baby to push – a baby to carry. Everybody had a purpose – all she could do was watch and carry shopping.

Hermione Folkard put the rectangular container down. She looked inside it again - she looked for a long while, and then, quite suddenly, picked it back up. The next time she'd have to put cans out, there would be no paper on them – they would be as she'd always asked for, made a fuss over, pristine and clinical and steel-like – steel-like, like her. The paper-wrapped cans were evidence that Walter once existed. If they were taken away, she'd be letting him go all over again. The cans had to remain. They could be useful.

It was raining now. Hermione set about filling each can about half way up with soil from the flower beds – the grass was growing already – spring was coming. In each papered can she planted a small plant – a small plant – another small plant – and there they all stood – smack bang next to each other on the outside kitchen windowsill, like targets. She'd be able to see them from the inside of the house, sitting alone on her chair looking out – searching for Walter. She could shoot them with her eyes or laugh sorrowfully.

Hermione looked up at the window – looked through the window. Like a Moore sculpture they stood freeze framed. Darcy was to the left, Harry was to the right, Zita was in the middle – she was the only one crying and being at almost eye level it was difficult to ignore. They were two feet away from her, on the other side of the window but in reality they were far, far away. Their needy red eyes beckoned her indoors but she didn't want to. She put her hand to the wet window. All three responded. They were there but she couldn't touch them, not really – she wasn't entirely sure she wanted to touch anything or anyone again. Walter was on the other side of a wet and cold pane too. Unreachable. Untouchable.

Had she remained at the castle that Valentine's weekend, they would have embraced – closely - a memory to keep her going. Instead she was filled with regret – empty – empty forever – a pointless physical longing that could never be fulfilled.

The mud was gathering around her naked feet now – it was cold. February had almost passed but it did right to remind her that winter was still about – grasping, freezing, seizing. Her right leg stung – the nettles – she'd told Walter about the nettles. Inside, confined. Outside, liberated.

She thought about it before she did it – small consolation – still able to make choices. She knew the children couldn't see – she was sure; there had been no point going indoors. The warm trickle defeated her, returning her to the earth – with Walter – like a wounded animal searching for the long rest.

She found a corner on the outside wall. She huddled in a puddle after sliding downwards into the mud – never to arise again – a woman in black – angry, defeated, revengeful.

A week on from the funeral, she felt no better – many said she would, but she didn't. She felt far, far worse – she wouldn't see tomorrow, she was sure. In her mind she had climbed inside with Walter – nestled into him – pulled his skin over - gone. Time ravages before it devours.

17

SLEEPING WITH THE photograph, the giraffe and all three cards under her pillow, Mara gets out of bed as soon as her father closes the front door with a slam. Although she has looked at the photograph many times, she knows she will not tire from looking at it ever.

Over the last few days Mara has felt confused and angry. More than anything else, she has been quite tearful. Mara has wanted to confront her father on many an occasion but she knows she will only be cruising for a bruising, although it may be worth it after all.

Mara is the girl with all the gifts. In Pandora's box she not only discovered the photograph, she also found a series of envelopes, a birth certificate and a will. Her birth certificate contains the names of both her parents; Morgan Bones and Maria Starling. They were unmarried. It also contains her name; Mara Aneka Bones, her date of birth: 02.12.2002 and place of birth, Southport.

Her father's place of birth is like her mother's: Southport. His date of birth shows he is four years older than her. Mara's father is now forty-four. Her mother's date of birth is on the birth certificate too; her birthday is on the twenty-eighth of March – next month she would have celebrated her fortieth birthday. It seems strange, not having known all these years when her mother's birthday was. For a while, Mara contemplates the date of her mother's death.

Mara is sure her mother is no longer alive. Her father once said she was buried in a graveyard near their last home. Mara is determined to see the grave – to see her mother come what may – to see the date on her gravestone – to learn the ugly truth. Luckily for Mara, the address her parents lived at. is listed just below their names: 24 South Road, Manchester, M22 0ND.

Under the heading *Occupation*, the singular word *Unemployed* is listed below her father's name. Her mother's occupation is listed too, *Nurse.* Mara's mother was a nurse. For a moment Mara pictures her mother in a nurse's uniform, working at a hospital, caring for the sick and the dying too. There are signatures on the page – her father's is merely a compressed nervous scrawl; her mother's, in comparison, is clear, legible, cursive.

In the box were a series of letters, all addressed to her: *My Mara (Happy 10th Birthday!)*, *My Mara (Happy 13th Birthday!)*, *My Mara (Happy 16th Birthday!)*,

My Mara (Happy 18th Birthday!), My Mara (Happy 21st Birthday!), My Mara (On Your Wedding Day!) and *My Mara (On the birth of your child!).*

Mara opened the letter for her 10th birthday that very same day. She only has her 13th letter left to open. Mara is sure she wants to read her next letter but cannot bring herself to open it, she is still savouring what the first letter said. It left her feeling whole, complete – it was then Mara realised how much was missing in her life. How much was wrong with it.

My dearest Mara;

When I was a nurse on the Children's Ward, I cared for a little girl who was ten years old. She was the bravest girl I ever knew, she was quite ill. She had thick dark hair, like you and a brilliant smile. I think you look like her now – wonderful, beautiful. I am so very proud of you.

I am sure you are working really hard in school. I loved school. Next year will be your first year in secondary school, don't be afraid, keep working hard, read lots, be kind to others.

The little girl I was telling you about used to like me reading her a book called 'The Water-Babies' by Charles Kingsley. I hope you like the copy I have bought for you, for your birthday. The drawings are mesmerising; they are drawn by an American lady called Jessie Wilcox-Smith. My favourite one is the one where there are two babies kissing and it says 'They hugged and kissed each other for ever so long, they did not know why'. I also like the picture of the baby in the net. I wonder which one will be your favourite?

I am sorry I am not there for you today, on your special day. Please never be sad, I am with you in spirit – I will always be close by, like a guardian angel, watching over you.

I love you my darling. Happy 10th Birthday my big, beautiful girl!

Mummy xxxxxxxxxx (10!)

Mara found seven more packages, none of them too large and in the same cardboard box; all of them have ribbon that go all the way round. She only removed the one with a number ten written on a sticky label. When she opened it, after reading her letter, she was elated. The first thing she did was hug the book, then she cried, then she looked up for some unknown reason and uttered the words: *Thank you Mummy.*

18

TAKING THE CHILDREN to school was Walter's job. Walking the dogs in the park was Walter's job. Basically, anything that kept life running smoothly and securely was Walter's job. How much harder life had suddenly become. So abrupt. So unexpected.

The urge to remain in bed on this Monday morning, was greater than anything else – the need to drink a glass of wine, even greater. Harry had returned back to his flat. He left shortly after dinner, on the evening before – Walter's place set at the table – nobody felt like desert. He hadn't cried much since his father had been taken so cruelly; he seemed to have drifted to a faraway place.

At the funeral, his uncle Philip made a remark about him being the man of the house. Both of them looked at one another for a short while. In reality, Hermione Folkard's only sibling was at a loss. He had been Walter's best man at their wedding; he loved him dearly. When he spoke at the funeral, he added that Walter had been the best man he'd ever known. Walter may have had small feet for a man, but his size eight shoes would never be filled by another. Harry knew that, everyone did. Like swimming in a sea of unconsciousness, life would simply go on, forever altered, forever dead.

Darcy had little to say. As usual, according to Zita, she was running late for school. According to Zita too, dad put mayonnaise in their sandwiches for their packed lunch – they were also allowed a chocolate treat. Hermione Folkard smiled. It really didn't matter now – she was never going to live up to their expectations but she would try.

The children had grown used to their mother talking to their father, as if he were still amongst them. 'You did, did you then? It's all coming out now! Oh well, no harm done, A chocolate treat isn't going to kill anyone.' For a moment the girls stopped in their tracks and looked at one another. Then they all laughed. It was a great comfort to them all, to continue their lives like war veterans, in the knowledge that Walter was somehow still amongst them. Hermione Folkard headed to the wrong cupboard before Zita lead her by the hand to the right one. It was filled with a selection of unhealthy snacks.

Hermione Folkard avoided the family portrait on the way out; the girls didn't. She needed to be strong, take control of her emotions – make it to work – be strong for the girls. In contrast, the girls needed to connect with their father, like he was at the door before they left, his smile wishing them a good day.

Together, they sat silently in the car for a few moments before Zita began to cry – Walter's red convertible on the drive.

It seemed wrong to push the girls back into an unwanted routine. She'd advised throughout her many years as a police officer, that this was the best way to help children adjust, following the loss of a loved one. She wasn't so sure now. What harm could it do if they were to opt out from normality for a small period in time? They could adjust when they were ready to do so and not before. Hermione Folkard wrestled with the thought of abandoning all routines and responsibilities at the point when she suddenly remembered that Darcy was now in Year Ten and studying for her GCSE's.

The engine turned over. They were on their way. A neighbour had offered to sell Walter's car for them; he said he would get them a good price. Hermione Folkard watched Walter's car in her wing mirror slowly disappear. She didn't need the money and she wasn't prepared to part with anything belonging to Walter. As far as she was concerned, his car would be waiting for her to arrive home forever.

***

It was raining heavily now. Inspector Folkard looked out from her office window, rain drops bouncing from the car rooftops, pounding them relentlessly – bleak as far as the eye could see. Sergeant Shakespeare entered, two mugs of coffee in her hands. Together they gathered, looking out, a sombre silence lingered.

'So - a phased return to work. Sounds sensible.'

Hermione Folkard did not reply. Catherine Shakespeare placed her free hand on hers – a therapeutic warmth failing to heal the broken.

'What time do you leave?'

'Twelve.'

'Well Hermione Folkard, we have work to do, and do it we must.'

Tears fell down Hermione Folkard's face before she spoke apologetically. 'I can't control them. They just fall on cue. It's so hard Catherine.'

'Time does help – you won't always feel this way. Like I said last night, one day at a time.'

'One hour at a time more like.'

'One hour at a time.'

It was unusual for both women to demonstrate any affection in the workplace. From outside the office, concerned colleagues looked respectfully away as they witnessed their captain allow herself to be held – near inaudible sobs permeating.

***

It was almost twelve when Chief Superintendent Reid entered the hushed incident room; soft conversations resembled those carried out inside a church – an atmosphere with secrecy. He stopped for a brief moment to glance at the board before he located Hermione Folkard by PC Cunliffe's desk. She had her back to him. For a moment he listened. He was pleased she had not taken any more time. Time was a great healer but it was also true, that keeping busy, at times like this, was a necessary evil. Douglas Reid knew the adjustment would be slow and painful; although everyone's journey would be unique, life after loss was inescapably predictable. His inspector's grief would be no different.

'So the toxicology report revealed nothing conclusive.'

'And Joseph's condition remains the same. If anything it is looking worse, the swelling has reduced very little – the chance of brain-damage more likely.' Hermione Folkard was about to speak again when Douglas Reid interrupted.

'Got a moment?'

Hermione Folkard looked unsurprised. She had been expecting him. She closed her office door behind him as Sergeant Shakespeare entered the incident room. A cut-throat gesture by PC McKenna informed her of his arrival. Sergeant Shakespeare had grown in confidence over the last few years; despite this, she kept her distance; she was pretending to read the incident board in depth.

'It's twelve. You leave at twelve. I want you to go home and take this time to do whatever you need to do. Sleep helps.'

Hermione Folkard's composure was fooling no one, least of all him. She sat behind her desk. There, she could present herself with some composure, keep her hands hidden and fidget when she wanted. Douglas Reid pulled a chair towards hers. When he placed his hand on hers, she was taken aback. For a moment she pictured Walter's hands, larger than hers, smaller than his, protective. She missed them. Hermione Folkard's throat began to feel uncomfortable; a tightening sensation followed.

'It's been almost fifteen years this summer since I lost my son in a car accident. It's hard to believe, but what they say is true – it does get easier - you never forget - but it does get easier.'

'I'm sorry. I didn't know.'

For a moment they sat in silence – she had joined a club – a secret club that only mourners could join – could possibly understand – the grief, the loss, the loneliness, the pain. A pang of guilt afflicted her.

'It's my only consolation, that I haven't lost one of the kids - that keeps me going. God knows what losing a child must be like? I'm so sorry.'

Douglas Reid removed his hand slowly. He got up and headed towards the window that they all seemed to favour that morning – a Blue Peter moment.

'You have an appointment with Occupational Health at twelve on Friday. Get the all clear – and you can return full-time next week. I've approved your request to start after nine until after the children's schools break-up for the summer.'

'Thank you.'

'You know where I am.'

When the Chief Superintendent exited her office, Sergeant Shakespeare pretended not to notice. Despite her coolness, an uncomfortable anxiety nibbled inside her ribcage as he passed. She hoped he would be patient. He was the type that expected progress to be measurable on a daily basis.

Sergeant Shakespeare's concerns were unfounded; Douglas Reid had experienced much since the death of his son. Recently, his brother had died of a heart-attack; he was only forty-eight. Life could be cruel. Going on, deprived of loved ones by your side, was hard. The death of his only son hit his wife the hardest – six months after his death, she took a large dose of sleeping pills.

***

The cemetery on Liverpool Road could be seen in the near distance – its location on a notable hill – closer to heaven; beyond it, was an open view of the sea. The altitude of many tombs and gravestones, on the face of it, towered well above anyone's height – solemn angels and archangels erupting from marble memorials supplicating with an arm raised to God, its dominating chapel to the centre of it all.

Hermione Folkard touched the odd sculpture with its intricate carvings as she wandered along the path; it was as though she were wandering through a museum or a park, at home with her tranquil surroundings. It was comforting to see how they flourished, in particular, over the graves of children, protective messengers from God watching over them in their parents' absence.

One archangel stood out amongst them all, it had large triangular wings, their tips almost touching the ground itself. It held its right hand as if raising a soul towards heaven. In its left it held a bunch of daisies. Hermione Folkard paused over the grave to read:

SARAH
DAUGHTER TO JOHN & ESTHER BARNARD
AGED 5 YEARS OLD
DECEASED 7 OCTOBER 1785

The little bed is empty now, the cloths laid by.

Hermione Folkard arrived to her final destination; she paused over the excavated soil now returned to its origin. The newly laid turf, a patchwork quilt, was a lighter shade of pale green – the contrast obvious against the rest of the grass surrounding the nearby, more established graves.

The wreaths and bunches of flowers spread far and wide; where the headstone should have been - a mound of flowers, roses, lots of roses. Hermione Folkard crouched down before falling down to her knees. She spoke to Walter for a long while, then, as she had done several nights before, she lay flat on her stomach across the tomb, conscious that her body should lay as if hovering exactly above Walter's – keeping him company, warming him.

It was a red admiral that awoke her about twenty minutes later. It had at first landed on her shoulder before it had brushed the side of her cheek. It seemed half-suspended in the afternoon moonlight before it quickly disappeared. Hermione Folkard woke from a much needed slumber; it was time to pick the girls up from school, time to rejoin the land of the living.

19

MARA'S EMOTIONAL ANGER has gradually grown over the last few days to a crescendo; it is a seemingly inexorable march that can only end one way.

She knows that sometimes parents conceal information from their children for what they call *their own good*. To Mara, it seems wrong to treat children like idiots, although to an extent, and in some circumstances, it is almost understandable. For example, if Mara's father felt unable to share details about her mother, because she was so young when she died, Mara can understand. But Mara is now fourteen years old; in nine months she will be fifteen.

To Mara, it all seems wrong, very wrong. Her father has concealed so much. Her father must pay. Take for instance last Sunday, the day after she opened the first letter. Never before had she listened so intently at what Father Stephen Smith had to say on the subject of forgiveness. He urged the congregation to *search from within* stating that we had all the power to correct our mistakes in our life journey. He added that our moral ethics required personal growth, that *today was the day to make some sort of an amendment, even if it was only the one*. Mara thought long and hard. She looked towards Joseph's empty pew. She wanted to correct her mistakes yet truly felt she was unable to change anything.

Mara then thought about the birds and the pestle and mortar and the Borax and her father who likes to drink whisky. She looked ahead to the glossy blue and white statue of the Virgin Mary who was holding her child tenderly in her arms, their hypnotic eyes fixed upon one another. Mara then looked diagonally across to the left of the altar; the statue of Joseph was of a similar size to that of Mary's. In his arms, he too, held closely a small child.

As parents go, they seemed dedicated, elated in their roles, loving. Mara looked towards her father, his face downwards as if in prayer; he was slyly glancing at the time on his mobile. It was a mystery to her why her father bothered to take her religiously to church every Sunday.

***

Mara has never seen a will before. She has heard about wills in school but never actually seen one – wills that are left by people who die – rich inheritances to be had. For a moment Mara thought about the word *Will* – it would make more sense to call it a *Want* or a *Wish*.

When she opened her mother's will, she was confused as to what it really was; she even took it with her to school to find out more information on the internet, in the library. At one point, Mara asked Mrs Cassidy what an executor was; when she looked it up on the on-line dictionary, she was confused. Mrs Cassidy's smile put her at ease straight away before she told her that it was usually a person who carried out the wishes of someone, as laid out in a will, who had died and on their behalf, following his or her death.

It began with her mother's full name, stating she was of sound mind – then, a few subheadings followed. Her mother, having inherited enough money to have bought her own home, had left her only living child, herself, everything that was hers. Under Section III she had requested that the child's father should take care of their daughter, homing her until the age of eighteen, when she would inherit the house that they lived in.

There were conditions attached, Mara's father had to make sure she remained in full time education until the age of sixteen. He was also to take their child to church every Sunday. When Mara reached her eighteenth birthday, then and only then, would he receive a lump sum of £20,000.

Mara was shocked. The image she has of her mother is quite different now; she seems shrewd, calculating and wise. No wonder her father had hung on to her.

For years he scorned at her resentfully – she never really understood why he hadn't got rid of her, put her in care, abandoned her. He certainly never made her feel wanted.

Her mother's will explained too their Sunday ritual. But when, when was he planning to tell her any of this? On her eighteenth birthday? Moreover, was he ever going to give her the items so lovingly prepared, by her mother, to her? After all, he hadn't bothered passing her the card and present meant for her tenth or thirteenth birthday.

***

On the way home, Mara thinks about her thirteenth birthday present and the letter. She decides she will try to hold on – wait a while longer.

In the distance, as Mara walks, she spies the back of her terraced home – her home. It is in between the corner house, belonging to Mr and Mrs Stone, and the purple-painted terrace belonging to Mrs Tanner and Mrs Lexton. It is her home. Not her father's. Hers. It was once her mother's and now it is hers. It all belongs to her. Mara's anger rises, her hands make a fist.

Empowered, Mara straightens her back and lifts her chin a little higher so that unknowingly her head rises a little. She takes confident strides around the corner, past Mr and Mrs Stones' bright yellow gate, into the cul-de-sac, that is, until she spies her father's silver car on the drive. Mara's stomach lurches. She hopes there is not going to be another police visit.

Mara's father is leaning over the kitchen sink as she enters. Even before she opened the front door, she heard him vomiting. The sounds of retching should be concerning – it seems as if he were gasping for air at one point – but they are not. Mara smiles. Her father lifts his head a little. He moves it a tad to the right; he knows she is home, standing there, watching him.

'Food poisoning!' he shouts.

Mara feels herself wince. She only stands at the kitchen door but the smell's repulsive.

'Probably didn't heat the lasagne up properly. That's what comes of rushing and eating on the job!'

Mara cannot think of anything to say. She is about to head upstairs when she spies some blood on the tea-towel he holds in his right hand. Mara pauses dead in her tracks.

'And Lou, she's dead! I came home and found her dead! There's only ten bloody canaries left! Ten! Last year I had near thirty!'

Mara's father's voice is getting louder. But Mara does not care. His anguish is welcomed – it is a black hole of solipsism. The pain he experiences both physically and mentally is incomparable to what her mother must have encountered in her last few months – cancer conspiring before taking hold of her forever.

On the kitchen top, by the breadbin, by the back door, her father's favourite bird, a female he has reared from near birth, lies there on its back – stiff. It's hind claws are curled, the legs erect, pointing upwards; it's chest streaks are chestnut-red - a whitish supercilium feature to the head. Her father will bury her somewhere special, no doubt.

At the first opportunity, either on a school day or on a Saturday, Mara plans to get a train to Manchester, to visit her mother's grave. She has already looked on the internet. An off-peak return is £5.40 on a coach, whereas on a train, it will cost her £8.15. The financial dilemma is solved because a coach journey is almost three hours each way. Mara needs to find her mother and get back before her father returns home. Her only dilemma is the money. Maybe now is not the time to ask her father.

***

Every night before bed, every night without failure, Mara has read a whole chapter from the book that was given to her by her mother. When Mara opened *The Water-Babies*, she was pleasantly surprised to find an inscription inside wishing her a happy tenth birthday. There was also a quotation. It was one she had never heard before – so beautiful; *In every heart there is a secret that answers to the vibrations of beauty.* Mara researched the quote in the library and found out that it was written by someone called Christopher Morley. Mara likes it, even though she is not sure she fully understands it. She likes it because she likes secrets.

In Chapter One a little chimney-sweeper called Tom went up one chimney and came down *THE WRONG CHIMNEY*. Because the little girl awoke in her bed and saw him in her room, covered in soot, she screamed thinking him to be a burglar! Mara loved the illustrations although at first they didn't seem to match the story much.

In Chapter Two, poor Tom is chased by a series of different people at the property, also thinking him a thief. At the end of the chapter, he enters a wood full of rhododendrons. He pushes his way through them until his head collides with a wall!

On the third night, Mara's father came unexpectedly into her room as she lay reading in bed. Mara was so surprised she just froze on the spot. Of course, her father would have no idea what book her mother had gifted her; neither had he ever paid any attention to anything she had ever read. He left without saying a word, a glass of whisky in his hand.

Poor Tom was out all alone on the wild moor, with an Irishwoman hot on his heels, feeling ever so hungry. From the top of a small mountain he spotted a village called Harthover. On his way there he sang a song that Mara found hard to sing to herself. It had lots of references to the water in a river; her favourite line was the very last.

Play by me, bathe in me, mother and child.

There is a beautiful picture to the left of Chapter Four. It contains a naked baby with longish dark hair and dark eyes. It is lying on its back in shallow water belonging to a river bed. The footnote below it states; *He felt how comfortable it was to have nothing on him but himself.* Mara is stricken by the picture. It is filled with innocence and freedom – something she has never really encountered or even considered. It is true, that when she herself bathes, she is usually feeling fairly relaxed, although she has never liked the sight of her own naked body.

In this chapter, poor Tom becomes *CLEAN AT LAST*, as the title states. Before he does though, he arrives at a cottage. When he enters, hungry and thirsty, he is seen by an elderly lady by the fireside; she is surrounded by children. When they see him, looking all dirty, some begin to cry, others shouted at the black figure. The old lady took pity on him and gave him bread and milk. Later that evening, Tom headed for the river's edge. Everyone who was chasing him, believed him to have drowned.

Yesterday evening, Mara read another chapter. It was called *THE NEW WATER-BABY*. Tom was turned by the fairies into a water baby! Mara now knew why the book was entitled so. Tom lived in the water, with gills about his neck, drinking water-milk. There, he saw water-forests with water-monkeys and water-squirrels, all of them with six legs! By the end of the longest of chapters, Tom had met and spoken with many creatures, all who seemed both odd yet wise.

Tonight, Mara will read her sixth chapter. It is called *THE GREAT STORM*. Mara likes the sound of this chapter; it sounds as though something thrilling is about to happen.

Mara's father is vomiting once more. He still sounds rough. After a short while he consoles himself by watching television. For a moment, she thought he was calling upstairs to her, she is not sure. Moments later he is at her bedroom door.

'That kid, the one in hospital – news says he's dead, died this morning.'

Mara does not know what to say. She sits in silence on her bed, staring at him, then towards the window. For a moment, her father thinks she is about to cry; he closes the door behind him. He is going to be sick again.

20

INSPECTOR FOLKARD LISTENED intently, made a few notes, thanked the caller before hanging up. From the look on her face, she was about to communicate bad news – news they could do without. The investigation had been on-going for almost exactly a month; they were still no further on. Her voice lowered as she asked for their attention.

'Joseph Rawcliffe died peacefully at 08:31 earlier this morning; his parents and sister were at his bedside. MSSA Pneumonia. Apparently, this is quite common with coma victims following severe head trauma – the lungs, because they are inactive, fill with fluid, essentially the patient drowns.'

'Graphic.'

'Painless, I've been assured.'

Silence enveloped the room. This was broken by the sound of a clicking pen. PC Clark often did this, even when she didn't want to write anything down. After a few moments. Sergeant Shakespeare altered the incident board accordingly. They were now looking at a possible double murder.

They had known the chances of Joseph regaining consciousness to be small. Only yesterday, PC McKenna updated them on his progress; although his condition had not changed, a recent neurological scan had revealed that a considerable part of white matter belonging to his brain, had now turned grey thus his consultant concluding that his brain was dying – should he have awoken, he would have most likely needed twenty-four hour care.

'Can you prepare a statement for the press Catherine? Keep it brief and stick to the facts – pass our condolences onto his family. Finish by making another appeal to the public for information.'

Inspector Folkard was about to re-enter her office when she turned and spoke again.

'I'd like to re-interview the Rawcliffe family as soon as convenient; in particular, I'd like to ask Joseph's sister, Niamh, a few questions. She's only a year older – in the same school: Year Eleven. It may be that something seeming quite insignificant at the time might give us the break we need.'

Sergeant Shakespeare followed her into her office.

'I've got a meeting with Occupational before another with Douglas. Fingers crossed, I'll be back full-time next week.'

Inspector Folkard gathered her belongings. She had just about tied the belt to her navy raincoat when

Sergeant Shakespeare held her gently by her upper arm preventing her from moving forward.

'Are you ready? There's no shame taking it easy for another couple of weeks – even a couple of months.'

'It will be a relief to return full-time. The kids are in school. I'm on my own. Suddenly, there's nothing to do – nothing I want to do – nothing important. I find myself, most afternoons at the cemetery, talking to Walter, which is great as he rarely answers back.'

Both women afforded themselves a smile.

'Poor Walter's getting no peace – there's no getting away from me.'

At that Hermione Folkard's voice changed – altered into a muffled croak. Her eyes filled as her throat tightened. She squeezed her colleagues' hand before she turned to the window to wipe her eyes. Silence.

'I need to keep busy.'

'Busy is good. A day at a time remember?'

'A day at a time.'

Hermione Folkard was walking out of her office past Sergeant Boardley's desk when she was abruptly called back – a sense of urgency to her voice.

'Finally something from Social Services! Morgan Bones was visited by Social Services on a few occasions, all visits took place when Mara was still in Primary School. The main cause for concern was neglect. However, further visits to their current address ended back in 2010 when Mara was nine. Nothing since then.'

Sergeant Boardley handed Inspector Folkard a file.

'Might be worth taking a look at. Mr Bones was also prosecuted for animal cruelty. At the same time, give or take a few weeks, Mara's schoolteacher, Miss Bushnell, contacted Social Services because she had noted bruising on Mara's legs during PE.'

'Thank you Barbara. Anything else?'

'Yes. In your absence Catherine asked us to do a little digging on Mara Bones' family. Maria Starling, Mara's mother, died of cancer. Breast cancer. She was never married to Mara's father. Maria's mother died of breast cancer too. There are no grandparents to speak of. They have all since passed away. No extended family. Sad really.'

'His side?'

'Nothing. Hard to know without interviewing him. Mara was three years old at the time when her mother died; she's unlikely to remember anything. Her father has had a few on and off girlfriends but no-one serious. At home it's just Mara and her dad.'

'Julia? Can you do me a favour? Go back to *Stanley Secondary* and ask prudently, so that it arouses no suspicion, for the names of close friends belonging to a few students – include Mara on that list. I'd like to speak with any of her close friends. I have a gut feeling there will be very few to interview.'

Inspector Folkard was about to place her right hand on the door handle when she added.

'See if you can find out her reading age, current working grades and predicted grades. Tell you what, thinking about Zita's last school report, it's all on there. Get a copy of her last school report. Oh, and find out if her father attends parents evening.'

One for Sorrow,

Two for Joy,

Three for a Girl,

Four for a Boy,

Five for Silver,

Six for Gold,

Seven for a Secret NEVER to be Told,

Eight for a Wish

Nine for a Kiss

Ten for a Bird you Must Not Miss.

MARA RARELY SEES more than one magpie whilst she is out and about. Come to think of it, she often sees one in particular, swoop onto next door's rooftop before swish-landing into their tidy gnome-filled garden. Their neighbours, Robert and Louise Stone told their father, in one of their over-the-fence conversations a few weeks ago, that they've got a magpie that keeps visiting them daily. Apparently it does this because it likes the dry cat food they leave outside whilst they're out at work.

Mrs Stone prefers squirrels. When they lived in Formby, they had a red squirrel that often frequented their back garden. Mr Stone called him Squish, insisting *it* was a he, but Mrs Stone called the same squirrel Whitetip – she insisted *it* was not. Mara's dad hates getting caught in over-the-fence conversations with the Stones. He rarely talks to anyone – no-one ever calls round.

Mara likes magpies. They are intelligent for a bird. Their black and white plumage reminds her of penguins and nuns and Lara her Dalmatian. They also seem to know when she is watching them – they pick up on any movement even if she is indoors observing them from the kitchen window. The one that visits next door is quite large – a long tail like a ruler.

A nursery song she has recently memorised surpasses her lips once more. For as long as she can remember, she only ever knew the first four parts. Then she looked the song up in the library and was pleasantly surprised to learn the rest. Mara decides she will not sing past the ninth bird. The tenth bird is now dead anyway.

Mara sits up in bed. She had planned to read only the seventh chapter today but the news of Joseph's death is bothering her. It all happened a month ago, on the fourteenth, last month. A whole month has passed; it feels much longer somehow. Deep, deep, down she is secretly pleased. For herself, the white part of her, that is, if she were a magpie, she wanted him to live – she never planned for him to get hurt. But the dark side, the black part of her, wanted him to never wake up. Never tell.

Mara thinks of her mother. Her mother would not be pleased, but she'd understand. She's sure of it. Accidents are just that, accidents.

Her father went to work this morning, without calling in on Mara. He never calls in unless he wants something doing. Mara heard him rise in the night a couple of times to be sick. At one point they crossed on the landing as she headed for the bathroom that reeked of acid-like vomit. He looked deathly pale.

The rest of *The Water-Babies* book was a bit strange. The writer used the word 'and' an awful lot. He seemed to wander off whilst telling the story. Mara reminds herself that her mother chose that particular book from many others. She chose it especially for her. For a reason. Mara appreciates that.

It has to be said that the book is a bewitching read; she's never read anything like it before. After Tom drowns and becomes a water-baby he meets other water-babies and fairies. One of the fairies is called Mrs Doasyouwouldbedoneby. Mrs Bedobyasyoudid. Is the other fairy. Mara loves their names. They remind her of Mrs Tanner and Mrs Lexton next door.

Eventually Ellie, the young girl who screamed because Tom was dirty, becomes a water-baby too before Grimes, his old wicked master, drowns himself. Tom helps him see the error of his ways. It's all a bit like *A Christmas Carol*. Grimes, who is a lot like Scrooge, repents before the book ends.

Mara is heading for the bird shed when she suddenly diverts from the path and crosses the lawn, to stand before the wide pond. For a short while she looks at her reflection in the water. It is better than the one she sees daily in her mirror. She lowers her right arm below the surface and wriggles her fingers beneath the cold water.

It is sad that some adults let their children down so very badly. Conor's father did in *A Monster Calls*. Her father has let her down all his life. He most likely let her mother down too – he never married her. Her will suggests she did not trust him. Mara knows she is justified in wanting to teach him a lesson or two.

When Mara looks through the bird-shed window she sees two more dead canaries on the floor. On their backs. Mara whispers the tune through the thin metallic window bars before going back indoors.

'Eight for a Wish - Nine for a Kiss.'

22

A MONTH AGO, Hermione Folkard had arrived at Comlongon Castle and had spent the best part of the day enjoying her husband's company. She pictured herself nestled, spooned as they lay together watching television. before her mobile had rang. She could never correct that. If she could go back, she would have switched the mobile off – reception was awful out there anyway. She could have spent at least one more night by his side.

It had already been so long since they had made love. She couldn't even recall the last time they had been together. As usual, she'd been the one to delay things – too tired – the children would hear – the *wait until we are away* promise. Exorable Walter. Patient. Always patient. The weekend that had pledged so much, had in fact, delivered so very little. The lost weekend. The last weekend. Gone. Unlike a palindromic number, there was no going back.

Hermione Folkard ached for Walter. She ached for him so much. She had still not washed the bedsheets - his scent fading – the fear that one day it would no longer be there. When she went to the bathroom to find his aftershave, to spray her pillow, she found an array of them. Which one was the one he preferred? She didn't know. Had she really, in the last few years, paid that little attention?

Castigating herself wouldn't help. Neither would staying in bed - negativity transfixing her from every angle. It was just after six-thirty. Surprisingly, she had slept well; no waking up shortly after three in the morning. She rose to go to the bathroom, having no intention of staying up for long.

As she passed Darcy's bedroom, she spotted Zita sleeping soundly back to back with her older sister, both on the edge of the bed. They had slept together since Walter had passed away. Darcy was 'keeping it together' somehow, the resilience of teenagers admirable. Zita surprisingly was doing well in school too – only a few episodes – the school couldn't have done more. Once home, she still cried often. The whole unbearable exhaustible sorry situation had to stomached, grieved, travelled. There was no hiding from it.

It was later that afternoon, when Hermione Folkard was setting Walter's place at the table that she heard her youngest out chattering in the garden. Her arms swelled with goosebumps. She was talking to Walter.

'I know daddy. But I feel so sad without you. Won't you please come back home?'

Zita was stood in the rain, by the tin cans filled with nothing growing. She had her back to her, her right arm held ahead of her, her palm open.

'Take my hand daddy.'

Hermione Folkard looked in vain. She stepped out into the garden and was about to coax her daughter indoors when an admiral landed on her daughter's shoulder.

'I love you too daddy.'

Zita Folkard waved before turning around, a peaceful look about her smiling face, her hair moist from the thin rain.

'Daddy says I have to look after you mummy. He says I'm not old enough to make you a cup of tea but that I am to make sure you take your vitamins and inhaler every morning.'

Her youngest took her by the hand, back indoors before giving her a hug. Together they embraced for a while before Zita headed to the kitchen cupboard in search of her vitamins.

23

MONDAY EVENING AND Mara has stomach cramps. Mara often sits in her bedroom at night. She didn't often sit downstairs in the first place but since her father watches the news these days, she is avoiding the lounge. Mara doesn't want to know. Guilt consumes her like gigantic tidal waves; one minute she thinks she's fine, the next she's overcome with dread. It's best to keep reading – avoid thinking.

Her father enters the kitchen just as Mara takes out a box of paracetamol from one of the cupboards. Her left hand is on her stomach. Her father looks a little startled. He reaches into his pocket and hands her a £10 note. Mara thinks of thanking her father but changes her mind. He is gone anyway. He put the mug of coffee she made for him in the sink and left via the back door – to check on his birds.

On the kitchen table there are several familiar items. Her father has stuffed the odd bird or two in the past. When she was ten, her father asked her to assist him. He lay the same materials out onto the same table, a sharp knife, sewing needle with thread, a small plaster cast and a container of Borax. Her father must be planning to stuff his favourite.

Moments later, her father enters with the frozen bird in his hand; he places it onto its side, down on the table, its beady eye peering through the plastic bag. Mara looks nervously towards the tub of Borax before she asks him if he wants any help. Mara's father nods before he checks the tub. Mara's father looks perplexed.

'It's been a while, but I could have sworn I had near enough a full tub.'

Mara's father leaves the kitchen again in search of another. Five minutes later and he has returned with nothing more than a couple of rags. For a moment, he looks at Mara before he looks at his bird.

'I'll have to pop out and get another one. I'd best go now before it gets late.'

Mara's father has his head now in the fridge, under the counter. He is placing his bird in the freezer compartment, next to a small loaf of bread.

***

Mara has her money. On Saturday she will visit her mother's grave. The thought of finding her mother gives her goose-pimples. A large smile spreads across her face. Mara plans on making a special bunch of flowers from the garden to give to her mother. Her first gift.

From underneath her pillow, Mara takes out her thirteenth card. There was no present attached to this one but Mara knows there is probably a gift inside the envelope for her. It feels like a rectangular box - flat. Mara decides she wants to open the gift and card. It will cheer her up. It's so lonely having no-one to talk to in the evening. Her father is out; she can take her time reading her card – no-one will interrupt. Even during the day, she can go almost all day without anyone acknowledging her; until recently, Mara had never really valued her privacy.

Her form tutor, Mr Quinn almost always asks how she is. He has a mighty mound of curly long hair, the colour of an old English sheepdog. He peers over his spectacles as he reads the daily notices in different accents; he has a way of making her smile. There is something rib-tickling about him – even the bully boys like him, he brings old comics in for them. He can sketch a Denis the Menace on the whiteboard in less than ten seconds. His favourite superhero is Spiderman; when anyone in the class talks over him, he pretends to shoot webs from his palm to catch their attention.

If Mara hasn't got English, which she hasn't on two days of the week, Mara might go through the day without talking to anyone other than Mrs Cassidy. Mrs Cassidy is simply the best and she doesn't ask too many questions. In Year Eight, Mrs Cassidy started bringing in boxes of tights for her - said they were the wrong size for her daughter Alice. Mrs Cassidy has been bringing in the odd thing or two for a while now – she is very matter-of-fact about it. Mara knows she doesn't want to embarrass her. In Year Nine Mara plaited her dark hair at night before she went to bed - to make it crinkly like Mrs Cassidy's, but the kids in class made fun of her. Most girls she knows straighten their hair or have products to make it look shiny and smooth. Mara has given up trying to control her unruly hair. There is little point. She might as well be invisible. It is a sad state of affairs when you consider yourself closer to those that have passed away than to the living.

Earlier on today, Mara had English with Mr Carey. They have just finished reading *Jekyll and Hyde*. Mara loves this novella, despite the language being quite challenging. She once saw a cartoon where Bugs Bunny went home with a Dr Jekyll, whom he hoped would adopt him. Unfortunately, Dr Jekyll took a red potion that altered him from time to time. It was really funny. It took Bugs Bunny ages before he realised there weren't two men in the house. The best part was when Bugs Bunny locked himself safely in a cupboard with Dr Jekyll in order to keep Mr Hyde out. Bugs Bunny turned the light off so he wouldn't know where they were. Bugs Bunny was talking when Dr Jekyll's eyes started to change from a relaxing blue colour to a blood-shot red. Bugs Bunny's face was a picture when he turned the light on.

Mara's essay on the duality of man gained her an A. Mr Carey said she had a thorough awareness of the task, text and its audience. Mara understands the struggle between good and evil. It is hard for some more than others. Her mother was clearly good. Her father clearly isn't. Mara ponders on whether she is neither or maybe a bit of both.

***

The envelope that says *My Mara (Happy 13th Birthday!)* is now open. The photograph of her mother is by her side. Mara takes out a small grey box with the name of the jewellers written in gold on the front. For a moment Mara instinctively touches her ears. What if the box contains earrings? She hasn't had her ears pierced yet. Mara pauses for a moment before opening the box – takes in a deep breath. No-one has ever given her any jewellery.

Inside is a necklace with a cross. Made of gold. It is lovely. It is truly lovely; at the heart of it is what seems to be a diamond. It is a real diamond. It says so on a sticker in the box. Nine carat gold. Just lovely. Mara decides against wearing it, for now; maybe she will wear it under her uniform. For now, she will try it on before putting it away. Mara kisses her mother's photograph.

'Thank you mother.'

Mara takes out the letter from the envelope. It is a little longer than the last. For some reason Mara feels disappointed, downcast. Once the letter is read, there will be no others for a while, unless she reads them beforehand.

My dearest Mara;

Happy Thirteenth Birthday my darling young lady!

I try to picture you, what you are like right now. I know you are lovely, both on the inside and out. I am so proud of you.

It was difficult choosing a gift for you. Of all the gifts I have prepared, this was the hardest. I think it is because at the age of thirteen I found life at home, and in school, quite difficult. Let's see…

I suppose it is the same for most teenage girls. You will have most likely started your period by now. I was late starting mine. I was nearly fourteen! It was all a bit of a shock. It was a bit of a shock every month after! I am sure you don't need me to tell you this but I'm going to because I think it's sound advice, advice my mother gave to me.

Make sure you have plenty of pads and paracetamol in at home. You can get stronger medication from the doctor if the pain is awful – a hot water-bottle helps. Make sure you have a small bag with a couple of pads and tablets in case you're in school when your period starts. If you feel you need someone to talk to, ask to see your doctor or the school nurse – I know your dad isn't much good with these things!

I suppose it was at this age I started noticing boys too. To be honest, boys didn't seem to notice me. I wasn't very confident at school but neither is anyone else, even if it seems they are. It was in sixth form when I met my first proper boyfriend. I shall tell you more about this when I write you another letter. My mother told me that love was worth waiting for, and it was. Don't rush into any relationships Mara honey – concentrate on your studies. There is plenty of time for boys and love!

I know your dad takes you to church every Sunday. I asked him to do this for me. I wasn't a very religious person but I always enjoyed going to church with my mother. I don't know if you know this, and I hope this doesn't upset you too much, today of all days – my mother died too of breast cancer. She died when I was in my twenties. I missed her terribly. I still do.

I am sorry too, that I too, passed away from the same disease. But as a nurse, I know of the great advances, of the many lives saved through research. I also know that you too may be at risk yourself – so it is important that when you are older you follow the instructions given by your doctor on how to check yourself. Please try not to worry, that is a mother's job. You will understand my worry when you become a mother yourself!

My gift of a cross to you is because I believe there is something out there, something bigger than us. It may be a God, who knows. I always felt my mother was nearby, protecting me as I am with you. The diamond is you. My precious gift in life. Wear this cross and remember honey that I am always with you, by your side, especially today, on your birthday, as you blow out your candles, open your presents amongst your family and friends, I am with you, like a guardian angel, watching over you.

I love you my darling. Happy 13th Birthday my big, beautiful girl!

Mummy xxxxxxxxxxxx (13!)

Despite all her efforts not to cry, Mara cannot control the anguish she feels inside. There have never been any parties, friends and family – presents – everything her mother hoped she'd have – normality. Her father is the most selfish man she knows. He sees only to himself, in reality, and his birds. She knows he lives alongside her, rather than with her, for her. He clearly does not care about her – he never really did.

Mara is wearing her cross now. It looks beautiful around her neck, as her mother intended. When her father asks, Mara will tell him where she got it from, whom she got it from. It is time Mara started speaking up for herself. She has her mother by her side after all. All hope of a loving relationship with her father has now burst like a balloon.

24

DESPITE WALTER HAVING passed away almost a month ago, flowers keep arriving every three to four days. Big bunches – lots of white bunches – pale, colourless. The children welcome their arrival with open arms.

'The house is full of flowers. It shows how much daddy's loved.'

Darcy smiled at her sister who enthusiastically took indoors the latest arrangement left in the porch. Darcy didn't like the cards. She found them too difficult to read. Hermione Folkard agreed; she put them in a drawer to read at a later date.

'It's a good job none of us suffer with hay fever.'

Going to work reminded her of when she started an exercise regime, after Zita had been born. It was difficult getting up the day after but it was even harder on the second day. Tuesday morning and her second full day awaited her; Hermione Folkard was tired out before the day had really begun. She wasn't sleeping very well.

Last night at three in the morning she awoke following a vivid dream. Walter was in it. It was a dream she could no longer make sense of. In her dreams, they spent time together – at one point they argued. Hermione Folkard woke up crying - back to reality. Zita was by her side, her elbow close to her face. No Walter. She would never awake to Walter again. The simple things one took for granted are only appreciated once they are gone. It's a hard lesson.

At times she knew, had it not been for the children, she had no desire to go on living. She wasn't suicidal. She just didn't enjoy life anymore – there was nothing she enjoyed doing – no one she wanted to spend time with. Her brother had rang the previous night. He said this would pass. He sounded low himself, like he was trying to convince himself.

Twenty minutes later, Zita popped three vitamins into her mouth as she vacated the kitchen ready for work. She stood attentively whilst Darcy held a lilac inhaler to her lips before she huffed. Darcy counted to ten. Hermione Folkard puffed; she felt a little dizzy.

***

As soon as she entered her office Sergeant Boardley followed her with a file in hand. Hermione Folkard thanked her. From it she withdrew Mara's school report.

'Her Reading Age is above average. Mara is currently fourteen years and three months old; her Reading Age is sixteen years and four months, almost two years ahead. They don't do Spelling Age tests unless they attend SEN or have a statement of Special Educational Needs.'

'Thank you Barbara. This school report is quite similar to Darcy's. Attendance is excellent – only one day off. Can you find out when that was please? Might be something.'

'Of course. It's a good school report; she is on or above target in all subjects. I did notice though that almost all the teachers make a comment about her lack of interaction or holding back or not asking for help when she needs it, she sounds quite withdrawn, lacking in social skills maybe?'

Sergeant Boardley looked deep in thought.

'Oh. I almost forgot. According to her form tutor, Mr Quinn, her father attended Parents Evening in years seven and eight – hasn't attended the last two.'

'I rarely attended parents evening. Walter did that. The girls didn't seem to mind as long as I was there for plays and on sports days. God knows how I'll fit it all in now!'

'You'll manage fine. You'll manage better than you think. Just take one day at a time.'

Hermione Folkard sighed.

'Thank you again Barbara. Anything on the interviews with the Rawcliffes?'

'Sergeant Shakespeare has an appointment with them later this afternoon. Their daughter Niamh is still off school. They will try to interview her there and then.'

In the distance, Sergeant Shakespeare could be seen through her inside office window entering the incident room before she then approached the staff kettle. She instinctively waved at them both. Hermione Folkard smiled.

'I think I'll join her. I could do with a strong coffee myself.'

***

Later in the evening, Hermione Folkard was sat in the kitchen consoling Harry, when her work mobile rang. He had brought a photograph of Walter that he liked for the gravestone – one that would go in a waterproof oval frame and be placed centre-top. It was comforting sitting with Harry; he looked so much like Walter.

Hermione Folkard apologised before taking the call.

'It's Catherine, sorry Harry. Pop the kettle on; I'll be with you in a tic.'

'Say hi from me.'

'Catherine.'

'Nothing new from either of the parents. They seem to be dealing with things better than I thought they would – maybe the time they had with him prepared them in some way. They seemed worse before he died.'

There was a pause.

'Sorry. I wasn't thinking.'

'Makes perfect sense to me. They had a chance to say goodbye. Spent weeks crying, hoping, coming to terms with his demise. I'm almost envious. I never got the chance to say goodbye.'

Hermione Folkard caught Harry wiping his face with both palms.

'We never got the chance to say goodbye.'

'His sister Niamh didn't have much to add, other than she knew of Mara. If we hadn't asked if the name was familiar, she wouldn't have told us that she attends the same church as them – on a Sunday – sits nearby, on the other side of the church with her father. Apparently Joseph makes faces at Mara to make her laugh. Apparently Mara rarely laughs. She said she was one of the weird kids before she apologised.'

Hermione Folkard went quiet for a minute.

'Could have slipped her mind, I suppose. Might be worth interviewing the priest. Did you get the name of the church?'

'A favourite of yours. *St Patrick's*, on Marshide Road.'

Hermione Folkard sighed again. She had been the only person to attend Mr Rimmer's funeral a couple of years ago. She collected his ashes and together with his mother's, she spread them on his father's grave. His mother's wishes according to her will and testament. The Catholic priest, Father Stephen Smith, had been very accommodating. He was a tall, broad man with large blue eyes hidden behind his spectacles. His smile matched his friendly demeanour; he had once been an English teacher himself, like Mr Rimmer. He loved teaching but it wasn't for him.

25

FOUR DAYS LATER and Mara's anger has not subsided; she is careful not to let her father see her wearing her cross. Mara is not afraid to confront her father; she is more than happy to do so. Not confronting him has been hard. But now is not the time. Moreover, Mara does not want him to destroy any of her mother's cards or gifts, before she has opened them.

What lies ahead is inevitable now. She will not be able to treasure her gifts as her mother wished, open them as she hoped. There is no point shopping in the past. Mara mentally presses the eject button. Nothing has been as her mother willed.

Her father returned to work today. He kept vomiting on and off all of Wednesday evening. In the bathroom, in the washing-basket, Mara spotted traces of blood on his white work shirt.

Whilst he was off, he finished stuffing his bird. When Mara entered the kitchen, Wednesday after school, he was working on the skin.

'Borax is far better than dry preservative. The preservative dries the skin out fast – no stretch in it. Borax gives you time to sew the bird up first and align the feather tracks.'

Mara wanted to tell her father she knew a fair bit about Borax herself. In Year Seven, Mr McCuskey, her History teacher, told her class all about how the late Victorians adulterated foods, especially bread, putting chalk and Borax in the flour to make it look whiter; they put it in plaster too, to make the loaf seem heavier. They put it in milk as well.

***

When Mara got up this morning the bird was gone and so was everything else. The last bird he stuffed ended up in the bin. The skin tore just as he was sewing it – he was in a foul mood for days.

Mara is preparing her father's sandwich. The soup is already in the pan. Tonight they are having pea and ham soup, Mara's favourite. The evenings are lighter now; it is not as cold. Mara takes a walk down the path. Although her father is no gardener, he does mow the lawn and tidy the pond. In the beds are a few established trees and bushes. Surrounding them are many bluebells, daffodils, primroses – a wild meadow of sorts.

Tomorrow, Mara will make up a neat bunch of flowers from the garden, daffodils most likely – the others are likely to wilt. She will then catch the number nine bus that will take her straight to the town centre. There, at Southport's only train station, she will buy her train ticket to Manchester. She already has a green plastic bag ready with sandwiches.

Mara has been on the internet again. She is lucky. When she googled her previous home address she found only one church nearby. Mara knows there is a chance that her mother may not have been buried there. She also knows that it may be a very large cemetery and that she may not find her mother at all – a needle in a haystack. But Mara won't allow anything to deter her from trying. Mara won't let anything get in her way.

26

DARCY WAS SITTING in the back room reading. Hermione Folkard was comforted by the sight of her eldest lounging on the settee, feet up. She was wearing Walter's pyjama bottoms accompanied by a pale blue tee-shirt she had bought for him last Father's Day. On the cover of the book was a pretty young woman, probably a few years older than Darcy, wearing a large sky-blue ballgown – very frilly – dazzling.

'Good morning honey. Looks like a grown-up Cinderella story from the cover?'

Darcy continued to read before she mumbled morosely.

'I'm half-way through mum. I need you to get me the next one. It's one of a series of five.'

'I'm afraid I have to go out for a couple of hours, work. I'll try to call into a bookshop if I pass one.'

Darcy frowned and looked up.

'You look like you're only half-way through anyway.'

'You don't understand. Reading is stopping me from thinking. It's the only thing that works. If I don't have the next book, what am I going to do?'

For a moment, Hermione Folkard thought Darcy was going to begin crying, pain etched across her reddening face. She hadn't been eating properly either. But then, nobody really had. Her cooking wasn't up to much.

'I'll pick the next one up, that way you'll know it is there – when you need it.'

For a moment the two looked at one another with mutual affection. Hermione Folkard approached her daughter before sitting next to her. They said nothing. There was nothing to be said. Sadness had replaced anger. When sadness took a back seat, the anger would return – sometimes worse than before. Hermione Folkard had the number of a bereavement counsellor in the drawer of her desk. Maybe it was time for her to book an appointment.

'Are you sure you're okay to mind Zita for a few hours?'

Darcy nodded.

'We'll be fine. Please don't forget my book.'

'I won't. I'll be home for tea. We've got nothing in. I'll get something for tea too.'

Hermione Folkard called upstairs to Zita. The next half-hour was spent cuddling her youngest child; she didn't want her mother to go out. She was needed at home.

***

The weather had brightened; spring had most definitely arrived. Tree buds threatened to blossom along the scenic road leading to Churchtown's quaint village. Even the sight of St. Patrick's Church on Marshide Road did little to dampen her emotional state. Everything these days was easier once she ventured outdoors, though getting there in the first place was a daily struggle.

Father Stephen had remembered her; when he opened the door he welcomed her with a bright smile. He was only young, must have been in his early thirties but something about him seemed wise beyond his years. He beckoned her indoors.

'Just got back. Six hours from Essex. Such a lovely retreat. Haven't been there before.'

'Where did you go?'

'Bernadine Hyning. A monastery. Lovely.'

'Monks?'

'Nuns actually. Twelve of them.'

'Gone a bit off nuns since I saw *Philomena* last year.' Hermione Folkard couldn't believe she had spoken her thoughts out loud, although she'd said worse than that after she'd watched the movie. Father Stephen was laughing.

'Dreadful business. Embarrassing too, especially for the Catholic Church. Pope Francis held an audience with Philomena Lee you know? She said it helped her find closure. I'm glad it did.'

Father Stephen tutted to himself as he beckoned her in. They walked through his untidy hallway towards a back room on the right. It had a lovely view, a side garden, much tidier than anything she could see indoors.

'I'm sorry. I've forgotten your name; and you're not in uniform – Detective Inspector?'

' Folkard. Hermione Folkard.'

Instinctively, Hermione Folkard found herself touching her wedding ring. She turned it to the right twice before she realised she was being watched.'

'And what can I do for you? Cup of tea?'

'Yes please.'

'Milk? Sugar?'

'Milk please. No sugar.'

Hermione Folkard paused before she began.

'I'm making a few enquiries about a parishioner of yours.'

'Joseph Rawcliffe I suppose? Sad state of affairs. Attended Church every Sunday. The whole family did. Lovely family. I'm calling in on them, after mass.'

'Must be comforting for them – to have you call on them – reassurance I suppose.'

'It is. Death is devastating. The impact on a family and its relationships is something no-one is ever ready for.'

For a moment, Hermione Folkard seemed to be about to speak. She paused. Thought better of it.

'No actually. Another family in your parish – the Bones family. Can you tell me a little about them?'

Father Smith paused for a short while, as if deep in thought.

'Morgan Bones has been bringing Mara to this parish, almost every Sunday, since he moved into the area, about ten years ago. Mara is a lovely girl. Quiet. Went to our primary. I hoped she'd go onto the feeder school *Christ the King* but her father sent her to *Stanley*. More convenient I suppose. Doesn't make sense though. Coming to church every Sunday and then sending your child to a non-Catholic school.'

'I suppose not.'

'It's not as if the results are better. It's a rough school in comparison. Doesn't make sense. I tried talking to him but his mind was made up. Said the other was too far. Too many parishioners doing the same these days. Mara was the only child not to do her first Holy Communion. She attended all the classes. They were done in school, but on the day, he rang, to say she was sick.

Hermione Folkard thought better than to share her feelings about religion on the whole. She had been brought up a Catholic herself. When it was time for her to do her Confirmation, Hermione Cummings, as she was known then, decided she wanted to wait until she was older – it had after all, been suggested to the class that it was a life-long commitment.

On the day she announced her decision, to delay her commitment to the Catholic Church, her mother nearly fainted. She learned then and there to keep her opinions, doubts and *pointless curiosity*, as her mother had said that day, to herself - or more to the point, until she was old enough to stand up to her mother and father.

'How did she get on with Joseph? They were in a couple of classes together, in school, but I really haven't been able to find much more about either of them. Were they friends?'

'I'm pretty sure they got on well. I'd seen him making faces at her during Mass. Not much gets by me Inspector.'

'Hermione.'

'I didn't say anything. I didn't want her father telling her off. He's quite serious. And rude! I called a few times to the house when they first moved into the area but he clearly wasn't very happy to see me. Told me to my face not to bother calling again.'

'Odd that he goes to church then. Maybe he goes because Mara asks him too.'

'Maybe. I can't see it myself. I've seen him on his mobile during service. Spoke to him about it. He says nothing. No apology. Nothing. Poor Mara's face is a picture. She looks vacant most of the time. But when Joseph makes faces at her, her face beams. She has a lovely smile, when she smiles that is. That's why I say nothing. She comes to the house of God looking like she has the world on her shoulders. She leaves smiling. Small miracle don't you think?'

Hermione Folkard stood up. She glanced outdoors before turning away.

'Anything else you can tell me?'

'Not that I can think of. If I think of anything else I'll call you. I think I might still have your card somewhere.'

'Thank you Father.'

'What is it that is troubling you?'

'A gut feeling. A feeling that Mara is somehow involved.'

'No. Not that. What's troubling *you*? I hope you don't mind me saying – I do know of your own recent family bereavement. How are you coping?'

'I... I...'

Hermione Folkard put her hand out to steady herself. For a moment she felt dizzy. Father Stephen directed her back to her chair; his untidy yet homely lounge beckoning her to stay like a long lost relative.

'Sit down Hermione.'

'I'm sorry. I thought I'd slept quite well last night. I think you took me by surprise too.'

'No, I'm sorry. You look a million miles away, in comparison to last time we met that is – Bernard Rimmer's service. You've lost quite a bit of weight too.'

'I now realise that my loss of appetite isn't down to a lack of hunger.' Hermione Folkard lowered her voice. 'It's strange. All these years, dealing with families that have lost loved ones – feeling sympathy for them, when in reality – only a person who suffers such a loss can truly understand.'

'It's the difference between sympathy and empathy. When my own brother died, in a motorbike accident, my parents were at a loss. I was too young to understand. I was only eight. My brother was nineteen at the time.'

He paused for a short while.

'I was once married. My wife died in an accident too; we'd been married less than a year – she was pregnant. It was only then I truly understood the pain they must have faced all those years ago. I don't know how I would have coped without them.'

Hermione Folkard felt guilty. She was in some strange way pleased, pleased to share an unspeakable understanding with someone who truly knew what it was to feel a monumental loss in life.

'I feel guilty if I eat. I feel if I eat, I am accepting Walter's death – enjoying myself, eating that is. Going on with life. I know this probably sounds crazy. I feel guilty if I wear make-up - if I smile. I'm terrified one day I'll go to bed and have forgotten to remember Walter.'

'Far from it. Losing a loved one, especially unexpected, as you did, as you all did, is always traumatic. The death of a spouse is one of the most profound losses another human can ever experience. The transition from wife to widow is very real, a personal and painful phenomenon.'

Hermione Folkard began to cry. She sobbed. Trying to adjust to her new identity whilst a multitude of questions besieged her daily, hourly even, had taken its toll. The guilt of living consumed her. Only the children kept her going. She had to keep going.

'I feel so guilty returning to work too. But I know, if I don't pretend I'm coping, neither will the children. I cannot tell them to go to school when I won't go to work myself. I have to carry on. Walter would have wanted me to carry on.'

'Hermione, work can tame many things. It can tame your fears – it stops you losing control. This unstableness is not permanent. Life will never be the same but it will get easier. I promise. I know this. Unlike many, you have the ability to cope. Financially, you are better off than most. Get a cleaner. Hire a gardener. Do whatever you need to do so that you can give yourself and your family the space and time needed to grieve. The world won't end if your home is a mess. Look around. Mine hasn't.'

Hermione Folkard afforded herself a smile before she began to cry once more. This time, she allowed herself to cry out loud – the pain too much – her face grim like a carved mask.

27

MARA STRUGGLED TO sleep; she became restless like a storm-tossed ship. Because of this, she has awoken much earlier than normal. Her father is still asleep. In an hour he will rise to get ready for work.

Yesterday, Friday, had been the worst school day she'd experienced in a while. She hadn't realised she was humming to herself as she walked down the corridor, on her way to her second lesson. The mockingbird song was still on her mind, the song her mother used to sing to her.

Unbeknown, Sally Conway had passed her in the corridor. She caught her unawares. It was nothing really. She laughed at her. She turned to tea-leaf Tom, lolloping in a line of stragglers and said something about her singing a nursery rhyme. Then laughed again.

'A baby's nursery rhyme.'

A baby's nursery rhyme was all that Sally Conway had said. But when Sally Conway says anything, it has a way of travelling amongst her cronies like a Mexican wave - mimicking mockingjays but worse. There is something very, very irritating about Sally Conway's voice – it is both whining and nasal. It's in the way she impersonates others too. It has a grating effect on Mara. And of course, on cue, everyone laughs.

Mara won't have her mother's lullaby mocked. Mara won't have anything connected with her mother mocked. Both of Mara's hands have made a fist-like shape.

Later during lunchtime, Mara was heading for the library when she heard Sally's familiar voice along the corridor.

'Did your mama buy you a mockingbird then?'

Mara didn't want to cry, not in front of them, not in front of anyone but she couldn't hold back the tears. Thinking about her mother seems to have taken over her life. Her mother is the only thing she treasures. But thinking about how life could have been, had her mother lived, hurts the most. Life seems pointless without her.

***

Mara is sitting in the penultimate carriage wearing her dark-green duffle coat. For a while, Mara couldn't wear it, it smelled funny. She is sitting with her green plastic bag by her side. The bag contains sandwiches, an apple and a large bunch of daffodils tied with a yellow ribbon. She is holding a book that she is not reading.

Mrs Cassidy gave her a new novel to read for the weekend. It is like many dystopian novels she has read but a little too girly for Mara. Glittering gowns and elaborate jewels are not really her thing but Mrs Cassidy says that she is bound to like it; all the girls like it - there are apparently another four that complete the series. Mrs Cassidy said that she put it aside that morning, just for her; if it's not her cup of tea, then she can bring it back.

Despite trying to concentrate, reading just won't take her mind off what is troubling her now. The rocking sensation is comforting, but inside, her stomach is tied up in knots. What if, despite hours of searching, she cannot find her mother?

A young woman with long ginger locks sits opposite her now. She has a serious look on her face. She has been on her mobile the entire time. Her skin is almost as pale as paper – she has a pink splurge running along one side of her face. Mara is wondering whether it is a birth-mark or a burn when she suddenly looks up – a frown altering her pale complexion.

Mara deliberately looks out of the window. Her book is still held open but she is yet to read beyond the third chapter. Mara wishes she had an alternative book to read, something to take her mind off things. There was another book she liked the look of, one with circus-type lettering on the cover.

Depending on what you concentrate your eyes on, what you look at can pass so fast that you are not entirely sure if you saw anything at all. Close up, Mara sees very little – flashes of shape – streams of colour. There are no people out here to observe, a visual haiku. Nature is in its element – at peace.

But if you look to the distance, it is amazing how much detail you can take in, in those few seconds – 1 - 2 – gone - 1 - 2 – gone – 1 - 2 – house like cottage with a dog, maybe a cat and washing – something blue pegged onto the washing line – trousers too. The windows are like eyes in a film she once saw. It looks homely. Everyone that lives in that house is surely happy – 1 - 2 – gone - 1 - 2 – gone. A large field – lots of white sheep with black woolly heads and bulging eyes. No obvious litter. A hill for Jack and Jill – 1 - 2 – gone - 1 - 2 –gone - 1 - 2 – gone.

Most of the houses that the train now passes are in the wide green countryside. Mara has never been away – never been on holiday. Being on a train is almost alien to her; it is a holiday in itself – a short break away. On a couple of occasions, when Mara was much younger and Lara was still alive, she accompanied her father to take Dalmatian puppies to their new owners' homes; they had to take the train. Once they went as far a London. They descended the train – her father passed the pup over. Money and pleasantries were exchanged. They got back on the train.

She loved trains then. She still loves them now – rocking her, rocking her like a mother swaying her babe to sleep. Like in Harry Potter, the window frames contain moving images – 1 - 2 – gone - 1 - 2 – gone - 1 - 2 – a flat of water with lots of birds flying in circular movements – mesmerising murmurations - starlings boomerang before they rise - 1 - 2 – gone - 1 - 2 – gone – 1 – 2 - gone. Another large field – lots of brown cows, black and white ones too – small long-legged calves – calves nuzzling close-by – no moon for one of them to jump over – 1 - 2 – gone - 1 - 2 –gone - 1 - 2 – gone.

Mara knows which station she needs to get off at. She has followed the railway line picture that is on a sticker on the compartment's double-door nearby. Six more stops and she will have arrived to the town of Whitlag. When Mara looked on Google maps, she saw the town was on the outside of Manchester, four stops before Manchester Victoria. The pictures on the internet showed a small town; it has a population of 3126 residents; it was once an old coal mining town.

Getting to St Peregrine's Church should not be difficult, since the town is significantly small. If she has time, Mara would like to visit her previous home on Newbottle Road; she'd also like to see the back garden – to see if it jogs any memories of her mother pushing her on the swing. On the internet map, the address looked fairly close – possibly a ten minute walk, in the opposite direction to the station.

Although the train is not packed, it is still fairly busy. At the next stop there are many additional passengers that ascend the train coach. Mara is unsure whether to give her seat up for an elderly man with thick glasses who looks unstable. At the point when she decides she will ask him, the red-headed woman sitting opposite her offers him her seat.

It does not take long for his body odour to reach her, to reach all of them close by. He is a largish man. His raincoat seems too big regardless; it is not fastened and it has a few buttons missing. He wears an expensive unironed pale-blue shirt underneath a woolly emerald-green argyle jumper. His trousers are brown, like his coat. Mara has noticed he is wearing trainers. None of his outfit looks right - a bad interview suit.

Similarly, the disorientated elderly male who could be in his forties or even in his early sixties, carries a plain green plastic bag like Mara. His bag is stuffed with papers, magazines mostly. He takes out his chess set to show her. When Mara declines, he puts his train ticket away in a purse about his neck and tucks it under his jumper.

He smiles - a picket fence in need of paint. Mara is afraid not to smile back. Behind his thick-rimmed spectacles are two large grey eyes. Mara is unsure how she feels; mostly, she feels sorry for him. The train is slowing down. It is at this point Mara realises she has arrived to Whitlag.

Brakes screech as if resisting the inevitable cut-off point. Mara is now looking out through the double-door windows. It is like coming home. How quaint the town seems, despite the pink graffiti on the platform. Strewn in large letters are the words JESUS LOVES YOU. There is a red fish around the words; it is wearing a yellow crown. Only the letter U is visible through the slit-like window once the train stops.

Mara ascends the train and looks along the platform. A small crowd heads for the exit. As Mara follows, she notices each traveller is handing their ticket to the attendant. Mara looks for her ticket, an unnecessary panic building up inside her. Eventually, Mara finds it in her green bag – she was sure she had it in her pocket. The male attendant smiles. His tidy grey moustache hides most of his mouth; when he speaks to Mara, only his bottom lip can be seen moving. Mara is about to head off when she turns back.

'Excuse me. Could you please tell me in which direction should I walk to find the church?'

'That I can do. Left out. Then, right ahead, about a mile down the road. Keep walking straight. See? It's right ahead. Head that way.'

Mara can see a greyish-looking church with a spire in the distance. From here it looks close enough. She thanks the attendant. His eyes smile in return. Mara clutches her green bag, excitement bubbling inside. As Mara heads down the long road she notices the quietness surrounding her. This is where she grew up. Home. It is green and leafy and quiet.

Most of the houses are scattered here and there – lots of front garden, neat and interesting. In comparison, the houses are much smaller – mostly terraced housing blocks dotted here and there. A cat snakes its way around a gate to greet Mara. It is a large ginger cat. Mara bends down to stroke it. She is talking to the cat when the head of an elderly lady pops up unexpectedly from behind the walled garden.

'Hello. Ginger. His name is Ginger.'

'Hello Ginger.'

Mara smiles. The sun peeks from behind a cloud; as if a curtain had been drawn back, the place is awash with sunshine. Mara smiles once again before the short white-haired lady smiles back. Ginger follows Mara for a few metres before he stops and sits like a sculptured statue watching her on her journey. Mara waves to the cat.

***

Mara has been looking for her mother's grave for at least an hour. The cemetery surrounding the quaint church is large. At first she looked for her mother randomly before she decided to look section by section. Mara has decided she will look for a few minutes more and then take a break and eat her lunch. In reality, Mara somehow thought she would be 'led' to the right grave – like destiny. But Mara is now close to tears. She isn't even hungry.

Sitting on a bench with a plaque dedicated to Bernadine-Mary Lewis, Mara is eating one of her sandwiches. It is only when she begins eating that she realises how hungry she actually is. With every bite comes a greater determination to find her mother. The arched and studded church doors are closed but there is a small dwelling attached to the side. If all else fails, she could knock at the door and ask for help.

The main cobbled path has graves dating back to the 1800's. At the end is a section for infants. Mara looks for a while before she resumes her search – some babies are only days old. There is one solitary grave that catches her attention. It is like a stump, a square block the size of a shoe-box. FLORA. That was it. Nothing else.

The sandstone wall goes all the way round the cemetery. There is one other set of small iron gates at the back of the cemetery. Mara squints as she looks up. The sun shines on the slate roof. The church clock tower, with its pyramidal spire, is signalling twenty-to-twelve. It is only now, as Mara studies the layout, that she notices the cemetery is divided into four sections – not obvious at first – even the colour of the stones differentiate each subdivision.

Mara stands up. Her mother didn't die that long ago, in reality. She would be buried where the stone looks newish, glossy and marbled. How foolish she has been. Mara places the rest of her apple in her green bag, careful not to damage the daffodils. Ahead and east is where Mara is heading now – a new confidence in her stride.

Looking from one grave to another, Mara scans line by line, at times stopping to look at the toys and artefacts left by grieving relatives. Mara sees a few items she'd like to buy herself for her mother. Some graves have butterflies and dream catchers. Others have small statues – religious artefacts too. Most of the graves have nothing; they look lonely and abandoned, forgotten. Mara has decided she has done the right thing bringing her mother flowers. She does not like the artificial flowers left on some graves. The rain and sun have faded them.

Mara comes upon yet another grave that has the name Maria on it. For a moment her stomach leaps with a mixture of dread and excitement. But this Maria wasn't her mother either. This one is a mother and a grandmother. Her husband William is buried with her too.

When Mara does find the grave she is looking for, she is taken by surprise. She double checks the name. She is here. She has found it.

Mara is both incredulous and relieved. Her eyes fill unexpectedly with tears. Mara looks around before she sits on the dry coarse grass before the headstone. Her smile slowly disappears.

SALLY-ANNE TAPIA-BOWES

IN

LOVING MEMORY OF

MARIA STARLING

Devoted Mother and Dear Daughter

December 8th, 1975 – January 26th, 2005

AT REST WITH HER UNBORN CHILD

28

'ITS CALLED The Sea Star Programme. It's a bit like a youth club. It is largely for children, teenagers too - a Programme for those have lost someone close to them.'

Hermione Folkard paused momentarily. She wasn't entirely sure they were listening.

'I'd really like you to go to their next meeting, tonight. There are other children there, who've lost a dad or a mum or a sister or brother.'

Remarkably and to her relief, both Zita and Darcy half-smiled. Their father's death had brought them closer – not that there had ever been much rivalry between them in the first place. They were both kind, good-natured girls. They knew their mother meant to help. Darcy put her arms around Zita in a motherly way although Zita looked confused.

'We haven't lost daddy. He is with us all the time.'

Zita paused before she glanced towards the back garden. For a moment, Darcy and Hermione Folkard looked too; it was hard holding back the tears. How bleak the weather was in comparison to yesterday.

The wind was wild and the branches battered about furiously in the garden; they would need their raincoats today. The girls trundled off to gather their belongings whilst Hermione Folkard simply stared out into the garden.

Walter was lying low, low down in the ground all alone, interred and cold. It had become a habit to think of him like this; his quarantined body surrounded by the cards, pictures and soft toys the children had placed inside the coffin. Hermione Folkard had taken something new each time she visited him; she hadn't planned it – mostly photographs. There were many times since that she had regretted not having had him cremated. It would have been better to have kept him at home, amongst them all, dry, warm, portable and close-by.

'Okay. Well today, after school, I want you to take Zita straight to St. Patrick's. Father Stephen will take you himself and I will pick you up at six. We'll go to McDonalds after, you can tell me all about it then.'

The girls smiled robotically. It was time to go; if they didn't leave now, they would all be late.

Father Stephen had passed her the details before she left on Saturday. She had completely forgotten about Darcy's book. It was the colour on the Sea Star Programme that suddenly reminded her that she had forgotten, despite Darcy's urgent plea. She arrived to the bookstore just in time, five minutes before they closed.

***

Inspector Folkard entered the incident room just as Sergeant Shakespeare had finished updating Chief Superintendent Reid on the case. He neither looked displeased nor otherwise. Something in his manner communicated an understanding for the complete state of affairs. An invisible net had been cast upon them all; it was holding them temporarily together until normal duty would one day be resumed.

'And have we interviewed the librarian – this Mrs Cassidy?'

'No sir, but we intend to pay Mrs Cassidy a visit today. We only learned of her relationship with the librarian Friday afternoon. We called straightaway but everyone had gone home.'

Superintendent Reid acknowledged Inspector Folkard's arrival with a slight nod of the head. He half-smiled in Sergeant Shakespeare's direction before he headed for the door.

'Good morning Sir.'

'Good morning. I'll leave you to it; thank you Sergeant Shakespeare.'

As soon as the door closed behind him, Inspector Folkard called her colleague over to her office. She seemed deep in thought but driven all the same. It was comforting for Sergeant Shakespeare to see a glimpse of her former colleague, even if it was only presently in intervals. Whether she'd ever return to her former self was doubtful; only time would tell.

'Do you mind taking Omar with you today Catherine? I'm going to read over witness statements – see if I've missed something –when I was off, I mean.'

'Not a problem. That's how you got your reputation in the first place – seeing something that would have gone unnoticed by most. Happy hunting!'

By twelve, the day was proving to be fruitless; so many statements seemed to read like one another. On top of everything else, when Sergeant Shakespeare returned, there was little else to learn about any of the teenagers connected with the case.

Mrs Cassidy knew very little of the boys because they never really used the library. She knew a little more about Mara but Mara, according to Mrs Cassidy, was 'a closed book'.

'Mara has been going to the library every day, almost every break and lunch-time. In her opinion, Mara is a troubled child, neglected even – has no real friends – a social pariah. Mara reads a lot. Mrs Cassidy gives her posters for her bedroom. At first Mara avoided the library if Mrs Cassidy spoke to her; it is only in the last year or so she has started to open up more.'

'Interesting but of little use. Did you check her reading material?'

'Yes. Most of what Mara has read has been on the back of Mrs Cassidy's recommendations.'

***

Curiously, both girls had plenty to say about the meeting. The older children had been separated from the younger ones after a ten minute talk about a possible summer trip to the Lake District in June. From Darcy's face and lack of make-up she had been crying at some point; despite this, she looked on the whole more relaxed.

'We sat in a circle, the older ones. We only had to share if we wanted to. It was hard to share, for some more than others. There were more girls than boys.'

'Did you share at all?'

There was a pause.

'No and yes. I didn't at the meeting. I listened. I couldn't have anyway. My throat hurt. I felt like I was chocking, listening to everyone. I spent most of my time trying not to cry. Made me feel less sorry for myself. Then, afterwards, Father Stephen introduced me to a girl called Niamh. We talked a bit. She lost her brother only a few weeks ago. I've got her number now – we're going to keep in touch.'

They weren't far from Macdonald's when Hermione Folkard overheard the tail-end of a news item - *fatally struck by the oncoming double-decker - in what authorities believe is a tragic accident.* Hermione Folkard turned the radio off.

29

One for Sorrow,

Two for Joy,

Three for a Girl,

Four for a Boy,

Five for Silver,

Six for Gold,

Seven for a Secret Never to be Told.

MARA IS IN the bathroom when she hears her father swearing profusely. From the sound of it, he is still feeling unwell. The doctor says he has a stomach virus. Her father doesn't want Mr Luca, his boss, to know, he has been advised he should not be handling food. It may take up to three weeks until it fully clears.

When Mara descends the stairs for breakfast, she is surprised by the sight of the stuffed bird, now mounted sideways on a branch, on the window-ledge, to the left of the front door. It is so life-like. It is the size of a chess piece – a Queen that has been captured in her finest moment.

Mara nears the bird to look at it closer. Her father has done a good job. The female's glass eyes are a ruby red – shiny. Unlike most creatures, she is much prettier in death than life. On her perch, she looks important – not like the trophies collected by hunters, many now in galleries like the ones in the film *Night at the Museum*. She, is a preservation of a beloved pet – evidence that her father has yet to come to terms with the loss of this animal. Evidence he cares.

A poem she studied earlier this year, from her GCSE poetry anthology, *Porphyria's Lover*, tells the story of a man who strangles his beloved by wrapping her long hair around her neck three times. He was sure she would have approved – that she would have wanted this – to be with him forever. He never asked her. He just did it. One minute they were embracing, the next, she was dead. By the end of the poem, they sit still, by the fire, together – now inseparable.

Mara loves this poem although she is not entirely sure why. It is exciting, when so many other poems are not. Mara feels sorry for the lover whom her English teacher referred to as a monster. It is true, he has obviously become unstable over time, but that is only because Porphyria keeps saying she'll leave her husband, then doesn't. She wanted to have her cake and eat it.

Her father probably placed her here, by the door, so that he can say goodbye to her as he leaves for work. She will be there, ready to greet him, in the window, as he parks his car on the drive, on his return journey. She will be there every day, when he heads off to work.

Mara is about to head for the lounge when she spies from her right eye something beginning with B. Expectedly, on the kitchen table lie two more birds; there are now only seven left.

Seven is Mara's favourite number. It has been her favourite number for as far back as she can remember. There are seven days in the week. Sunday, the seventh day, is her favourite. Mara used to see Joseph on the seventh day. Mara also likes a book about the seventh son of a seventh son, although the film didn't do it justice. There are seven continents and seven wonders in the world. Everyone knows there are seven colours in the rainbow. There are also seven deadly sins. These are pride, greed, lust, gluttony, wrath, sloth and envy.

Mara thinks about one of the deadly sins – it begins with the letter E. Her mother is AT REST WITH HER UNBORN CHILD. Scans these days inform parents whether the unborn child is either female or male. Mara has wondered if her parents knew the infant's gender. How far in the pregnancy was her mother when she died of cancer? Mara is glad that it was UNBORN. That means her mother only ever held her.

For some reason Mara feels very agitated, angry even. The UNBORN is buried with her. At the cemetery, she had to share her time with her mother and because of the shock, she forgot to leave the daffodils. She returned to Flora's grave and lay them there. Like the book she is presently reading, she feels bitter that her mother's love was shared, however briefly with another child.

For days before she found her mother's grave, Mara felt truly sad that her mother was lying in a grave alone, cocooned and so far down. She also felt they had a lot in common. The thought of keeping her company, becoming re-united, had warmed her. Now Mara is not entirely sure how she feels. The baby was never born; her mother will have never looked into its eyes. Mara thinks on her mother's words – how much she loves her. One of the letters may reveal more but she is not entirely sure she wants to know.

***

Sitting in the library is best at lunch-time; Mrs Cassidy's smile is a much-needed blanket. But Mrs Cassidy has her own daughter. She knows Mrs Cassidy cares about her but not enough to take her home. Mrs Cassidy probably feels sorry for her. Maybe in the staff room Mrs Cassidy makes jokes about her. Maybe everybody knows she buys her tights out of pity.

It is raining outside and the wind is making a wailing-like sound. Mara has been on the verge of tears all day. Every time Sally Conway passes her she makes whistling sounds in the attempt of imitating a bird. Sadly, many other kids have joined in. At one point, across the yard, at least thirty other kids joined in – they probably had no idea what the joke was but they knew she was the butt of it. It is only when incidents like these happen that you realise how vulnerable you are. And like the flip of a coin, how angry you can become.

At the end of the school day Mara is heading for the bus. The wind whips up a frenzy. Many girls scream as their skirts rise; the boys return their shrieks with gaudy laughter. The crowd moves forward, in bulk, before it stops ready to cross the road.

A double-decker.

The smell of sweat and smoke intermingles. There is shoving and pulling as teenagers wrestle playfully amongst themselves. More screams – more laughter. Shoving.

A double-decker.

Shoving. Screaming. Laughter.

A singular sharp shove.

More laughter.

More screaming.

Screaming.

Less laughter.

Screaming.

***

Back at home, Mara is now crushing and grinding glass; as usual, she does this downstairs on the kitchen table. Mara has been doing this for almost an hour now - the right powdery consistency has been reached.

In front of her is the red recycled paint tin containing the bird seed. Mara taps the dark-green granite pestle lightly on the side of the small and matching mortar bowl, before she re-checks that the content has been reduced into a fine, white powder. Her father's whisky bottle is on the kitchen top next to the kitchen sink. Mara will put it away in the same place she found it.

ZITA WAS LAST to be dropped off. Today was the first day she had not complained about having to go into school. Small steps. From a minute at a time, to an hour at a time. The one day at a time would follow – one day.

According to the weather report on Mighty FM, a mini heat-wave was on its way. Hermione Folkard momentarily smiled as she headed for work. Everything was easier to bear when it wasn't raining. She would take some flowers for Walter later and sit on the ground with him; the last time she did so, she fell asleep for a good while whilst the sun blanketed her face.

The student from Stanley Secondary has been named as Sally Conway from Marshide, Southport. She was fatally struck in what authorities believe was a tragic accident. Reports state that there was some harmless pushing and shoving between students just before the accident. The student fell onto the oncoming path of a double-decker that failed to stop in time. The victim was pronounced dead at the scene.

When the traffic lights changed from amber to green, Hermione Folkard hesitated before engaging first gear; she couldn't remember where she had heard the familiar surname before. Then she recalled the Conways that lived on Marshide Road, opposite *Stanley Secondary* – neighbours of Mr Rimmer.

What a character Albert Conway was? Not only did he resemble Norris Cole from one of the most popular soaps, he behaved like him too. He was President of the Neighbourhood Watch Scheme, or something like that. He knew how to keep an eye on his neighbours alright, after all, everybody needs good neighbours. He used to live with his mother. Hermione Folkard could not recall her name.

Albert Conway had an ex-wife and only one daughter, from what she could recall. She never learned her name, nor her age. Coincidence. All a possible coincidence. Regardless, as soon as she arrived to work, she was sure to learn a lot more about the accident, after all, foul play could not always be ruled out.

Only a couple of years ago, in Sydney, Australia, a school student had deliberately pushed another in the path of an oncoming bus. The student died. There was plenty of media coverage. Not long after, the same happened in East London, after a squabble over a mobile phone. There were convictions both times.

By the time Hermione Folkard arrived to work, a separate incident board was being prepared for another possible investigation; Sally Conway, daughter of Albert and Miriam Conway – now divorced. Sally Conway had died within twenty minutes.

As many students as possible, present at the scene, had been interviewed. There had been lots of pushing and shoving. There was no evidence of any motive. Sally was with her friends. There had been no confrontations of any sort, no arguments beforehand. According to one of her close friends, Amanda Wells, who was stood beside her at the time, 'Everyone was shoving, even Sally. One second she was there, the next she was gone.'

Inspector Folkard and Sergeant Shakespeare looked through the statements together. There was nothing to indicate otherwise. A third tragedy for *Stanley Secondary* in less than two months. Despite this, Hermione Folkard wanted to explore any possible links to their present case. One never knew. The statements had taken place immediately after the police had arrived on site. Few students had continued home. Of those that didn't, most came forward or were identified by others.

'Can you do me a favour Juliet? Can you and Luke interview a few of Sally Conway's friends? Find out if she knew Joseph or Jacob. Find out if she was in any of their classes - if she was in any lessons with Mara Bones. What was her relationship with any them?

Sergeant Shakespeare smiled. It was good to see her colleague thinking outside the box again – thinking on her own two feet.

***

Later that evening, they were sitting at the table when Darcy's mobile made a sound that resembled an ascending piano.

'It's Niamh. '

'Oh yes? Is she ok?'

'Since the accident yesterday, all anyone wants to talk about is the girl who was hit by the bus – apparently not a nice person. People posting stuff they shouldn't on the internet.'

'Not sure I'm following love.'

'I didn't know until she told me last night that her brother was one of the boys that died in the park just before...'

Darcy came undone just as Hermione Folkard realised what she had said. Of course, Niamh, Joseph and their parents attended *St Patrick's Parish Church.* Father Stephen was bound to have suggested the Sea Star Programme to them as well. Why wouldn't he?

'I didn't realise Darcy. How is she?'

'She said she didn't spend time much with him although they got on well. I have Zita – and Harry – when he bothers coming home. But Niamh misses him a lot – I can tell – she has no-one else. It must be like being an only child now.'

Hermione Folkard nodded; she was deep in thought. Fate had brought their families together. It seemed strange but not unusual. She would, of course, have to inform Douglas Reid – any conflict of interest that arose in the line of duty had to be reported, however inconsequential. She couldn't see any reason why Darcy and Niamh should stop meeting or communicating. They were both gaining so much already, having so much in common.

One for Sorrow,

Two for Joy,

Three for a Girl,

Four for a Boy,

Five for Silver,

Six for Gold.

DECEMBER THE 8TH is her mother's birthday. Her mother's birthday is six days after her own. Her mother was just thirty when she died. It must have been a sad funeral – just after Christmas, freezing cold too.

Mara is lying on her bed chewing what is left of her nails. Her stomach hurts; she is also feeling nauseous. Her stomach pains come and go, come and go. She places one of her coarse hands across her stomach; the hot water-bottle helps a little.

For a few moments, Mara wonders if she herself attended the funeral; like the Inspector's youngest daughter, did she get the chance to place a flower on her mother's grave? They must have moved not long after the funeral, maybe the same year. Her mother must have bought the house before she died; maybe they were about to move. After all, she'd left Mara the house in her will. Mara thinks about the solicitor's stamp on the will. Maybe if she visited them, they could clarify a few things. Maybe they'd let her father know too.

Mara smiles. Until now, she had not realised that her mother must have been present in their home, in order to buy it. It is a comforting thought. Maybe even her mother decorated it. She should somehow bring it up in conversation with her father – maybe offer to paint her bedroom in the Easter break.

Before she returned on the train last Saturday, Mara visited their old family home. It didn't take long to find it. She again passed the house with the ginger cat. The house looked empty. Ginger meandered back and forth along the windowsill, on the inside of the lounge window.

When she arrived to the train station, she asked a stranger the way; he was walking a sausage dog whom he called Winnie. Mara had not seen one of these dogs before, well, strictly speaking, she had seen one on television, in a cartoon. Seeing one for real is thrilling; its body is really quite long in comparison to its short stubby legs – the droopy eyes and ears are elongated and comical. Mara was about to stroke it when it began growling.

It didn't take long before she found South Road, a ten minute walk in the opposite direction to the church. The small dwelling was half way down on the left. It looked no different to any other house in the area – a semi-detached brick house, the right half, probably two to three bedrooms – net curtains in every front window. There was a wooden, tall gate to the side; it was open.

Mara thought about ringing the doorbell but she did not. There was little about today that had felt right – gone to plan - nothing ever in life goes how she imagines. Stupid Mara. Head in the clouds. Or in a book. Welcome to the real world.

A lettuce-green humped-back car was parked in the drive. She could near no noise coming from the back garden. As she passed it, she saw two car seats in the back. One was clearly for a baby – a pastel Beatrix Potter musical mobile attached.

The sky was darkening. It was just after five. Mara needed to get back home, home before her father returned, home to make his soup and sandwich. As Mara treaded carefully past the open back gate, she spied a square back garden, much smaller than their own. The lawn needed mowing – a washing line halved it diagonally.

There was a swing, a slide, and a sand-pit by the back fence, facing her. The older child could have only been about the same age as when she herself inhabited the home, once upon a time, with both her parents – a time when she was probably happy and totally unaware of what life had in store for her.

Unexpectedly, an unaccustomed sound startled her. Upon turning around, Mara discovered a navy blue pram. From where she stood, she could see nothing. But the noise was now familiar; it was the cooing sound of a baby.

Mara leaned over the pram before looking to the open back door. There was no sound coming from the inside. The pram was below the kitchen window. Mara peered inside. Through the kitchen was the lounge. There sat a small girl, somewhere between the age of two and four. She was watching television. Mara could not see the television but she could see colourful patterns reflecting on and off the coffee table. The child looked amused. She was still in her pyjamas.

A young woman was sitting close-by, slumped – an untouched mug of tea ahead of her. She looked fast asleep in the armchair. Mara could not see the mother's eyes but her head was tilted backwards - her mouth slightly ajar. Mara looked at the mother for a few more moments.

The baby had a golden bangle about its tiny wrist.

It was difficult to tell whether the baby was a boy or a girl; it had no hair and it was all dressed in white.

The bedding was all white too.

The baby was very small.

Its tender elongated head lay on a petite pillow that had a frill along its perimeter.

The baby's fingers looked like bones; its nails sharp and feathery.

Mara lifted the small pillow from under the baby's head.

Moments later, she was heading for her train - the train that would take her home, home where the heart was not.

32

'DO YOU TAKE sugar Father?'

'None thanks. I'm sweet enough!'

Hermione Folkard emerged from the kitchen with two china mugs on a slender tray. Until today, she had not managed to complete a full shopping trip around the local supermarket since Walter had passed away, another job he used to do week in and week out – another job that she had taken for granted.

Last time she entered the store – she left without half the items needed, the shopping list still in the car.

'I've even got some biscuits. The girls will be shocked when they open the cupboards. Okay, I didn't actually go shopping; I ordered online.'

'You know you can save your shopping list as well – so you don't have to start all over again next week. It remembers what you order consistently. Clever really. My wife did all those things too. I have managed to survive after all.'

'I hope you don't mind me saying. It seems unusual to come across a priest that was once married?'

'It is unusual but not unheard of – especially in America. A bit like a second career. I was ordained just over three years ago. I still think about Beth every day. I'm human after all.'

Hermione Folkard paused before she spoke again; this time she looked sombre.

'On television, when a family member passes, you see neighbours calling round for weeks, passing endless casseroles over the doorstep. I could have done with a few of them. Not one. Not a single casserole has come my way!'

For a moment Hermione Folkard felt like laughing. How difficult even a laugh had now become. Father Stephen smiled and she in turn reciprocated.

'Yes, the girls seemed to settle well Monday evening. I told you they would. How's Harry?'

'Busy. It's his way.'

'I feel a bit better for having gone back to work. But I feel guilty. I feel guilty all the time. Every time I enjoy something, without Walter, I reproach myself. Every time I do something, or see something, and he's not here to see it with me, I feel guilty. I'm even grateful that the kids are coping better than I thought they would. I feel guilty about that too.'

Father Stephen was about to speak when Hermione Folkard interrupted him.

'I've stopped seeing him for what he was. He's just Walter, alone, underground. Even my memories of him are distorted. And in my dreams - sometimes we get to spend time together whilst I'm asleep. I wake up, knowing he is no longer there but feeling like I've spent a whole night in his company. On those mornings, I don't ever want to wake up. I sound crazy, don't I?'

'It's all normal. The dreams will continue. Get the photographs out, remember him as he would have liked you to think of him. He is still here to a large extent. He exists in your children. When you look at them, you are also looking at him. When you do something for them, you are also doing something for him. It is God's way.'

'I don't mean to offend Father, I'm not quite an atheist. I believed in very little in the first place. It is at times like this, I envy those who have strong beliefs, like yourself. The sheer mention of God and I can feel myself switching off, angry. I'm sorry. I must seem very rude, after all you've done for us.'

'I'm here regardless. What you are experiencing is perfectly normal. All of this takes time.'

Together they sat looking out towards the back garden. It was raining lightly now. Two small sparrows playfully flicked water from a small pool that had gathered between the flagstones.

'Darcy has made friends with Niamh Rawcliffe, Joseph's sister. I had to inform my line manager today.

I'm glad they've met, to be honest. She seems to get on well with her. Death is an exclusive club. No-one truly understands, unless they've experienced it.'

Hermione Folkard suddenly began to cry. Father Stephen placed his hand securely over hers. From time to time he patted it in succession, then rested it again.'

'It just happens. Tears just literally fall. I have no control over them. It all hurts so much. If I didn't have the children – what would be the point of going on?'

Father Stephen sat silently. There was little he could say that could comfort her. He knew first-hand what that pain was like - the physical relentless pain that could drive one insane. He'd often wondered himself what would have become of him, had Beth and he had children.

Hermione Folkard looked to the clock on the shelf. It was nearly six. Soon, the girls would need picking up from their singing lesson. She needed to wash her face. They'd know she'd been crying, again. That wouldn't do.

Slowly and with care, Father Stephen rose from his seat. Two biscuits had gone and she hadn't even noticed him consume them. Once upon a time, nothing happened without her filming it with her eyes for the playback – these days she seemed to waver through fog. Nothing was obvious anymore. No matter. Catherine Shakespeare was more than capable. Life went on, whether one liked it or not.

'By the way? Mara Bones. The young girl you asked me about?'

'Yes. She was in a couple of the boys' classes.'

'I'm hoping to pay her a visit tomorrow, whilst her father is at work. I heard she is off school – sick.'

Hermione Folkard recalled asking the team to check out any recent absentees following Sally Conway's accident.

'Will you call me if you manage to get to talk to her?'

'Of course. But remember, anything said to me privately, cannot be repeated – sacrosanct and all that.'

Both Father Stephen and Hermione Folkard smiled simultaneously as he exited the porch. This time, she didn't avoid pausing by their family portrait. Walter looked so handsome. He was the handsomest man she had ever met. She smiled and in return, he smiled back.

33

MARA'S FATHER ARRIVES home. He calls out her name, even before he closes the front door, whatever the reason, it must be important. Mara is in bed; she is choosing to ignore her father. Usually, he would find her downstairs; she would be in the kitchen, warming his soup, the sandwiches ready - but not tonight.

Uncharacteristically, Mara has decided to not prepare anything for her father; she may not prepare anything for him again. On this occasion, Mara has decided she will say she is ill – been vomiting – it's not too far from the truth. Mara has also decided that she will be taking a few days off school.

After her father has called a couple more times, he is heard ascending the stairs two at a time. The speed at which he climbs tells her it is not an emergency. Mara is lying sideways under the covers when he enters her room without knocking.

'What's going on? Mara?'

'I'm sick. I don't feel well. I keep being sick. And my stomach hurts.'

Mara's father is about to speak but thinks better of it. For a short while, he looks around her room; it is as if he has never really taken any notice until now. He is looking abstractedly at one of her posters when she speaks again.

'I don't think I can go to school tomorrow.'

Her father has now moved; he is now looking at her most recent poster. It is fixed to the back of her door facing her bed. It is an advertisement for a new best-selling book about a group of teenagers at a boarding school. The poster is mostly turquoise. The title is in large letters: KILLER GAMES. The poster is in the style of a horror movie; blood drops fall in the shape of tears from a large metallic knife. It is much different to the others in her room. At the bottom are the words; *She likes collecting losers and loners. Here, everyone is to blame.* There is a silent pause before her father speaks again.

'You've probably got what I had. I still don't feel right. I would have taken more time off but Mr Luca said he'd dock my pay. If I'm not shut of this virus in a fortnight, I'm going to make another appointment at the doctors. When I went last time, Dr Merridew was on his holidays again. Have you eaten?'

'Very little. I haven't prepared anything for you. I haven't been downstairs much today.'

Mara's father pauses for a moment before he speaks again. There is a familiar tone of excitement in his voice now. Before he speaks, Mara is quite sure what the topic of conversation will be.

'Says on the news, a girl in your school was killed after being hit by a bus right outside the gates! Luca's wife says everything comes in three's. That's three deaths, one after the other – and from what the news says, all in your year!'

Deep down, Mara knows she is responsible but her father's news has little impact; hearing about it, in the way she always does, like second-hand news items, hearing about it, allows her to detach herself from some of it – like stepping to the side. It is like dreaming – you wake up – did it ever really happen?

Something has changed in the last few days, probably since Mara found her mother's grave – a grave that had obviously been rarely visited – neglected, like herself. Death is a means for an end in many cases – an end that needs to sometimes happen in order for something new to begin – sometimes better – sometimes not.

In Romeo and Juliet, the family feud between the Capulets and the Montagues only ended as a direct result of the lovers' deaths. Fate intervened. Maybe fate could lend her a hand too.

'Dad.'

The unfamiliar monosyllabic word is an alien in the room but it has the desired effect. Mara's father seems uncomfortable all at once. His cheeks are pinched pink – embarrassed.

'Yes?'

'I was thinking I might paint my room, during the Easter holidays? Would you mind if I painted my room? I'd be happy to paint yours too.'

Mara's father looks confused. For a moment he glances about her room before speaking.

'Looks okay to me. Bit outdated maybe.'

'Did you decorate my room when we moved here?'

Mara's father is thinking. For a moment his hands are on his hips. He releases one of them before he lifts it upwards to touch his chin; for a moment he resembles a teapot.

'Nope. I think it was like this when we moved here.'

For a few moments, Mara's father looks like he is about to speak again. He looks at Mara's eyes. Although they are purple underneath and she looks weak, there is a new-found confidence that has grown out of nowhere – something he cannot put his finger on – something he finds untraceable.

'We'll see.'

Mara's father has now left her bedroom and almost closed the door.

'We'll see.' Mara echoes.

***

Tonight Mara hopes she will sleep better than the last two nights. The dream from last night has bothered her more than any others. In her sleep, Mara keeps hearing the sound of a baby crying. It is a strange sound. It is also irritating, the crying gets louder and louder – angrier and angrier – the baby's face contorts, becomes ugly like an old doll.

Yesterday, she awoke just as the baby's mother entered the garden to console it. Last night, no-one came; once again the baby's crying got louder and louder. Mara wanted the baby to stop crying. But the baby didn't stop. It became more agitated with each cry. As each cry intensified with its screech-like demands, Mara became more distressed. In the end, Mara picked up a pillow and placed it on the baby's face to shut it up. But each time she removed it, the baby would begin to cry once more.

As each day passes, Mara feels she is walking on a tight-rope. Everything in her life is altered. Nothing is at it was. If her life was empty before, it is even emptier now. There is nothing to look forward to anymore, literally. Mara has nothing to lose.

Mara's father is now calling upstairs again. Another bird is dead. But Mara will not answer. If he wants her, he knows where he can find her.

One for Sorrow,

Two for Joy,

Three for a Girl,

Four for a Boy,

Five for Silver.

Tomorrow, when her father is back at work, she will open all her letters and gifts. There is no point waiting any longer. Any delay is pointless. Mara repeatedly wipes tears of frustration rapidly away; her coarse fingertips work their way across her cheekbone in whisk-like waves. Mara's mind is restless; her shoulders sag like heavy clouds.

It is dusky outside now. It is also raining heavily. Mara rises to look out of her window. There is blood seeping through her lemon nightdress. Her lower arms bear the scars of cuts that have seen better times. Fresh incisions now replace them. Self-harm is no label; few know anything about this religion. It is a tattoo on the soul, an understanding – a physical self-communication, not mutilation – a spiritual yoga.

Mara runs two of her fingertips across her chapped lips. She remembers a few lines from a poem she once memorised before she inaudibly cries; *we are mosaics – pieces of light – stars glued together with magic and music and words.*

The sky is a mosaic itself, darkening greys for as far as the eye can see. Grey Matter, does any of it matter? Grey is usually one of her favourite colours. Grey is the colour of dust and squirrels, of elephants and metal, of stones and feathers. Today, grey is the colour of gloom and fears, of graves and tears, of death and the-too-many-to-mention lost years. A silver-white lightning bolt forks the sky ahead. Everything is silent before a rumble in the sky quakes.

34

HERMIONE FOLKARD DETECTED a familiar flurry of activity taking place around Sergeant Shakespeare's desk. She didn't know why, but for a moment, she felt a tad excluded. Everyone was either smiling or laughing loudly. It hit her. Sometimes, it is only when someone does *that* something that you realise it has been a while since you last experienced it. *That* was laughter.

For a while, no-one around her had laughed much. No-one had laughed out loud. Not in her presence anyway. Could it be, that her own misery had oozed and spread so widely that it had flooded the ark itself? Right now, they were all visibly content; yet there she sat, watching, like a child outside a sweet-shop looking in, experiencing the very opposite.

Catherine looked over her shoulder, as if sensing she was being watched. In turn, others followed. They weren't laughing as much now, as if they'd forgotten themselves. Some looked guilty. Most half-smiled. A few looked at her with pity. That was the pits. One person headed back to his desk, avoiding all eye-contact - his white styrofoam cup had teeth marks along half the circumference by the time he'd sat back down. For a moment Sergeant Shakespeare hesitated before she waved her over.

Absurdly, Hermione Folkard had forgotten all about Catherine's wedding plans that summer. Of course. Had Walter not died, she would have probably deliberated almost every decision with her, especially as they travelled about in their unmarked car from one daily duty to another. Now it all seemed so obvious. Catherine had avoided the entire subject during their time alone. Their whole time had been consumed by her own grief.

Hermione Folkard raised a smile before she joined those left around Sergeant Shakespeare's desk. Although some were communicative – their exchanges could have been filed under the category of phatic language - the sort that often centres around the British weather.

'The wedding cake, what do you think?'

Before she could respond, a sketch of a three tier cake telling a story all of its own instantly caught her eye. Straightaway she laughed – a small laugh, like a cough. The more she looked at every detail – the more she laughed. It presented a scene of a female police officer at the altar whilst the wife-to-be was busy protesting on her own wedding day outside the church – placards in the guests' hands both inside and outside the church. It was brilliant – cartoon like.

'A friend of Wendy's is making the cake. It's brilliant isn't it!'

'Brilliant. I love it.'

A few minutes later and Hermione Folkard wanted to retreat back to her noiseless enclosed office, close the blinds. But this, she could not do. She remained there amongst her valued colleagues like a redundant sail waiting for a gust of wind, waiting for the right time to move effortlessly away without causing any form of disrespect. All Hermione Folkard could do was ignore the mental images of her own wedding day that flashed now before her. She swallowed hard. Her throat was dry again.

'Ok. That's it everyone. I'll keep you up-to-date with the whole saga of there-is-not-a-chance-in-hell-I'm-wearing-a-wedding-dress and the what-do-you-think-of-this-instead, that is after I've been window-shopping with Wendy for the fortieth time! I fear though that we'll end up looking like an Elvis support act if we go ahead and wear matching white trouser suits!'

Hermione Folkard turned away and looked towards the incident board.

'Have you set a date yet?'

'We have. August the 15th, Bartle Hall in Lancaster at 1pm. We were very lucky – a cancellation. We're going on Sunday to take a look – only just booked it. I took the liberty of booking you a family room, for you and the children. I knew you wouldn't be up to it.'

Hermione Folkard swallowed. Her throat hurt more now. It was hard holding back the tears. The word 'family' took her by surprise, a sharp cake knife. Were they still a family as such? For longer than a moment, she pictured a scene in a Carol Ann Duffy poem that she had always loved. She pictured herself looking into a full-length mirror – unrecognisable – in her wedding dress. Once upon a time she could have recollected the entire poem. Now, all she could remember were a few lines.

The slewed mirror, full-length, her, myself.

Who did this to me?

Puce curses that are sounds not words.

Some nights better, the lost body over me.

A red balloon bursting in my face.

Don't think it's only the heart that b-b-breaks.

Catherine Shakespeare had followed Hermione Folkard back to her office. She left the door slightly open before she began to speak using a more formal voice. To everyone nearby, everything was on the mend, the ship was still sturdy – the choppy waters calming. What the others couldn't see was that for a few seconds, Catherine Shakespeare had held her friend's hand very lightly before letting go at the right time.

In reality, Catherine Shakespeare was the wind that, from time to time, directed Hermione Folkard's sail – an invisible, inoffensive much-needed gust of wind. Without her, Hermione Folkard would have most probably taken much longer to return to work. The investigation was moving slower than a tortoise, a relentless and unwelcome plodding – but work was a *safer* place to be. It mopped up time. Before she knew it, the day's shift would come to an end. Night-time, once her favourite stretch of day, lasted – dragged like a heavy corpse. Sleep refused her every attempt.

'The new guy taking over, Mansell Beattie, I think that is his name, has finished conducting the post-mortem examination on Sally Conway.'

Hermione Folkard sat behind her desk, swivelled her chair so that her back was to the inside window.

'Sally Conway, as you guessed correctly, is in fact the daughter of Albert and Miriam Conway. Mr Rimmer's nosey neighbour.'

'Albert Conway, our incredibly valued but incredibly annoying nosey neighbour!'

'President of the Neighbourhood Watch; crime prevention for the Marshide community no less!'

They half-laughed. Outside, the sky was darkening. Grey listless clouds moved pedantically across the sky, a monochromic exhibition.

'To be fair, from the many reportings of suspicious circumstances, on two occasions, these lead to an arrest for burglary.'

'Yes. And now his estranged daughter is *dead.*'

Hermione Folkard paused after she had uttered the last word. She stood up and headed for the only window in her office that overlooked the staff car park.

'It's going to rain. Looks stormy. So what did this Mansell Beattie have to say. Still sticking to the accident theory?'

'Yes. Agrees with the first response crime scene report. SOCO arrived shortly after the ambulance. No visible evidence of any suspicious circumstances. No significant eye-witnesses either. One minute she was there; the next she was gone.'

'Have you interviewed all the children present at the scene? Do you have a list?'

'I do. I've already checked. Mara's name is not in the list.'

'Doesn't mean she wasn't there. Can you ask someone to interview a couple of her close friends again? See if the two knew each other. It's a long shot I know.'

'Oh – I meant to add, toxicology report – Beattie said there were traces of alcohol in her system – may go some way towards explaining why she wasn't paying attention? Little comfort to her family, I know.'

'Alcohol? From the night before or consumed on the school premises?'

'Same day. Probably a can of cider shared behind the bike-shed! Anyway, Sally Conway, like most children in the year, knew Joseph and Jacob. They were in four classes together. Including Mara, all four students, three deceased, share four Geography lessons a week. Remember? You asked a couple of days ago for us to cross-check?'

'Yes. I did, didn't I? I also asked if anyone could check who was absent from school immediately following the accident?'

'You did. Sorry. I'll get onto that. Luke McKenna was looking into it. Back in a tick.'

'Hope you don't mind, I'm going to head home Catherine. I'm not feeling so well, banging headache. Call me if you need me.'

Hermione Folkard squeezed her friends lower arm as she passed her on the way to retrieving her personal possessions behind her desk. She was about to head for her office door when PC McKenna knocked on it.

'List of absentees Sergeant.'

'Thank you Luke.'

Sergeant Shakespeare paused momentarily before she spoke. The right hand side, from her philtrum to her upper cheek, raised itself momentarily. Hermione Folkard knew instinctively this would result in the bearing of good news.

'Think you might want to take a look at this before you go. First name on the list – hasn't returned to school since Sally's accident – guess who?

UNUSUALLY, IT IS quite hot today, for a day in March. According to her father, Africa and Spain are responsible for the sudden heat wave in the North-West. Her father hates the heat. He doesn't hate it because he works in a restaurant – that would make sense. Instead, he hates the heat because the canaries don't like it. Heat causes stress. Heat also breeds flies, and flies, female flies according to her father, bite his birds – suck on their blood, to aid reproduction.

Mara is sitting on a buttery-yellow blanket; she usually keeps it on top of her wardrobe for the winter months. It is one of those blankets that replaces human touch. It hugs, warms and comforts. Next week will be April – April showers. Mara intends to make the most of her time off. Returning to school seems more impossible as each day passes.

Little by little and over the last couple of weeks, Mara's appetite has dwindled. Her father hasn't even noticed. Her stomach still hurts; it is an ache that comes and leaves in waves. At times it feels like it has been scratched by a wild cat from the inside. Sickness has resulted in Mara looking pale and gaunt; below her yellowing eyes are patches like purple pools. Visible threadbare veins fork her delicate gossamer-like skin, the fabric belonging to the rest of her face thicker and more obscure. Mara is unaware of this. She has ceased looking in the mirror – afraid of whom she has become.

Mara's unbrushed hair is tied to the top of her head; her high ponytail is short and untidy. She hangs her head forward so that her chin almost touches her chest. The afternoon sun warms her snow-white swan-shaped neck. It is one of those lazy days when everything seems to happen in slow-motion – time almost standing still. A day for snapshots.

Her mother's gift, the gold necklace bearing the Christian cross, is about her neck. On the internet, it said that the meaning of a cross was death – after all , it is an instrument of execution. Her primary school had presented the death of Jesus very differently. It masked the realism and horror now understood by Mara. In reality, crucifixion is a slow and excruciating way to die, hanging there, nailed. She also learned that at the time, the Israelites were commanded to sacrifice an unblemished lamb and smear the blood in order to protect their loved ones.

When we eat this bread and drink this blood – Mara thinks about the communion ritual. It is requested every Sunday, by Father Stephen, that they partake in the eating of Jesus' flesh and the drinking of his blood. Mara wonders why nobody stands up and shouts something. *Are you kidding me? Have they all been brainwashed?*

Transubstantiation, the act of changing the substances of bread and wine into flesh and blood, is in reality, a magic trick, the emperor's new clothes. Mara lets out a wry laugh. Why doesn't somebody just shout out that he's naked? Mara decides, if she ever goes to another service, that she will no longer partake in communion. Maybe she should stop going to church altogether.

Mara was once sent out of class for asking why God didn't ever go first. Her RE Teacher had been explaining the meaning of the phrase *Do this in my name.* Undoubtedly, there is no God. There is no saviour, to save her.

Mara checks her cross is on the right way round before kissing it. She has decided to wear it from now on, come what may. At some point, her father will ask her about it; she will reply herself by asking him some uncomfortable questions – questions that needed answering a long time ago. Mara knows he will become angry and challenge her but Mara is ready for him.

The heat is so uplifting. Today of all the most marvellous days, it seems impossible that her future could be so uncertain – hanging in the balance. Mara is still wearing the same sleeveless yellow nightdress that she wore the day before, and the day before that. Although the blood has dried around the midriff, fresh lacerations to her lower arms have painted a new story on the canvas. It is a story of woe. And neglect. And demise.

Killer Games has lay unopened for the last hour on the blanket. Mara has decided not to read it anymore. It seems every story has a thread of hope, a silver lining – a dream that is in some small way realised. Friends. Love. Adventure. Unlike her own story which is friendless and lonely and uneventful.

Reading no longer helps. Mrs Cassidy would disagree, but she does not understand – no-one does. There is no reading material that does not remind Mara of what she has not got, of what she will never have. She is beyond healing. Beyond hope.

In contrast to her reading book, her sixteenth and eighteenth letters lie open; one of the pink envelopes moves staccato-fashion across the blanket like a ballerina *en pointe*. It is a welcomed breeze. Mara leans forward and catches it before securing both letters under her new diary, a thoughtful present for her sixteenth birthday.

Her mother wishes her to record memories. Something she wishes she had done herself in the past, so she could have passed *her* diary to Mara. Her mother says she would have been able to get to know her better – see her as a young person – relate to what her mother called *the pains of growing up.*

The cover of the diary is really beautiful. It is a bright glossy pink with a large majestic peacock's head to the forefront. The emerald-green fowl spreads its long feathers across the front and back cover, a bit like the phoenix did on one of the covers in the Harry Potter series. The eyespots on each wing have gold eyeshadow glitter to them. Inside, her mother has written something on the first page taken from a Dr Seuss children's book:

>*You're off to great places.*
>
>*Today is your day.*
>
>*Your mountain is waiting.*
>
>*So get on your way.*

At first Mara thought she would subdivide the diary into Primary and Secondary School memories. But Mara couldn't think of anything truly interesting, or eventful to write. Mara was sure there was nothing about herself or her life that anyone would ever want to read about. Then she thought she'd write about her mother. After a while, Mara decided it was pointless. It would end up like a Tracy Beaker journal – a fabrication based on hopes and wishes and dreams. In reality, only her father can tell her the truth.

Instead, Mara has begun writing her confession. She might as well use the diary to record what is real – what her life has suddenly become. The truth. It is addressed to the Inspector who knows about loss.

Mara is also wearing a gold bangle on her right wrist. On the inside it says, *To my darling Mara on her 18th Birthday – Love always Mum x.* The message ends just before it began – a bit like her relationship with her mother – short but sweet.

Mara looks at the cross. Another cross. Another symbolic symbol – a binary code, this time one signifying love and affection, a kiss. Mara sees these symbols sprinkled liberally across many walls and pages – random, meaningful. Few have ever come her way. In fact, until recently, none had ever come her way. Mara smiles gratefully. A red admiral settles on her buttercup blanket before her. She was once loved. It is a comfort that few would understand. No-one should go through life unloved.

When Mara first read the message, she cried. Her throat tightened. She felt guilty - guilty that her petty jealousy over an unborn child had affected her so much - guilty that it consumed her to such an extent that she became so enraged and behaved so badly on the very day she found her mother.

For too many years, Mara has been feeling like a frightened animal. If she were a dog, she'd keep her tail tucked between her back legs; Lara often did so when her father was around. Mr Pinnington, her science teacher, has fingers like toes – bluish in colour. He says that ducks pretend to be dead when they are caught by foxes, this is their only coping mechanism. He says humans, with the exception of autistic people, can control pain; so in reality, intense fear is worse for birds than intense pain - this is why so many die of heart attacks.

Mara is not sure if she prefers intense pain to intense fear. A dark cloud has not only hung over her entire life but devoured her bit by bit, year upon year, like a foul dementor from a magic book who walks the earth feeding on human happiness in order to reduce her to something that is soulless, hard-hearted and evil.

Sadly, Mara is now closer to the dead than to the living. If she were to believe in God, then hell surely awaits. But Mara does not believe in such things. It is peace that awaits her. Her mother will be waiting, her arms wide open – she is sure of that. It reminds her of one of the final scenes in the story of *The Little Matchgirl*. In the young girl's final vision, before she dies, frozen to death, she sees her departed grandmother, arms wide open, waiting for her.

Mara thinks back to the time she was last held in an embrace. She had hoped, even imagined many times, Joseph would be the person to keep her safe, hold her, love her. Ridiculous. Her whole life has been one ridiculous event after another. She has been ridiculed all her life.

In primary school the children sometimes remarked that she smelled of urine but they still sat and played with her, on occasion; there were other kids who smelt the same – mostly boys. Once she reached secondary school, things got worse; students did more than voice their opinions about her lack of hygiene, a frightened rabbit caught in the headlights most days, from form time to the end of the day - eight long hours - exposed – no safety net but for the library.

Thinking back, Mara is sure that her form tutor, Mr Quinn, had spoken to the school nurse. He gave her some free deodorant after speaking to her about the importance of washing regularly.

Mara was about eleven when she stopped wetting the bed. Her father rarely changed the bedding. Mara started washing the sheets in the sink when she was in primary school but the mattress was the most difficult to clean. Mara has slept on the same mattress for as long as she can remember. Her period has made matters worse. One of the stains resembles the shape of the continent of Africa. She was about to turn the stained mattress over a couple of days ago, when she decided there was no point. A popular song, playing on the charts, entered her head at the time; one of the lines talks about *lying in your bed of lies.*

Mara liked reading both letters, although they seemed to say so little, despite their length. Both letters made Mara feel sad. Her mother had such high expectations. She didn't mean to become so little in life. Had she had the letters earlier, would she have been inspired? Become more confident as a result? Made more of herself? Mara is not sure. It is difficult being anything other than Mara.

One thing Mara is sure about is her father. He clearly couldn't be bothered about being *her father*. The hierarchy at 25 North Lane goes like this. Top – the birds. Middle – Mara. Bottom – Lara. At least she is treated better than an animal. Poor Lara – bottom of the heap. Dead. Dead as charity.

By sixteen, Mara's mother is sure she will have a sweetheart and have achieved such good grades in school that she will go on to study A Levels. By eighteen, Mara's mother is sure she will have had many sweethearts. She speaks to her about heartbreak and the importance of University – becoming a woman – financially independent of others. If only her mother knew. If she does, she'll be turning in her grave, as they say.

Even the thought of going back out-of-doors terrifies Mara; communicating with the outside world seems surreal now. The thought of going onto any further education, having any admirers, being independent in any way, is most certainly impossible. Mara will not ever be able to depend on her father. She is ill-at-ease everywhere. Mara knows she is a freak, a misfit. She has violated the law – in time, she will have to pay.

An hour has now passed. Bees fuzz from one flower to another. There is a faint aroma in the air – it is both sickly and sweet. Often Mara raises her hand in salute to shade her eyes. She squints, even smiles from time to time. Smiling was something that Mara did when she read – or was in the library. But laughing is alien to Mara. Mara laughed plenty as a child. Her mother used to tickle her daily and make her shriek with laughter. But Mara does not know this.

Her remaining hand steadies her. Rays thrown like a fishermen's net entrap her on the spot. Everything is so hot and rosy. If you squint with your right eye you can squash closed the clusters of the blue-belled-shaped flowers. If you squint with your left, you can close down upon the milky sap of a large, open poppy.

***

It is the sound of *arguing* that wakes Mara, almost an hour later after she drifted off to sleep. Accusatory sentences are flung back and forth in quick succession. Her neighbours to the left are having their daily debate in the back garden. Only to strangers would it appear far more serious than it actually is. Mara is used to the exchanges between these two sisters who are not too dissimilar in age or size.

Mrs Lexton refers to her sister as Mrs Tanner, and in return, Mrs Tanner refers to her sister as Mrs Lexton. They talk like they are shouting most of the time. Each sentence is a statement or an imperative. Sometimes, when their voices are raised, it is hard to tell which sister is which.

Mara cannot see the women but they are easy to picture. They are both just over five foot in height and shaped like an apple. Mara would have to watch from the upstairs window if she wanted to see them. For a moment Mara is sorry to have had her sleep disturbed; she has not been sleeping well recently.

But their exchanges are so humorous and dealt with such blows that Mara finds herself wishing they would go on for ever. All the world is a stage or in this case, a table tennis competition.

Mrs Lexton has lived next door for a very long time; she lived with her husband until he mysteriously vanished one day – according to Mr Stone, the neighbour to their right. A couple of summers ago, Mrs Lexton was having one of her debates with Mrs Tanner when Mara heard her say that she FUCKING REGRETTED MOVING IN with her. That is the only time Mara has ever heard anyone cry next door. Mr Stone told her father, who was not listening, that Mrs Lexton had taken her in after Mr Tanner had died of a violent heart attack. He also laughed after he said that Mrs Tanner had probably worn him down and near enough killed him herself.

In reality, Mrs Tanner and Mrs Lexton are very close. All the neighbours are frightened of them in some small way. Neither of the sisters bother to say hello anymore as they pass. Their grunts and grumbles, as they waddle off daily to the village of Crossens, are a barrier designed to warn any passer-by to keep their distance. Even the bible-bashers don't attempt calling on them.

Today, Mrs Lexton is shouting out from a downstairs window to Mrs Tanner who is sitting on a kitchen chair by the back door. Mrs Tanner is smoking her pipe - Mara likes the smell of it. Mara has many times spotted them smoking a pipe in the back garden. They hold the pipe with their teeth when they talk; they even smoke them when they peg the washing out.

The frames of every door and window in their house are painted purple. It suits their house. Mara wonders if the inside of their home is purple too. Their garden, in comparison to theirs, is a haven. Mara can see very little to the left from her father's bedroom window but what she has seen is tidy and colourful – lots of neat beds – not a weed in sight. There are different gnomes about the garden too. Mara thinks of Mr Hyde. Yes, the sisters are dwarfish in many ways. But they are not malicious and wicked. Not like her.

'I TOLD YOU Mrs Tanner!'

'And I told YOU Mrs Lexton!'

'You told me WHAT MRS TANNER! WHAT DID YOU TELL ME?'

'I said, THERE'S A CUP OF TEA WAITING INSIDE!'

'Then WHY DIDN'T YOU SAY SO MRS TANNER?'

'MRS TANNER! MRS TANNER!'

'MRS LEXTON!'

'I'd like my cup of tea here PLEASE MRS TANNER.'

'THEN COME AND BLOODY GET IT YOURSELF MRS LEXTON!'

36

'MARA'S FATHER Didn't ring the school to report his daughter's absence. However, he was aware of it. When the attendance officer rang, he said Mara had a stomach bug, that he himself had been ill with the same virus. He still doesn't feel right. She's been vomiting too.'

'Sounds plausible. Maybe just a coincidence?'

Inspector Folkard failed to reply. She looked at Sergeant Shakespeare before tapping the incident board with a pen.

'Is Juliet still re-interviewing Sally Conway's friends? Are you sure there is no CCTV?'

'Yes and none.'

'All videos on student phones and media checked?'

'Yes, but, I suppose officers checking all media were only looking for any evidence of foul play. They weren't looking for Mara directly. Might be worth taking a second look?'

'Yes. Although most of the filming, if not all, will have taken place after the incident. Regardless, get them to look through again.'

Inspector Folkard was looking intently at the photographs of Joseph Rawcliffe and Jacob Lamb when PC Cunliffe entered the room.

'Mr and Mrs Conway are downstairs collecting their daughter's personal effects.'

'Thank you.'

For a moment, Inspector Folkard hesitated before heading downstairs. It seemed odd to be meeting under such sad circumstances. She couldn't help feeling sorry for Albert Conway and his estranged wife. There was another sibling, a younger sister, still in primary, but for Albert Conway, Sally had been his only child. From what she had read in the report, Sally and her father were not on speaking terms. Now, there would be no chance of a reconciliation.

PC McKenna's right hand gestured in her direction before he opened the door. He was unusually red in the face, like had been running for a bus. He smiled kindly before his facial expression changed into one that recognised his line-manager's confused expression.

'Wind burn. I know; it looks awful! Potholing with Juliet this last weekend.'

Inspector Folkard's mouth avoided making an *O* before she stopped herself from turning around and searching out his colleague. For many reasons it was difficult to imagine PC Clarke potholing. She had once and only once tried it herself with a past boyfriend, when she was in her early twenties. It was an enjoyable experience in many ways but when the water began to rise later in the day, she found herself feeling a panic she had never experienced before.

'On my way to find you actually.'

'Oh yes?'

'Six of Sally Conway's friends confirmed Sally and Mara knew each other. Not unusual. But when asked about their relationship, all of them confirmed that Sally used to bully Mara. One Thomas Rice, known as Tea-Leaf Tom, stated Sally had bullied Mara for as long as he could remember. He was quite forthcoming with information on Sally - sounds to me like she was quite a horrible young lady – had made his life a misery in primary too.

Apparently, Sally used to have regular fights to keep her status as the cock-of-the-back-of-the-Crown secure. She earned and retained the title through fighting other girls, outside school, in the carpark at the back of the Crown pub in Churchtown.'

'Classy. I need you to re-interview him again. I need to know of any incidents between Mara and Sally prior to the accident. Every detail. And thank you Luke.'

'Oh. Anything on her mobile?'

'Nothing other than some very unpleasant comments about various other girls. Maybe we should check them out too?'

'Maybe. The investigation is closed on this one but I want to be sure. A hunch, that's all it is.'

***

Albert Conway looked surprised when Inspector Folkard approached him from a side door. He looked no different to the last time she had seen him, only paler; he had dark circles below his eyes, as did his wife. He smiled to see her familiar face. Before Inspector Folkard could speak, he introduced his estranged wife to her.

'Miriam, this is Inspector Folkard. I once assisted in solving one of their cases. Mr Rimmer. Next door. All very unpleasant.'

For a moment he looked as though he was about to say more. He looked at Miriam's unimpressed face before pausing.

'I read about your recent loss Inspector. I'd like to offer my sincere condolences.'

'I wanted to personally offer mine to yourselves. I am very sorry for your loss. Losing a child, and so young, is a loss no parent should endure.'

Miriam Conway began to cry. Albert Conway placed his arm around her shoulder at the same point she shrugged it off. She was a large woman with frizzy bleached blonde hair. In comparison, Albert Conway looked dwarfish in stature. He must have been half her weight.

'Do you have everything you need?'

'Yes. We have her things now. Funeral to arrange.'

'Yes.'

Hermione Folkard wanted to say more but was afraid she would lose her iron-maiden composure.

'I believe there is a younger sibling?'

'Stephanie. She's with my mum. I have to get back – she's eight. She's so upset – keeps crying. Next minute she seems normal – going about her business – then she's crying again, asking questions, like she's forgotten what's happened.'

Miriam's face contorted; for a moment she looked hard and angry like a woman ready to take on the world, then quite suddenly, like a scene from Conan Doyle's *Hound of the Baskervilles*, her face altered, tragic – broken, her shoulders loosened, defeated, tired - a Stapleton moment - a face scored with vile passions.

Eventually, Mrs Conway allowed herself to be helped out of the reception area by her estranged husband who looked somewhat defeated too. Inspector Folkard held the door open. She couldn't help feeling sorry for him. She suspected Miriam had once made his life a misery. It was too late for him to make amends with his daughter – too late to turn the clock back.

In some strange way Hermione Folkard felt a little relieved. In reality, she had little to regret. In comparison, Walter and herself had lived harmoniously for most of their time together. She missed him so very much. He looked so handsome that first time she had seen him at work. So serious. His hair had since turned mostly grey. He looked better as the years passed, refined. Yes, they had much to be proud of, much to celebrate. She needed to remind the children of that - share her memories with them, make them smile, laugh-out-loud. She needed to share treasured memories even when she felt unable to – share the mental photographs that she feared on a daily basis she would one day forget, never again to be remembered.

***

'How's the second book going Darcy?'

Hermione Folkard shouted from the open-plan kitchen into the silent lounge where both girls loafed reading.

'At the end of it. When's dinner going to be ready? Did you make the cauliflower cheese?'

'Five minutes and yes. I picked up the other three Cass books for you on the way home – and the next Harry Potter for you Zita.'

Zita was engrossed. She was now half way through the third in the series. In her eyes everything was possible, wondrous and magical. For her last birthday, Walter had bought from the internet the exact replica wand belonging to her favourite character. Zita often spoke to others in the voice of this character by saying things like *You've got the emotional range of a teaspoon* and *I don't want to break rules, you know.*

Since Walter had died, Zita had rarely made reference to her favoured character, hadn't even picked up her wand. Come to think of it, Darcy had stopped singing; she used to sing spontaneously and powerfully, often, every day - like birdsong. The house was far too quiet – listless - weighty. Every aspect of its existence grieved, struggled, like the roof had become too heavy for the structure to subsist. The walls held it up bravely. The storm would pass, the edifice, although scathed, would surely survive.

'Food's nearly ready. Can you both set the table?'

'Niamh has started reading these too. I've texted her to tell her I have the rest for us to read - thanks mum!'

Hermione Folkard began serving spaghetti into their bowls. Walter's place was set but no bowl had been put out for him, just the place mat, serviette, spoon and fork. No glass either. Zita looked over at the bookcase, at a more recent photograph of Walter. It had been taken in France, a couple of summers ago. In each arm he held one of the girls. They were all smiling for her; she held the camera and captured the moment, forever.

'I wish our own photographs moved like they do in my book. I wish they spoke too.'

For a moment they all fell silent. Hermione Folkard began to serve the accompanying salad onto each plate. They collectively looked towards Walter's photograph before staring back at his empty chair. It didn't seem right to ignore it. The girls abandoned their bowls, as did she – their mouths chewing on lettuce, like it tasted of frost.

'I've been thinking; we should go on holiday this summer. Dad always wanted to go to Florida – to see the Kennedy Space Centre mostly – and there's a Harry Potter World Resort there too. I think we should go there and see all the things he wanted us to see. Have a special family holiday – take Harry and Mark too. What do you think? I know dad would like us all to do that. He wouldn't want us moping around. He'd want us to make the most of the summer. What do you think?'

The girls looked towards Walter's chair before they looked back at their mother. As if he himself had approved their plans. They instantaneously beamed.

'That's a good idea mum.'

'It's a good idea mum. I'll ring Harry.'

'After dinner please. Mind, we have to be back for Catherine and Wendy's wedding – August the 15th. You are bridesmaids after all girls!'

Hermione Folkard held back the tears that threatened to surge regardless of her best efforts to repress them. The girls were smiling now. Zita had already managed to smear enough red sauce outside her lips to resemble a circus clown. Darcy placed a warm hand on her mother's before kissing her on the cheek.

'Florida it is!'

LIKE YESTERDAY, The heat wave clings to the seaside town of Southport like a petulant child. Aggravated drivers, hungover from a restless night's sleep, use their horns frequently as they curse the heat in the same manner they cursed the rain only the week before.

It is early afternoon, Mara is sitting once again in the overgrown spring garden. She lounges languidly on the same buttercup yellow blanket – the intense sun bearing down upon her furrowed forehead. Tall globe-shaped thistles are ahead of her – their spiky leaves and bristly metallic-blue flowers are an architectural backdrop to the unruly garden; behind, her father's much-loved bird shed. It is difficult to hear their distinctive birdsong now there are only four canaries left:

One for Sorrow,

Two for Joy,

Three for a Girl,

Four for a Boy.

Mrs Tanner and Mrs Lexton are indoors baking. From the smell wafting in the miserly breeze, they are making bread. There is nothing like the smell emitted from the dough during the fermentation process - its chemistry is unique. Despite the tempting aromas, Mara does not feel hungry; her appetite has dwindled – she has eaten nothing since yesterday evening. Her father brought her two pieces of margarined toast; one piece lies listless on a plate on her dressing table.

Deep down, Mara hopes Mrs Tanner and Mrs Lexton will, at some point in the afternoon, hold one of their verbal table-tennis matches outdoors. Mara smiles. It is difficult not to smile when thinking about her neighbours. Mr Stone on the other side of the fence can be quite entertaining too. He has told her on a few occasions that he is a big fan of *Echo and the Bunnymen*. A few weeks ago he tried to get her to sing a few lines from a song called *Rescue*:

Won't you come on down to my

Won't you come on down to my rescue.

Things are wrong.

Things are going wrong.

Fortunately Mrs Stone came outdoors and rescued her. She apologised before coaxing her husband back indoors; he was still humming and singing the lyrics at the top of his voice as he entered the back door. Mrs Stone, feeling a tad embarrassed, had to laugh in the end.

Today, Mara missed a trip to Blackpool. It is one of those reward trips arranged for students who have maintained or exceeded the target attendance of 95%. Mara has rarely been absent from school since she was an infant. Every year, for the last four years, she has been invited to attend the same reward trip. It is subsidised; the parent need only contribute fifty percent towards the total cost.

With the exception of this year, Mara usually leaves the school letter on the kitchen table, only to find it has been placed in the bin not long after her father returns home from work. In Year Eight, Mara asked if she could go in exchange for her Birthday come Christmas present. Her father agreed after a long pause. He said he'd leave the money on the kitchen table. On the morning of the trip, Mara flew down the stairs in her own clothes only to find the tin of bird seed on it.

The students who remain behind on the day for trips are poorly organised into lessons. Most are led by teachers who refuse to teach them on a trip day. Some scowl at them for not having stayed at home. Almost all of them make some reference to them having been denied the privilege of the trip because of their poor behaviour. Many students are relieved by this, they do not want anyone to know that, in fact, it is because they are just poor - full stop.

Earlier on in the year, Mara attended a trip to John Moores' University in the centre of Liverpool. Almost all of Year Ten attended; it was compulsory. Mara was delighted. The coach ride was exciting in itself – the views heading towards the heart of the city engrossing. Mara sat at the front. She told herself that no one sat by her because they didn't want to sit near the teachers. By the end of the journey, Mara had forgotten her solitary journey: the shapes of the city, almost all made up of triangles, burned everlasting photographic images that have since been resurrected, usually when admiring an interesting building or skyline.

The day entailed various activities. She couldn't believe the size of the lecture theatre – the buzz – the enthusiasm to achieve and become something. The library was something else. There didn't seem to be many books on the entrance floor – there were computers everywhere, a real technology hub.

What Mara liked the most were the halls of residence. The bedrooms had their own bathrooms. The area and hallway were decorated in a really trendy way, dynamic oranges and greens - all dark wood furniture – all grown-up. The lounge area had astro-turf for a carpet. Mara knew there and then she was going to go to university – escape her life – make something of herself.

Having finished reading her twenty-first letter from her mother, Mara reflects on going to university. Her mother believed she would make it. Mara did want that for herself, once upon a time. Her mother hopes she has not yet settled her heart on someone, that she is studying hard and making something of herself. Mara's smile has changed, dwarfed. In her hand she holds her gift, an envelope with the deeds to the house, in her name. Mara has six and a half years until she has some control of her life. Mara cannot wait that long. Time is running out.

Two letters and two gifts remain. One is for her wedding day; the other on becoming a mother. Mara has decided she will not open these today; she may never open them. After all, she will never marry. She will never be loved and become a mother.

Today, she was grinding her glass when she accidentally lacerated the top of her thumb, although not badly; it throbbed even after the bleeding stopped. Mara has found recently that glass can also have a healing effect, when cutting oneself. The external pain kills the internal anguish – draws it outwards – blood spills and the pain eases. An exorcism of sorts.

Mara is yet to change her nightdress. The air surrounding her is thick with the smell of urine and sweat; her hair is matted – tied into an untidy bun on the top of her head. On the inside of her lower arm, fresh cuts, just below the cubital fossa, spell the word MUM. Tomorrow would have been her mother's fortieth birthday.

Suddenly, and quite unexpectedly, Mara hears a rhythmic succession of rat-ta-tat knocks on the wooden gate behind her – to the side of the house, Usually Mara would have heard the echoes of footsteps ahead of their arrival. The mystery caller has advanced without being heard. A familiar voice calls over the tall gate. For a moment Mara sits perfectly still, unable to move and unwilling to respond.

'Hellooo? Maraaa? Anyone theeere?'

Father Stephen's sing-song-like voice sounds friendly but Mara feels startled, exposed. Suddenly embarrassed by her appearance, she looks down at her soiled nightdress before she unintentionally covers the word MUM with her right hand. When the kindly voice speaks again, she nervously reaches up with both her hands to tidy loose strands behind her ears. She does so even though she has no intention of opening the gate.

'Hellooo? Anyone theeere?'

'WHO'S THAT CALLING?'

'Oh! I'm sorry!'

'WHO IS IT I SAID? WHAT DO YOU WANT? WHY DON'T YOU USE THE BLOODY FRONT DOOR LIKE EVERYONE ELSE?'

Father Stephen is now nervously rubbing his hands together. He is stood in the tunnel that runs between the two terraced houses. To the left, the tall wooden gate leading to Mrs Tanner's and Mrs Lexton's back garden – to the right, the gate belonging to Mara's –

ahead a wooden wall. Although he tries, it is impossible for him to see through any of the slats.

'I was looking for Mara Bones? I used the door-knocker at the front, several times, but no-one answered. I thought, it being a fine day, I may find her in the garden.'

'MAYBE SHE DOESN'T WANT TO BE FOUND!'

Father Stephen is about to speak when Mrs Tanner shouts again from her back garden.

'MAYBE SHE IS DELIBERATELY NOT ANSWERING THE DOOR TO MALE STRANGERS BECAUSE HER FATHER HAS TOLD HER NOT TO. YOU DIDN'T THINK OF THAT, DID YOU?'

'WHO ARE YOU SHOUTING AT MRS TANNER? WHAT'S ALL THE RACKET ABOUT? ANYONE'D THINK THERE'S A BLOODY FIRE!'

'THERE'S A PERVERT AT THE GATE AFTER MARA, MRS LEXTON!'

'I'm not exactly a stranger. I'm –'

'IF YOU'RE NOT EXACTLY A STRANGER THEN WHAT THE BLOODY HELL ARE YOU? DOES MARA KNOW YOU?'

'My name is Father Stephen – I'm –'

'A BLOODY MORMON MRS LEXTON. THERE'S A BIBLE BASHER AT THE GATE AFTER MARA!'

'TELL HIM, MRS TANNER THAT IT'S TOO LATE. WE'RE ALL GOING TO HELL, WHERE THE DEVIL'S GOT ALL THE BEST TUNES AND ITS WARM AND FRIENDLY!'

'WHAT'S YOUR NAME AGAIN?'

Father Stephen looks at the closed back gate belonging to the Bones household. He hesitates for a moment thinking he has heard the faint laughter of a female – most likely Mara. He is about to speak when he decides to call back at a later time. Her waspish neighbours have suddenly grown silent. The familiar smell of pipe tobacco reaches him. For a moment he closes his eyes and inhales the air.

'MRS LEXTON, I THINK YOU'D BETTER CALL THE POLICE. I CAN STILL HEAR HIM BREATHING BEHIND THE GATE. GOD BLOODY KNOWS WHAT HE'S DOING BEHIND THERE!'

38

INSPECTOR FOLKARD And Sergeant Shakespeare gathered around PC Stanfield's desk. He removed a red pen from between his teeth before using it like a wand on the monitor screen before them.

'This was filmed moments after the accident. Look, here. See? Mara Bones walking away - proximity from the scene is two minutes walking distance. She doesn't appear on any other footage. That's all we've got.'

'At least we know she was there – close to the scene. Can you check if she's returned back to school? Either way, contact her father. It's a long shot but we'll pay her a visit later.'

***

The stimulating drive along the coastal road was especially beautiful that morning. Although, not unusually, the sea was nowhere to be seen, the variety of landscapes and rich diversity of wildlife enthused Inspector Folkard sufficiently enough into opening her car window to take in the fresh air. The views across the water were crystal clear; the Irish

Sea and North Wales to the left – Lytham and St Anne's and Blackpool to the right. For a moment they both looked away from the coastline, right, along a wide long road that did not seem to end, spongy marshland rich with wild birds at either side.

Although neither spoke, they were both recalling a case they had worked on a couple of years earlier. A few weeks ago, Inspector Folkard had spotted a well-wrapped Mr and Mrs Chambers trundling along Cambridge Road in matching biscuit-coloured coats. They looked thin but well enough. Mr Chambers seemed to be chatting away to his wife: a positive sign that his Alzheimer's disease was thankfully progressing slowly. His wife in turn nodded, a vacant expression on her face.

The weekend heat wave had refused to budge – the early sun was already bronzing the faces of retired couples walking closely together. Energetic dog-walkers appeared more enthusiastic than their four-legged companions, their draping tongues protruding sideways from their mouths – heads hung low – an occasional wag of the tail.

'I didn't thank you for booking us a room at Bartle Hall. Thank you.'

Hermione Folkard paused. The chosen venue had reminded her of Lyme Park; its glorious grounds, surrounded by gardens, moorland and deer park famously used for the period drama *Pride and Prejudice*. For a few seconds, painful images flashed before her – Walter holding her hand before he kissed her tenderly in the Edwardian Rose Garden. Since his death, she had longed to revisit the place; she had longed to return to Comlongon too; she had longed to return to many of their favourite haunts. Metaphorically, she was walking a tight-rope; the desire to return to places that mattered to them both as strong as the desire to never see them ever again.

'The girls and I looked the venue up on the internet last night. Looks magnificent. The girls are ecstatic about their bridesmaid dresses. I had to stop them from calling you last night; they wanted to know the exact colour of them as they insisted it was paramount that they practice their make-up routine several times before the big day!'

'Of course! There's only four months to go after all!' replied Catherine sarcastically.

'You went yesterday to take a look? How did that go?'

'We did. It's perfect in every way. Even nicer seeing it when the weather is as fabulous as it is today. They asked us to call by early in the day then we could see the set-up for an open-air wedding taking place later that afternoon. Beautiful. Just beautiful, Wendy wasn't fussed about the whole outdoor thing – says we might as well marry in the back of the garden and save ourselves the money!'

Hermione Folkard laughed. She could have guessed that. There was no doubt that Wendy was the more practical of the two. There was also no doubt how much Catherine meant to Wendy. Catherine was likely to get her own way in almost anything she had set her heart on. She paused. Her bridesmaids had worn gold dresses; they had wings and wands too!'

'Cerise.'

'Sorry?'

'Cerise. The bridesmaid dresses. I think they're going to be cerise - a bright fuchsia pink.'

'Ah! I shall let the girls know!'

'Honeymoon?'

'New Zealand. Ever since they passed same-sex marriages, Wendy's wanted to get out there. I've always wanted to go there myself. Our parents are paying for the flights and hotel as our wedding gift; that gives us a chance to save up for the holiday. Time's flying and we have no money saved for it. We seem to have spent it before it even makes its way into our bank accounts!'

Hermione Folkard smiled. She glanced at her colleague, radiant with the weekend's gaieties. She wished she could oppress the swelling envy she felt. There was no part of her that resented her friend's happiness but she did begrudge no longer having a piece of it herself. Loss. She had heard that loss could make you bitter, twisted and cynical. How true this was of some she knew. She hoped she would never succumb, even in her darkest hour.

The end of the coastal road was in sight - the Crossens roundabout ahead of them. The faint outline of St John's spire could be seen spiking into the sun like an olive on the end of a cocktail stick. Hermione Folkard squinted before she raised her right hand to shield her eyes. Half-way down Rufford Street and they turned right onto North Lane - in the cul-de-sac to their immediate left, the Bones household was in sight.

Catherine Shakespeare turned the engine off. She'd parked outside on the main road; they had arrived a little early. She removed her seat-belt at the point when she saw Mr Bones drive down the cul-de-sac having arrived home to be with his daughter for their informal meeting. At almost the same time, Hermione Folkard answered a call on her mobile.

'Ah! Father Stephen, what can I do for you? – you did? - No! - Really? – Thanks for the warning! Yes, yes, will do – ok – Yes, no problem. Thank you for calling anyway. Thank you Father.'

'That sounded interesting? Shall we go in?'

'I'll tell you later! Hilarious. Seems like the Bones have some very interesting neighbours. I think we'd better use the front door.'

39

MARA HEADS SLOWLY down the stairs when her father calls her. For a moment she thinks she is going to be sick. Her right hand instinctively rests on her stomach as she reaches the downstairs landing.

She saw *her* Inspector arrive, accompanied by the same policewoman as last time. *Her* Inspector has lost weight – too much weight; her face looked gaunt from the side. Mara knew *her* Inspector would look upwards towards her bedroom window as she approached the house; she had remained unseen but knew that she knew she was there, watching her.

Instinctively too, Mara checked herself in the mirror, checked her freshly-washed hair for no reason. She'd lost plenty of weight too; wearing all-black only served to highlight it more. She had no time to change. She looped her thumbs into the trims of each sleeve, hiding most of her hands, as most teenagers do. It was important no part of her arms were exposed. She felt physically cleansed after her long bath. Did she look like a killer? Sadly, Mara thought she did.

When Mara entered the lounge she found the Inspector and her colleague sitting on the pink and green floral settee to the right; her father sat nearby in a separate matching armchair. All three smiled and remained seated as she entered. In return, she smiled back. It was difficult holding eye-contact so she elected to look at her father before sitting down on a two-seater to the left of the door, just below the front window.

Mara sat back, trying to look relaxed. In response, the police officers did so too; only her father remained tense in his chair, his elbows slightly bent outwards, his shoulders hunched. His face looked rigid with pain, like he'd spent hours at a dentist.

'Hello Mara. I'm sure you remember us both from our last visit. I'm Sergeant Shakespeare and this is Inspector Folkard.'

There was a short pause. Mara looked at them both before quickly sharing a friendly half-smile.

'You've lost weight I see. I believe you've been unwell – not returned to school as of yet. How are you feeling?'

'I'm feeling much better, thank you.'

Inspector Folkard looked towards Morgan Bones before speaking herself for the first time. Although her face remained composed, her body language told another story.

'Has she been to the doctor?'

'I tried to get an appointment Friday – but the phone was constantly engaged. I was going to call in myself if I didn't get through today. I've been fairly ill myself – only now starting to feel better. A bug the doctor said – nothing he could do about it. I have been ill near three weeks. Mara's probably got the same.'

'All the same, it would be wise to get her checked out. I hope you have better luck getting through today.'

Morgan Bones shifted uneasily in his armchair. Inspector Folkard held her gaze before returning her attention towards Mara. In turn, her father attempted to sit back, only to lean forward again. He looked at Mara as though he were seeing her properly for the first time before he looked back at the officers, his face redder than before.

'I'll take her to the Walk-In Centre if I can't get hold of a doctor, as soon as you leave. Mara shifted uneasily in her chair, the last thing she wanted was to be examined. Neglect was something she had always been able to count on. His need to play the dutiful father was the last thing she needed.

'I'd like to speak to you Mara about an incident that occurred last week, outside your school; an incident we have spoken to many students about. Because you have been unwell, we were not able to speak to you in school like the other students in your year. As you know, this resulted in the unfortunate death of a girl we believe you knew, Sally Conway?'

Sergeant Shakespeare paused. Mara remained silent. He gaze did not shift from her speaker. Her hands remained clasped on her lap – composed.

'We are here to gain a better understanding of not just the incident in question but of also Sally herself. Several students have reported she was a difficult character – a bully. Some have named you as a victim and stated that she had upset you on the day in question?'

Mara looked like she was about to speak. She paused before talking. She kept her eyes fixed on Sergeant Shakespeare. For a moment her right hand let go of her left. Her middle three fingers lifted slightly upwards before they fell into place once again.

'Sally Conway upset everyone. She upset teachers and students – every day. She picked on me no more than she picked on others. Like lots of other students, I did my best to ignore her.'

'Did you ever confront her? Or fight with her?'

'No. I was afraid of her. I kept as far away from her as possible. I have never had a fight in my life.'

Inspector Folkard spotted a familiar novel on the shelf underneath the coffee table top. She smiled before interrupting.

'How are you getting on with the Cass novel. It's a series of five you know?'

Mara paused. She had to look at the Inspector now. She wasn't entirely sure why she had wanted to avoid her gaze. She looked at the book before returning a half-smile. A small part of her now wished she had not abandoned it so easily. It was a book that her mother would have approved of; maybe if she escaped intact, she would give it another try.

'I, I started reading it and stopped once I fell ill. I've been sleeping a lot. It was a good story. Reminded me a little of *The Hunger Games*.'

'Mara. You are not the only person we are directing this question towards; please think carefully before answering.'

Sergeant Shakespeare paused deliberately before continuing; she had everyone's full attention. Mara unclasped her hands and tucked invisible strands behind both ears. Her hands now rested at either side – tiny fists closed. For a moment, when her arms were raised, Inspector Folkard thought she saw a scratch along the vein of her left arm; she hoped Mara would repeat the involuntary gesture then she could examine the graze for a second time.

'CCTV in the area shows you were close by when the accident involving Sally Conway happened. Can you confirm that you were there at the time of the accident?'

Mara paused. She played the Sergeant's question carefully in her head before answering.

'I was nearby, like everyone else, but not near enough to see what happened. I heard a lot of screaming but did not even stop to look at what was happening. Kids scream all the time. I had no idea that something awful had happened. Some kids were laughing. It was hard to tell. I like to get home as soon as possible – avoid any trouble.'

'Mrs Cassidy, the school librarian, states that you usually stop behind after school, to get your homework done, almost every day. It seems unusual that on this day you chose to head home at the same time as everyone else. Where you going somewhere?'

'I wasn't feeling well.'

'Did you share this with anyone? Did you go and see Mrs Cassidy to explain? Did you speak to your form tutor, Mr Quinn, for instance?'

'No. I was feeling sick. I wanted to get home as soon as possible. I was sick as soon as I got in. I'm only now beginning to feel better.'

Morgan Bones shifted uneasily in his chair. He was not entirely sure why the questions which seemed routine had sounded accusatory for some reason. He checked himself before speaking.

'She's been sick the whole week. I never thought, my birds have been dying off – only got four left. Maybe we've all had bird flu.'

Her father could not think of anything more to say. Sergeant Shakespeare and Mara were now looking at him incredulously whilst Inspector Folkard held her gaze on Mara. Mara was about to raise her hands when he spoke again.

'Yes. I'm sure of it. Bird flu.'

40

'BIRD FLU. I have to say, I found myself speechless at that point.'

Inspector Folkard raised a smile. She too found herself dumbstruck. Mara's father had seemed utterly serious. Sergeant Shakespeare reassured him as best she could, reminding him that the birds in question were almost always poultry, the likes of chickens and geese, ducks and turkeys. A case of human bird flu outside the UK was very rare; within the UK, there had never been a case to date. Mara's father had nodded, reassured. Mara had remained impassive.

'Mara's left arm looked cut, or scratched – on the inside. It could be nothing. I only saw it once. I don't suppose you noticed?'

'I didn't. Did she seem hurt?'

'I don't know. It happened so quickly – when she raised her arms to tuck her hair behind her ears. I know teenagers often wear long-sleeved tops hiding their hands – disappearing into them – I – I just wondered if she was self-harming I suppose.'

'Or – you could be looking for signs that fit the profile of a troubled, guilty teenager who is internalising her anger and pain.'

'Maybe.'

'So we are no further on – nothing to go on.'

'Nothing to go on.'

'She looked to me like she has lost too much weight. I'm concerned. It's a gut feeling. Get in touch with Social Services – maybe they can make a discreet visit based on her falling attendance – a support worker-like visit.'

'Ok – good idea. I'll make the call as soon as I get back to the station.'

There was a pause – a long one. Catherine Shakespeare sensed her colleague's mind was uneasy. The investigation had not run smoothly, for a variety of reasons; they kept coming unstuck – making little headway.

'I know it's frustrating but the break we need will come. Don't beat yourself up. One day you'll look back and see how well you've managed – managed better than most – managed better than I could ever have done.'

'The children keep me going. How many times have we seen families come apart after the unexpected death of a loved one? More than most. And how many times have we seen those left behind struggle to adjust – even take their own lives. No-one understands unless they have lived it. No-one.'

'I'm sorry Hermione. I feel so helpless. I've known you and Walter longer than most. I feel guilty – for living – for having Wendy – for being happy. We did speak of postponing the wedding you know? But Wendy thought it would give us all something to look forward to.'

'Thank you but there really is no need. I'm glad it is going ahead – Walter would want it to go ahead. I do. Wendy is right. A celebration should never be postponed – and the girls are so looking forward to it.'

'You'll feel a bit better come this August. It won't be the same – it won't ever be the same - but you'll have the children with you. I'll be with you.'

'A widow.'

'Sorry?'

'A widow. That's what I'll be at the wedding. That's what I am now.'

Hermione Folkard looked out of the window. Her right hand followed the line of her brow before she dried her eyes with the back of her hands.

'I had to go to the bank and produce Walter's death certificate – to withdraw money – for a deposit for a holiday we would have taken the children on together. The bank manager referred to me as having been *abruptly widowed.* I hadn't even realised my marital status had changed. I am not classed as married anymore – even though in my heart I feel it. I am now- widowed.'

'It's easy for me to say but it is only a word. A meaningless word, if truth be told.'

Catherine Shakespeare pulled over. She placed her right hand on her colleague's left. Hermione's right hand was fighting a losing battle. Tears welled as soon as Hermione Folkard's eyes had dried.

'I'll drop you off home.'

Hermione Folkard did not protest. Two steps forward, one step back. Good days. Bad days. Today was a bad day. Yesterday had been worse.

Yesterday, she'd started moving some items belonging to Walter into a bag to move to the attic. Father Stephen had suggested she took her time sorting Walter's items – to not feel rushed. She thought of sending a few things to the local charity shop, but she couldn't – wouldn't. There was no way she could part with a single item belonging to him but she wanted to put something aside – she began by choosing what meant the least to her.

Hermione Folkard was packing a plain suit away when she heard a jingle. The jingle came when she brushed the suit up against his corduroy brown jacket, a jacket she had chosen to keep in the wardrobe. At first she didn't recognise the sound. Then, although she couldn't name the object, she knew there was a familiarity about it – something she should have remembered,

When she shook the jacket she heard the gentle sound of a cascabel. She searched Walter's pockets until she found the culprit, a heart-shaped metallic bell the size of a two-pence coin. She had given it to Walter many years ago. She thought and thought about it but she couldn't recall when she gave it to him. She once knew he kept it there but had forgotten already. She couldn't ask him when, how or why. She couldn't recall the memory that right then had meant so much to her – could have comforted her. Like many other questions, and memories, it went to the grave with him.

For a while she thought seriously about purchasing a notebook – a means of recording what she could remember now. Maybe in time the memory would flood back; the fear that it wouldn't, overwhelmed her. She cried herself to sleep.

The jacket hung in the wardrobe alongside some of her favourite ties and shirts – a pink shirt with a paisley pattern hung next to the corduroy jacket. Two hours later she had bagged half the contents up in bin bags. She was too tired to put them in the attic. She was grateful neither of the girls had walked in on her – she didn't want to have to explain – explain she was packing some of him away.

Now she could move her favourite outfits next to his; they could co-exist in the same wardrobe, his shoulders touching hers, his shoes by hers. She had inhaled deeply into the fabric of a favoured tweed jacket repeatedly. Walter. If she kept the wardrobe closed she'd be more likely to successfully retain his scent for as long as possible.

41

THE HEAT WAVE is now over. It came and went like a long lost lover leaving devotees alike bereft. It is April after all. April equals showers. Outside, the air has cooled and the sun hides shyly behind cloud-after-cloud. Momentarily he peeps from beneath his smoky veil before disappearing back.

Yesterday, Mara convinced her father that she would make an appointment at the doctors, to save him the time. Mara's father was in a rush to return to work. Mr Luca was furious that he had had to take more time off work. They seemed suspicious that the police were visiting his home again; he wished he hadn't mentioned their first visit. Mr Luca had looked at him as though he were up to something.

When her father arrived home yesterday evening, Mara told him she'd been to the doctors – that they had asked for her to come straight down and sit in the waiting area. The doctor – a doctor whose name she cannot remember but had a difficult surname to pronounce – the doctor told her she was over the worse of it – that she would be right as rain in a couple of days – to drink plenty of fluids.

Mara's father nodded. It was clear from his face he had had a problematic day. He had had to remain behind an extra hour. After visiting his birds he headed off to sleep – no shower – straight to bed. No goodnight kiss.

***

Mara can hear her father taking a shower before work. Care-free water falls in rapid succession until it is interrupted by a movement that momentarily stalls it. Mara's father rarely showers for more than five minutes. He will most likely be out of the front door within the next ten minutes.

Oddly, Mara's father has abruptly entered her bedroom, a towel about his waist. Mara sits upright; she did not anticipate this from him. It is obvious from his face he is unhappy. It is contorted – restless.

'Why aren't you dressed. You need to get back to school. You said yourself you were feeling better.'

'The doctor said I would be okay in a couple of days. I still don't feel right. I still feel sick.'

Her father looks at her unconvinced. He looks out of her first bedroom window to the left as if he is distracted before he speaks again.

'Tomorrow. No excuses. You're going back tomorrow. I'll not have social services on my back because you're not taking care of yourself – and not going to school.'

Mara lowers her eyes. Her father has made his mind up. He heads for the window to open it. As he does so, something catches his eye; from his angle, he notices the gold necklace about her neck - the cross cannot be seen; it is hidden beneath the front of her nightdress.

'What's that around your neck? Doesn't look like a bit of tat.'

Mara has prepared what she is about to say a hundred times. Right now, the words she had memorised and rehearsed so angrily and passionately fail her. But she will not lie. Her father is the liar. She may be many things but she is not a liar.

'It was a gift.'

'A gift from who?'

Mara pauses before looking at her father directly.

'A gift from my mother.'

Mara's father's face is incredulous. He takes one half-step forward before retreating. For a moment he stands still as if he were checking himself. Unbeknown to him, he is gritting his teeth and his hands are closed like fists.

Defensively, Mara puts both hands about her neckline. Her palms press downward on the cross. For a moment Mara fears he will grab her by the shoulders and snap it loose – take it away – but he does not. Mara's father grunts before he turns and leaves her room, stopping once to look upwards at the attic trap-door and once when he turns around before he speaks.

'I'll deal with you later.'

HERMIONE FOLKARD RETURNED Catherine Shakespeare's farewell wave of the hand. She looked at her watch 11:32. The children wouldn't be home from school for another few hours. She considered her family dwelling – more a house than a home now.

Directly above the front porch was Zita's bedroom window. Central to the semi-detached abode, her window possessed numerous pictures of her favoured Pokémon characters; twenty-something years ago Harry was as obsessed with the same fictional creatures as Zita was right now. She hoped the craze would soon pass, she could no longer keep up with all the new consortium paraphernalia.

Her garden looked untidy – the porch corners had crisp leaves stacked upon water-logged leaves. Cobwebs had gathered in every corner, even across the top of the door itself. She needed a gardener. She needed a cleaner too.

Hermione Folkard entered her home with a certain determination; today she would try to resolve some of the issues that had gone unanswered. Bills needed paying too. Direct Debits needed setting up; most of them were at Walter's bank. His life insurance needed addressing – the outstanding final funeral bill needed settling.

By nearly half-one she had sorted most of what could be done. Hermione Folkard felt pleased with herself – more in control. She put the kettle on. For the first time in a long while, she felt hungry. She opened the fridge just as her mobile rang.

'It's Catherine, sorry to disturb you but I knew you'd want to know straight away. Might be the break we need.'

'What is it?'

'A young woman, fitting the description of Mara Bones, was seen in the town of Whitlag: CCTV from both Southport and Whitlag train station is on its way. For the past fortnight, there has been an ongoing investigation following the death of an infant – found with a pillow over its face.'

'Doesn't make sense.'

'Do you remember you asked me to contact social services, for an informal visit, to check Mara is ok? Well, I rang them – asked for previous addresses. Whitlag is a town outside Manchester, the previous place where the family lived before her mother died of breast cancer. 24 South Road, was the address where the infant was suffocated, Mara's previous address.'

'Call me as soon as the CCTV is in. If it's Mara, contact CAMHS and set up a meeting room – we'll bring Mara into the station first thing – before her father leaves for work.'

'Sure. By the way, happened on a week day – when Mara was absent from school.'

'Unbelievable. Why did she return? I wonder if her father had any knowledge of her visit? Maybe they often go there – have family still there.'

'The suspect is believed to have stopped outside a house to ask directions to a nearby church: St Peregrine's Church. Maybe she spoke to a priest or someone.'

'Does it have a graveyard?'

'Not sure. Probably, why?'

'Her mother. Her mother is probably buried there.'

43

IT IS DARK now. Mara thinks for the umpteenth time about her father's parting words: *I'll deal with you later.* The words are bad enough but the tone of his voice was far worse. It was a loud whisper enveloped in a threat – a promise never to be broken.

Her father will be home soon enough. Had she been in school, Mara might not have worried as much – kept busy. The bells would have summoned her from one lesson to the other. Time would have passed quickly – writing, reading, listening. At lunch, she could have visited Mrs Cassidy, asked about the Cass books – maybe given the first in the series another go. Instead, at home, time has played a series of merciless tricks on her all day. Mara has played out many scenarios in her head. None of them are pleasant.

In the first scenario, Mara's father comes home and heads straight upstairs, to her bedroom. Mara is sitting on her bed waiting for him; she can hear him coming, thundering up the stairs, two-by-two. Mara's father bursts through her bedroom door. He does not stop to talk to her. He grabs a fistful of her hair with his right hand whilst his left palm heads for her face.

Instead of striking her though, he grasps her cross and chain around her neck, yanking it from her, snapping the chain. Mara is left devastated, crying. Her father leaves.

Something similar happens in the next scenario, except as the hours have passed Mara has found herself feeling more fearful. In this second scenario, Mara has removed her cross and hidden it under her mattress. When her father grabs her hair he yells at her, his face close to hers. Mara's father's breath is hot and angry; the more he screams the more fearful she becomes. She wets herself. Mara has no choice but to tell him where the cross is. He takes it away, sneering, laughing – his face the very picture of evil.

By mid-afternoon Mara is feeling brave. She won't remove her cross; she will shout back and threaten to speak to social services and the police, if he touches her. Her father's anger will lessen and she will be in control of the situation. She will shout at him then. How dare he keep secrets from her, lie to her, deny her from her mother's gifts?

The second scenario begins to crumble at the point when her father apologises and begins to share some much-needed information about her mother. This would never happen. Her father would never back down, let alone express regret.

The afternoon hours have passed slowly. Mara has been grinding her glass for over forty minutes but a large shard from the old greenhouse remains untouched on the kitchen table. Mara's new scenario before tea encompasses both her fear and her growing anger. She is still fearful but almost ready for the confrontation. If her father hits her repeatedly, as he often did when she was younger, she will defend herself as best she can. She will not let him take anything belonging to her, meant for her. Her mother wanted her to have it and have it she will.

By early evening, Mara has worked herself up into a frenzy. She has re-read all her letters with the exception of the last two that remain unopened. She hoped they would give her courage. Mara is now sitting on her bed, waiting for her father in the dark. Downstairs, awaiting him, are the last four canaries, on the kitchen table – dead. Mara has cut their tiny throats with the shard of glass. They are on the table lined up like chicken drumsticks, blood pooling on the wooden surface – their red eyes wide open.

Once upon a time her father's bird-shed was filled with the sound of music – alternating high-pitched outbursts according to their mood and the time of day. There were so many birds, before she started grinding her glass. Mara is now thinking about Lara, her Dalmatian. What began as revenge, following Lara's death, not long after Mara's tenth birthday, ended up giving Mara an uncontrollable sense of satisfaction.

At the vets Mara refused to leave Lara, even after she had peacefully passed away, lying on her side, on the floor, legs spread-eagled. Lara's eyes were red-rimmed, tired, large like saucers at first before they gradually slackened. Even to the end, Lara held her gaze on Mara – loyal – loving – a grey film forming in the corner of each eye.

Mara wouldn't stop crying. Her father had to tear her away – her hair all matted across her wet face. The vet allowed them to leave through the back; Mara's father was embarrassed. When he was given the bill, his anger returned; he yelled at Mara all the way home – slammed the brakes on at one point so hard that her small frame flung forward and she smacked her face on the dashboard.

That evening Mara cut her long dark hair.

Ten for a Bird you Must Not Miss.

Nine for a Kiss

Eight for a Wish

Seven for a Secret NEVER to be Told,

Six for Gold,

Five for Silver,

Four for a Boy,

Three for a Girl,

Two for Joy,

One for Sorrow.

But there are no magpies left now. There is only Mara. Her life has been black and white – maybe white then black. When her father discovers the last birds on the kitchen table, his tenderness and affection for his birds will be replaced with an uncontrollable anger following disbelief – she knows this. It is a porthole that they must both pass through because now there is nowhere else to go.

Mara is ready, ready for it. The headlights belonging to her father's car travel along the bedroom's longest wall, opposite the windows. He is home.

Mara is sitting up on her bed leaning against her tessellated metallic headboard. She is not only wearing her cross and chain about her neck; she is wearing all of her mother's gifts. Her diary is written. It has been carefully wrapped in brown paper and addressed to her favourite inspector. Mrs Stone next door, kindly agreed to take it to the post office for her. Mara has glued in all of her mother's letters into the diary – including the two she never opened.

She is waiting in the dark, facing the closed door.

Silence.

Her father closes the front door.

There is often more in silence than in what is actually said.

44

SERGEANT SHAKESPEARE SQUINTED. Close-up shots had failed to show a clear view of Mara's facial features but her clothes were distinctive enough. She was positive that in the footage, Mara was wearing the same dark-green duffle coat she saw hanging on the stair banister at home. Her hair, size and stature fitted perfectly. She was sure it was Mara. She called Hermione Folkard.

'Manchester police received a phone call from an elderly pensioner, a Mrs Robinson. According to her, the nice girl with the large dark eyes, fitting Mara's description, had got on famously with Ginger, her cat.'

'Any particular reason why she called the police?'

'No. Not really. She'd telephoned on a whim. A local news report urged any residents to call the station if they had come into contact with anyone unknown to the area. Had she not called, Mara would have most likely gone unnoticed. For days CID have been looking in the wrong direction – women who've lost children, miscarriages – even the mother's been questioned.'

'I didn't think her capable. I should be at that point in my career where nothing surprises me anymore. It's such a cold thing to do. We'll bring her in as planned first thing tomorrow. Is everything set up?'

'Yes. We have enough circumstantial evidence to get a warrant tonight, and search for the clothes in question.'

'I know, but we'll pick her up tomorrow. She's unlikely to be in any danger. She's too young, in my opinion, to remove at this late hour; if it is Mara, as I suspect it is, it will be her last night with the only parent she has.'

'It is just after nine. I don't mean to contradict you Hermione but ask yourself this, if the suspect were male, would you be making the same decision?'

Hermione Folkard paused – a Pinter-size pause. Sergeant Shakespeare heard her inhale – take a deep breath before she finally spoke.

'There is no evidence that she has committed any crime. DNA taken at the scene will confirm one way or another. We'll pick her up tomorrow.'

A pregnant pause was returned. Catherine Shakespeare couldn't put her finger on it. Her superior's decision to not act until the following day was both understandable and reasonable but for some reason, she did not agree – not on this occasion. If Mara was culpable for the infant's death – it was murder. That meant she was capable of a lot more. In essence, Mara could be responsible for a further three deaths. As serial killers went, Mara was not only intelligent but cunning too.

45

IT IS NOT long after half-past nine in the evening. The house is in near darkness. Mara's father locks the front door, takes his coat off and hangs it at the bottom of the stairs before heading to the lounge. Both his shirt and tie have been loosened – it's been a long day, unusually busy for a Tuesday. In his hands, he has a glass of whisky.

Mara's father quickly drains another glass; he wipes his forehead with his right palm before he heads to the kitchen sink. He washes his hands and cools his face with some water scooped together - both hands held together in the shape of a canoe.

For several moments, he stands at the sink looking out of the window. Directly ahead, in the distance, is the outline of his beloved bird-shed. He shrugs his shoulders, takes a deep breath and heads for the back door. Mara's father has walked the garden path in the dark, many times before. He can always detect the mood of his birds beforehand; in the evening, when it is dusky, they are usually silent. They are silent now.

The quietness as he enters the bird-shed is unusually eerie – unnatural even. Ordinarily he will hear some movement, a flutter of wings – the twitching of tiny legs – occasionally a tweet. Dread fills him. He taps the metal mesh to stir them but there is no response – no sign of life. He taps it again, louder this time, less hopeful. His eyes are now squinting in the near darkness, searching the floor for their tiny corpses. He cannot see anything. He heads to the house for a torch; he has one in the kitchen drawer – the middle one – the one with the batteries and the lightbulbs.

Mara's father crosses the kitchen diagonally before he reaches the light switch. He blinks a few times; his eyes are sensitive after the obscurity. His vision adjusts slowly.

Immediately to his left is the kitchen table. He usually finds his supper on it. Mara's father takes a step back. For a few moments he stands stunned, rooted to the spot – a pre-meditated carnage before his eyes. His birds. Four of them – lined up like soldiers – a clear foot between each one. There is a small dark pool underneath the head of each bird. Their almost severed heads have been manipulated so that they are looking upwards, their necks exposed. For some reason he tries to pick the nearest one up but its feathers are stuck to the table, glued to the wood with blood.

Mara's father looks towards the hallway. He moves slowly forward – incredulous. He turns left and looks up the stairs before he turns the light on and ascends. His hands are the shapes of fists now. Unknowingly, he is gritting his teeth.

For a few seconds, Mara's father stands rigid outside her bedroom door before he turns the door handle and pushes the door wide open. Mara is sitting in the dark – in her right hand, the shard of glass. She can hear him breathing heavily as he moves towards her.

'You evil little bitch. You killed them didn't you? You've been killing them all along.'

Mara remains silent. She has not eaten properly for days now. Nauseous, she is unrepentant. Her father takes her by her hair and drags her quickly out of bed and into the landing below the attic's entrance. Mara releases the shard of glass from her grip. It is covered in blood. Her father is so furious that he has not noticed she has cut her tiny wrists; he has not even noticed her jewellery.

Deliberately, each time Mara stumbles, her father yanks her to her feet before he shakes her and throws her against the nearest wall. He then picks her up like a basketball before the next bounce. He repeats this until he sees that she is bleeding – her nightdress is bloody; she has blood all over her hands.

Before too long, she stands facing the music - the dead birds ahead on the kitchen table. Mara is about to pass out.

Her Father

'You evil fucking bitch. I've given you everything. I'm the only parent you've got. You evil fucking bitch.'

Still incredulous, Mara's father is unsure what to do with his daughter. A cut to the side of her head, caught on a window-ledge on the way down, is bleeding profusely. Mara's father drags her along the unlit path – her rough finger-tipped-fingers fail to cling to anything along the way. The night-sky is clear enough. There are many stars above.

The air is filled with the scent of spring. Mara's bare feet burn against the concrete flags like a match being struck. She passes out as he throws her into his bird-free bird-shed, slamming the door behind her.

Once indoors, Mara's father sits down in the lounge. He sits in the single floral armchair facing the television. He thinks of the recent visits from the police before he takes out once more his bottle of whisky from a nearby side-cupboard.

***

It is daylight now, the dawn of a new day. Regaining consciousness only once, Mara thinks of her mother lying below ground with her brother or sister. Slumped in a corner, blood is now seeping from her mouth. Her arms are outstretched.

Tiny white feathers cling to her wrists.

Outside, the sound of birds awaken her momentarily. It is the sound of love and light and liberty.

Yesterday, she replayed many scenarios of how it would be when her father discovered the truth. He didn't even bother to ask about the truth – the fact is, he never cared – never, being the point.

That is why, the many scenarios that she had played in her mind leading up to his arrival home, were filled with outbursts depicting her as strong and brave and finally standing up for herself. Brave like her mother must have been.

In her final hours.

In her final moments.

In reality though, as the hours passed, she knew her chances were more than slim. An ignominious defeat awaited her. So Mara added more Borax than normal to her father's whisky. Sure, he had started bleeding out the last few weeks but should she not make it – she didn't want to make it – should she not survive, she was dammed sure he wasn't going to neither.

With difficulty, Mara lifts her heavy head, managing only to hold it to one side. She looks diagonally right, out through the only window belonging to the bird-shed. Perched on a branch, looking in, free as a bird is a lonesome magpie.

The air smells fresh.

To Mara it smells of dancing and cherries.

Mara can hear a soft voice now.

She is singing to her.

Hush little baby don't say a word,
Mama's gonna buy you a mockingbird,
and if that mockingbird don't sing,
Mama's gonna buy you a diamond ring.

Her mother is now pushing her to and fro, from behind, whilst she is on a swing in the back garden of their old home.

This time, she does not fall forward.

There is no need to cry.

Her mother's voice is comforting.

Hush little baby don't say a word,
Mama's gonna buy you a mockingbird,
and if that mockingbird don't sing,
Mama's gonna buy you a diamond ring.

Mara smiles for the last time.

She smiles for the last time before she closes her eyes.

Forever.

46

IT WAS RAINING when Sergeant Shakespeare awoke. April showers. She liked the pitter-patter of rain. She'd prefer the pitter-patter of children though. She checked the time on her mobile; it was nearly six. She needed to get up, Hermione Folkard would be round at seven sharp. They had a busy morning ahead of them.

Like every other morning, Catherine Shakespeare would arise an entire hour before her fiancée; she didn't resent this – not for a single second. In four months they would be wife and wife; she hoped in time, their marriage would be one that had been made in heaven – one that would last as long as the Folkard's.

Wendy stirred only to turn over. She looked peaceful sleeping on her side – her dark hair was just long enough to tie back into a ponytail; by August it would be the right length she had aimed for. Catherine smiled contentedly before she headed for the shower.

By ten-past seven, Catherine Shakespeare was grinning mischievously to herself. Hermione Folkard was rarely late. It would give her some pleasure to pull her colleague's leg. But by twenty-past seven, she had begun to grow worried. Where any of the children sick? It was not like Hermione Folkard to neither text nor telephone if she was running late.

Catherine Shakespeare began to dial her colleague's mobile. It rang out. No answer. She dialled again, two more times. Still no answer – no explanation – no text.

At seven-thirty, Sergeant Shakespeare headed for the station. She was late. She would wait there until Hermione Folkard showed up. Catherine Shakespeare hung her coat up before heading for her desk and logging on. She looked towards Hermione Folkard's vacant office. A visible brown package, already opened, as is customary, was on her desk; inside a brightly covered book of some sort – a metallic blue or green. Curiosity was about to get the better of her when Superintendent Reid entered, his face stern. He looked about for Hermione Folkard – a look of disappointment etched across his face.

'Sergeant Shakespeare - CAMHS need to get going. They have a court appearance this afternoon. Take Sergeant Boardley with you this morning. Can you brief her in five?'

'Yes Sir, sure.'

'Take the lead. Ask Inspector Folkard to drop by my office before the end of her shift please.'

'She is probably caught in traffic – a few accidents reported on the road this morning. I tried calling. She's left her mobile at home no doubt.'

Superintendent Reid did not respond. He looked towards Hermione Folkard's office once more before he exited the room. Sergeant Boardley smiled supportively.

'That's the last thing she needs – him on her back.'

Had they not been stuck behind a fleet of fire-engines, prior to reaching the busy coastal road, they would have arrived at least ten minutes beforehand. Southport's solitary shoreline looked especially beautiful – the Irish Sea hugging the semi-circular butter-cream coastline for as far as the eye could see.

Sergeant Boardley was not paying much attention to the interactive conversation taking place between the two officers from CAMHS in the back of the car. She was admiring the extensive sand dunes stretching for miles ahead of her. Shooting intermittent marram grass camouflaged basking sand lizards busy protecting their eggs. Their green flanks, as a result of the busy mating season, made them all the more difficult to spot.

Heath-dog violets appeared with more frequency now, before marshland pooled with salt-water took over. The rain had ceased in the last hour and the sun was now magnificent – not many clouds obscuring its pathway across the blue-trimmed sky.

Sergeant Boardley pointed towards the national nature reserve on both sides of the road now. As a member of the Wildlife Trust, she was keen to share with her companions that, amongst the fauna and flora, there were nationally important and rare species of mammals and butterflies amongst the marshes – especially insects. Catherine Shakespeare was not really listening; from time to time she interjected with the odd comment or two but on the whole was busy thinking about her colleague's absence.

Hermione Folkard's mental health had been understandably shaky of recent. Was it possible that she had returned to work too soon? Had it all got too much? In reality, and in a crisis, who would know how best to cope? Catherine Shakespeare had found it hard to empathise but was resolute in what to do next.

The best thing she could do right now, for her friend, was bring about a result – wrap the investigation up – put it to bed. When Hermione Folkard resurfaced, she would be able to pick up where she left off. Catherine Shakespeare was determined in her purpose - to ease the pressure and bring about an arrest.

'Napoleon Bonaparte lived in exile for two years on Lord Street during the eighteen-hundred's you know? He spent most of his time walking this shoreline.'

For a moment their attention was spent on Sergeant Boardley – the picture of a short, stout male, in his French naval uniform, comically wearing a black bicorne hat on his head, strolling along the sandy beach.

'You're kidding?'

'Not at all.'

The roundabout was ahead now; they had arrived to Crossens, a small village on the outskirts of Churchtown and the shore of Martin Mere. Not long after eight-thirty, they had arrived outside the quiet cul-de-sac. They exited the car in unison, the sun still burning brightly.

Almost instantly, upon turning a corner made up of many tall hedgerows, two resolute head-scarved women came trundling towards them. Dwarfed not only in stature, Sergeant Shakespeare detected the strong aroma of pipe tobacco as they approached. Although not a smoker herself, she liked the smell, her father used to smoke a pipe.

Every evening, following his tea, he'd take to the lounge and sit before the coal fire, to smoke his pipe – the much-cherished cherry-wood device kept besides the carriage clock he received upon his retirement from the police force. It is still there now. How strange that these two women reeked of it.

'Good morning.'

Sergeant Shakespeare stepped aside on the narrow side-walk to allow the women to pass. Instead, they chose to ignore her; without looking up they crossed the cul-de-sac together. The one walking ahead spat over a nearby hedge following a noise that could only be described to anyone interested as repulsive and unladylike. Immediately after, the other followed suit. All four officers were too astounded to make any remark, a crew of hang-mouthed adults.

Like ants on a mission, they waddled purposefully away towards the village, one with a plastic bag in her hand, the other with a tatty umbrella, spokes like broken ribs. Their red pinafores were still attached to their waists – their long black skirts, rigid, boots unpolished.

Mr Morgan Bone's silver car was still on the drive; it seemed they had arrived just in time. They sidled past it before Sergeant Boardley stepped ahead and sparingly rattled the door with its brass knocker. No response. Several knocks and a few minutes later, there was still no reply.

Sergeant Shakespeare made her way along the tunnel that ran to the left of the terraced house. Upon reaching the back gate, she failed to see anything whilst peering through the few gaps within the fence adjacent.

She called over the gate – behind her, the rest of the team had followed. No answer. She raised herself above the gate by placing her right foot sideways whilst pushing on a protruding piece of timber near the lock. From there she could only see into the empty lounge – a half-empty whisky bottle on the coffee table. The back garden was deserted too - quiet.

As she was about to lower herself, she noticed a solitary magpie on a tree branch above a small pond. Behind it, a wooden shed. Sergeant Shakespeare waited a few moments to make sure that neither Mara or her father were in there. After a few minutes, satisfied that neither were likely to emerge, she lowered herself back down.

'One for sorrow.'

'Did you say something?'

'Nothing. I can't see anyone.'

'Maybe they've gone to the shop?'

'Maybe. Let's wait in the car a while. They'll show up soon enough, I suppose. It may be that we may have missed Mara and that she has already caught the bus to school.'

'I'll ring the school in a bit – check if she's there. We can always pick her up there. Maybe the father is ill again – in bed.'

'Maybe, but unlikely. There's a half-empty whisky bottle on the coffee table. It's no wonder he can't hear us.'

In the ten minutes that followed, an unlikely conversation about what to make with and how best to use pipe-cleaners took place. This was regrettably interrupted by a call on Sergeant Shakespeare's work mobile. Her cut-throat gesture informed Sergeant Boardley that it was Superintendent Reid on the other end of the line. For a few moments she listened intently before responding.

'No sir. We are about to set off to pick her up at the school.'

Catherine Shakespeare appeared momentarily absorbed in whatever Superintendent Reid had said.

'We are to go back to the station beforehand.'

'Maybe they've heard from the father already – did he say why?'

'No. He didn't. It's hard to tell – he sounded irritable. Oh well, we'll soon find out.'

Sergeant Boardley was about to ask if there were any news on Inspector Folkard's whereabouts but Catherine Shakespeare's face already bore the look of someone worried. She decided against it and instead telephoned *Stanley Secondary*: Mara should have been registered by now.

Already Catherine Shakespeare had had to fight her natural instinct to call in on her colleague on the way to the Bones home. Having three others in tow, she had decided against it. Right now though, she felt an urgent need to call in on her once more. She looked in her centre mirror. Both CAMHS officers were chatting away. She would be passing close enough in the next ten minutes. A little detour.

It would have been better for Catherine Shakespeare if she had returned directly to the station as her superior had ordered. On her approach to pass by Hermione Folkard's property, she was redirected to an alternative route – fire engines apparently fighting a couple of houses ablaze.

Panic consuming her, Catherine Shakespeare pulled over and abandoned her car; she ran along the road before turning the corner on her left. Hermione Folkard's house and the adjoining property were on fire. The intensity of the blaze was obvious to all standing helplessly close by.

'Is everyone alright – what's happened? My friend – she's police – Hermione Folkard – her children – are they ok?'

A nearby firefighter in his full tunic undid a long zip about his synthetic collar before he motioned for her to sit on a nearby wall. His red face was expressionless; he removed his gloves. As he spoke, he placed a rehearsed hand on Catherine's arm. She was shaking all over.

'There is no-one left in the buildings as far as we know. Residents from both houses have been removed and taken to hospital.

I am sorry to say, two adults did not leave the property alive – a young child is in critical condition – smoke inhalation. That is all I know. I am very sorry.'

Catherine Shakespeare looked about bewildered. Dead. Two of them dead. Adults. Darcy? Zita? She was sure Hermione had mentioned that Harry too was calling in on his way home.

Of the two houses, the Folkards' was the worse to look at. Everything along one tall wall had been blackened – the windows and doors singed – Zita's life-sized Pokémon illustrations gone. Even some nearby trees had caught fire.

There were no flames, as such, coming from indoors – just a monstrous dark smoke billowing through every possible outlet. It was the roof that was on fire now. Flames ripped diagonally across both households. Despite the fire's greatest efforts, the buildings clung onto one another. Numerous firefighters worked quickly in unison to smash and tear away parts of it. In time, their strategy would pay off; they would win their battle.

'Where are they now? Southport Hospital?'

'Yes ma'am. I'm afraid so.'

Sickened and confused, Catherine Shakespeare took a deep breath before she began to cry. She took a couple of steps forward before she began to run back to the abandoned car – her bemused colleagues following close behind.

Songs of Innocence

Infant Joy

'I have no name:
I am but two days old.'
What shall I call thee?
'I happy am,
Joy is my name.'
Sweet joy befall thee!

Pretty joy!
Sweet joy, but two days old.
Sweet joy I call thee:
Thou dost smile,
I sing the while,
Sweet joy befall thee!

William Blake, 1789

Songs of Experience

Infant Sorrow

"My mother groaned! my father wept.
Into the dangerous world I leapt,
Helpless, naked, piping loud;
Like a fiend hid in a cloud.

Struggling in my father's hands,
Striving against my swaddling bands;
Bound and weary I thought best
To sulk upon my mother's breast."

William Blake, 1794

ABOUT THE AUTHOR

Sally-Anne Tapia-Bowes graduated from Hope and Liverpool University with a B.A. in English Literature and Contemporary Art followed by a P.G.C.E. in English and Drama. She has been a full-time English teacher for as long as she can remember.

HIS MOTHER was her debut novel, with sequels HER FATHER and SISTERS, released in 2017 and 2019.

Sally-Anne's first children's story-book *The Star that Lost Its Sparkle!* was published Christmas 2015. She has since gone on to write several other children's stories. She is a proud member of the SFS – *Society for Storytelling* and *Patron for Reading* at a local primary school.

Sally-Anne lives in Hightown, England, with her husband, children and two cats.

Official website: www.purplepenguinpublishing.com

Praise for Sally-Anne Tapia-Bowes

★ ★ ★ ★ ★

'A fascinating thriller with a complex, intriguing protagonist.

This compelling, beautifully written tale, deserves a place amongst the best contemporary psychological fiction.'

Bob Stone: Author of

A Bushy Tale* and *The Brush Off & The Missing Beat Trilogy

★ ★ ★ ★ ★

'The writing in this novel is woven with a thread of complete honesty and empathy.

The reader will be left questioning whom the real victims are.

Sally-Anne Tapia-Bowes has absolutely captured what it is like to live in today's fractured society.'

Stephen Beattie: Author of

Between the Lines* and *Treading the Helix

Printed in Great Britain
by Amazon